Before the Storm

Susan E Jones

For Rehanna and James

1

"Just one letter today," Mr Wright announces, waving an envelope at me. "It's addressed to Mrs Fielding of Meadowside Cottage, Hawthorn Lane."

The local postman has a big smile on his face. He leans his bicycle against the privet hedge and unlatches our front gate.

"Who did you say it was for?" I ask before I can stop myself.

"For you, of course!" He laughs and hands me the letter. "Tell me, Mrs Fielding, when will you begin to know your own name?"

"Oh, Mr Wright, I don't blame you for teasing me. I should be used to my married name by now, but it still sounds strange when I hear it spoken aloud."

I feel embarrassed. I've been married to Lionel for nearly a year now, yet each time I'm addressed as Mrs Fielding, it surprises me. I suppose it's hard for me to get used to the fact that I'm no longer Miss Bessie Hardwicke; after all, I answered to that name for thirty-nine years.

Mr Wright and I chat for a few minutes about the fine weather and how long it's expected to last, as it's not yet officially summer. Also, being a keen gardener, he gives me some advice on the fuchsia and dahlia plants I'm trying to grow in pots on the far side of the coalhouse. He appears to be in no hurry to continue on his rounds, but I need to get a move on with my morning chores, so I don't prolong the conversation. I've carefully placed the envelope in my apron pocket, as I won't open it immediately. I can tell from the handwriting that it's from my nephew Walter, and I shall enjoy reading it with a cup of tea when I've a moment or two to relax and properly savour his news.

It's a beautiful May morning and the dew-laden grass – a bright shade of green thanks to the recent April showers – sparkles in the sunshine. The magnolia tree, resplendently occupying its own corner of our front lawn, is still boasting a few of its magnificent pink and white blossoms, and the flowerbeds bordering the garden path are getting ready to explode into colour in the next couple of weeks. Closing my eyes for a moment, I let the sun bathe my face, while inhaling the sweet Devonshire air that I cannot appreciate enough. But household tasks await me, so I take one more deep breath and retreat inside.

Of course, life in the countryside is not new to me. Apart from one year in London, I lived all my life in the small Somerset village of Ferndell, surrounded by farmland, copses and rolling hills. But that single year in the big city – even though it eventually changed my life for the better – continues to haunt me. I still wake up each morning wondering why it's so quiet. Where are the menacing sounds of automobiles and omnibuses, Hansom cabs and other horse-drawn carriages, all competing for space on the busy streets of Wandsworth? And why am I no longer inhaling the dust and smoke that one could never really escape from, even indoors with the windows tightly shut or while strolling in one of the city's many parks?

When I come to my senses, I breathe a sigh of relief. I can now begin my day without the sense of dread I used to feel each morning. Life in London was an experience I shall never forget, nor regret. After all, it led to my marriage with Mr Lionel Fielding, a well-regarded pharmacist with whom I fell in love, but I felt blessed beyond measure when we moved out of the city and I was able to enjoy a more peaceful lifestyle in the beautiful county of Devon.

"Another letter from Walter?" Lionel asks me when I return to the kitchen and place my envelope on the table. He's finished his breakfast and is putting on his jacket, ready to leave for work. He now runs the pharmacy in the small town of Brampton-on-Sea, about half an hour's walk from our cottage.

"Yes," I say. "I'll read it in a little while, once I've washed up these dishes. You should know by now that I like to save his letters for when I have enough time to sit down and fully digest every word he has to say."

"I hope you'll do the same with my letters, my dear, if ever I have cause to write to you."

"Of course, Lionel. What a thing to say! How could you think otherwise?"

He chuckles, gives me a peck on the cheek, and leaves the house.

We moved here shortly after we were married last year; on the 3rd of June, 1911, to be precise. When I first met Lionel, he was running a much larger pharmacy in Wandsworth, close to where I earned my living as a companion to Mrs Fanny Grist, a widowed lady of substantial means, and his was the only friendly face I would encounter for days on end. I used to visit the pharmacy several times a week, as my employer was something of a hypochondriac and would complain continually of maladies for which she needed Lionel's expert advice and, more often than not, one of his special tonics.

I soon became aware that Lionel was starting to look upon me as more than just a frequent customer. Having suffered from a lack of self-esteem for most of my life, it took me some time to accept that he was serious in his professed fondness for me, even though there was no doubt in my mind about my feelings for him. Thankfully, he was persistent and a courtship developed. After just a few months of our getting to know one another, he asked for my hand in marriage. As a spinster soon to turn forty, I could hardly believe my good fortune.

Lionel knew how much I yearned to leave the turmoil of the city – which used to make me nervous and irritable – and, surprisingly, he admitted that he too was ready for a slower pace of life. He thus had little hesitation in agreeing to a timely proposition made by his fellow pharmacist and good friend, Mr Cecil Bradshaw, that he replace him upon his imminent retirement, due to poor health, from his Devonshire pharmacy. And so, by the end of the year, we had moved out of London and settled here in pretty Brampton-on-Sea, where the charms of both coast and countryside are practically on our doorstep.

Mind you, although Lionel said he was ready for the change, it did take him a while to get used to working in a country town where life is so much slower than in the city. The locals, although suspicious at first of such a suave outsider, are now so much at ease in his presence that they are often ready to reveal not just their ailments, but their whole life stories as well – romantic entanglements included! Lionel found the relaxed, familiar ways of his customers exasperating to begin with, but is now so amused by their conversations that he often regales me at mealtimes with the latest piece of local gossip.

As for me, I am used to the customs of small towns and villages, so for once, I can educate Lionel, which is a rarity indeed. But I must admit that it's taking me some time to adjust to my new status as a married woman. I spent most of my adult life in service at Farringdale House, the West Country home of Lord and Lady Radcliffe. When the Radcliffes' eldest daughter, Lady Sophia, with whom I was especially close, married an Italian count and moved to Rome, there were rumours circulating that the house's domestic staff needed to be cut. It was then that I decided it was time for a change. Encouraged by my close friend Patty, who had been living in London for more than a year, I applied for the position of companion to Mrs Grist, although I was convinced that my application would not even be considered. No one could have been more surprised than I was when Mrs Grist wrote to inform me that I'd been selected for the job.

My new position, however, was not one that I particularly enjoyed. While there was very little 'work' to be done in my new role – at least not in terms of the physical toil I was used to – I did find it mentally exhausting. Mrs Grist was not an easy person to get along with, and I was full of doubt as to my ability to be a worthy companion. But fortunately, Lionel came to my rescue. He was a godsend in those first difficult weeks, chiding me for my lack of self-confidence and encouraging me to believe in myself. His friendship and support helped me overcome my frequent bouts of anxiety, which would often make me so tense that I had difficulty engaging in coherent conversation with Mrs Grist. I'd then become quite panic-stricken, as the ability to converse was, after all, one of the main requirements of my job!

I cannot believe that so much has happened in such a short space of time, when for year after year, my life witnessed no changes from one day to the next. In fact, being so unaccustomed to it, I was terrified of change. But Lionel taught me that change is part of life and we need to be prepared for it. During the months when we were getting to know one another, I could not overcome the fear that I would end up with my reputation in tatters and be dismissed from my job. Even though I enjoyed Lionel's company and trusted him, I could not believe it possible that his intentions towards me were honourable. After all, as a widower who was respected throughout the borough, he might have taken his pick from any number of eligible ladies with whom he regularly came into contact. Thankfully, all my fears were unfounded. But the fact that he chose to marry someone as unrefined and timid as myself still continues to amaze me.

For the first part of the morning, I potter around the house, doing a bit of dusting and polishing, then I peel the potatoes, carrots and turnips for the beef hotpot that I'm making for our evening meal. Lionel takes sandwiches for a quick lunch break and closes the pharmacy at five o'clock sharp. Wednesday is the exception; it being half-day closing, he's home by half past one and we are able to enjoy a leisurely lunch together. It's the day of the week I look forward to most of all, apart from Sunday, of course.

Our cottage is not a particularly large one, at least not by London standards, though compared to the dwellings in the village where I grew up, it's a mansion. We have three bedrooms, a modern kitchen, and a bathroom with a water closet, which is quite a luxury for me. As there are just the two of us, it doesn't take a lot of work to keep the house clean and tidy, but being a housewife is still so new to me that I feel I have to 'earn my keep' by finding chores to do throughout the entire day, either inside or out. But, as I tell Lionel when he says I should slow down, it's not drudgery at all; it's a pleasure to be cleaning and cooking in my own home, having lived and worked for so long in the houses of other folk.

A sizeable vegetable patch at the back of the house keeps me busy for an hour or two most days, as I'm having to relearn the gardening knowledge that Father taught me when I was a girl. And since the flower borders in the front garden also require my attention – as my city born-and-bred husband claims not to possess any horticultural skills whatsoever – my afternoons are often spent out of doors. Lionel tells me time and time again to pursue my interests rather than devote all my time to household tasks, but it's not in my nature to take things easy. If I do put my feet up during a rainy afternoon, then I will usually occupy myself with knitting or sewing. I love to read, but rarely indulge in that favourite pastime during daylight hours. In the evenings, though, while Lionel is reading the newspaper or absorbed in one of his medical journals, I'll often pick up a popular novel and lose myself in a page-turning saga – a sticky romance more often than not.

For me, our peaceful evenings together are one of the highlights of married life. The quiet companionship that exists between us is something I've only recently learnt to appreciate. Growing up with three siblings in a small cottage, and then going straight to work at Farringdale House, I seldom had the opportunity to enjoy tranquillity or time for reflection. At the 'big house', as we called it, I used to share a bedroom with one or more of the other domestic staff, and they were usually ardent chatterboxes. But they were kind, big-hearted girls, and I missed them terribly when I left for London. Before my acquaintance with Lionel made life in the city tolerable, there were times when I felt so miserable and friendless that I cried myself to sleep.

Every other Sunday, however, I would take tea with my friend Patty and her husband Robert in Clapham, visits that I looked forward to with much anticipation. But seeing Patty so happy and content, along with her mother Celia, in their small but cosy terraced cottage, made me feel more alone than ever when I returned to Mrs Grist's spacious but unwelcoming three-storey house. Not that I would ever have begrudged Patty her happiness, as her life before she met Robert had not been an easy one and, like me, she was well into her thirties by the time she found happiness in marriage.

By mid-morning, I feel I've done enough to justify being able to sit down with a cup of tea and a biscuit, and open Walter's letter. Walter is the only living child of my late sister Ethel, who died in childbirth when he was just five years old. My eldest brother Edward and his wife Mabel took him into their home after his father, Frederick Blanch, left Ferndell – never to return – shortly after Ethel's death. Over the years, Walter has become like a son to me, although I couldn't see him as often as I would have liked to because of my work at Farringdale House. Nonetheless, we did spend most Sunday afternoons together throughout his childhood, and those were special times for both of us. He is now twenty-one years old and works independently as a stonemason, travelling wherever his skills are needed and dutifully writing me letters, or sending postcards, from every new location. He has a sweetheart in the village – a young lady by the name of Miss Blanche Goode – and they've recently become engaged. She's a sweet girl and I'm glad that Walter has found happiness again, as his heart was broken when his earlier courtship with the lovely Miss Edie Bancroft ended on a sour note.

As I've said, he writes to me regularly and, while there's seldom much that is newsworthy in his letters, I love to hear about his and Blanche's day-to-day lives and the current goings-on in Ferndell. Slitting open the envelope with a knife and pulling out a double-sided sheet of writing paper, I'm expecting a letter not so different from the ones I've received ever since moving away from the village. But this one is far from similar. The news that Walter conveys comes as a terrible shock and causes me considerable distress. He writes:

Dearest Aunt Bessie,

I'm afraid I'm the bearer of sad news, so I hope you're sitting down when you read this. I'm sure you will have heard about the terrible sinking in the North Atlantic Ocean of the passenger liner, the RMS Titanic, *a month ago. As you will recall, it struck an iceberg on its maiden voyage to New York, and many people lost their lives, although some managed to get into lifeboats and were eventually picked up by another steamship. Well, dear Aunt, I'm sorry to tell you that Blanche's Aunt Hilda may have been one of those who perished on that fateful night. I have waited a while before telling you this, as I was hoping and praying that we would receive news that she had survived, but to date we have heard nothing.*

We are led to believe, however, that a lot of the women on board were rescued, since many male passengers and most of the crew bravely sacrificed their lives so that the women and children could access the lifeboats first. But Blanche's aunt was travelling in third class, so it may have been difficult for her to reach the upper deck in time to secure a place in one of the too few lifeboats being launched.

I don't know if you have ever met Mrs Hilda Doyle, Aunt. She became a widow just before her twin sister, Yvonne Goode, Blanche's mother, lost her beloved Henry. Hilda was not well-off by any means, but she had been left a small sum of money by her late husband, so decided to embark on the voyage of a lifetime. She planned to visit her son Ernest, who was soon to be married in New York. As you can well imagine, the thought that she may not have survived the sinking is causing the family a great deal of anguish, but we haven't given up hope just yet. We are still praying that she was rescued and that we will soon receive a letter or telegram either from Hilda herself, or from Ernest.

I will write with more, hopefully happier news, in the coming weeks.

Your loving nephew,
Walter

I've been so busy digesting this terrible news that my tea has become cold. My hands are shaking as I place Walter's letter in my lap. I remember only too well the shocking 16th of April headline in Lionel's copy of the *London Evening News*, which read, *Titanic Disaster: Great Loss of Life*, and our feeling of disbelief that such a celebrated ship could sink on its maiden voyage. The distress that the Goode family – Mrs Yvonne Goode and her three daughters – must presently be suffering, not having received any news at all of Hilda's fate, is painful for me to envision. It's often worse when one doesn't have certainty; waiting day in, day out, for a letter or telegram to confirm whether a loved one is alive and well, soon to be tenderly embraced, or will never be returning home. My heart goes out to these good people, and especially to Hilda's son in New York, who is perhaps still waiting for news of his mother, on the eve of what would normally be a joyous event.

I can think of nothing else for the rest of the day and wish that Lionel would come home sooner. When he does return, I hand him Walter's letter.

"This is dreadful news, Lionel," I say. "Read it for yourself. I still can't quite believe it."

"I'm so sorry, Bessie," he says, handing the letter back to me after reading its contents. "The loss of life from that tragedy amounts to more than a thousand souls. Many bodies have not been recovered – and never will be – so those who were *not* pulled from the water and taken to New York for identification are presumed to be dead. Far be it from me to suggest that the Goode family cease hoping and praying that their relative has survived, but if they haven't received any news from America by now, then I really do fear the worst."

"Oh, Lionel, do you really think there's no hope at all that Hilda may be alive?"

"There's always hope, but the chances are slim. It's said that the names of the survivors – those who were picked up from the lifeboats by the RMS *Carpathia*, the rescue ship – have been published. Hilda's son, being in

America, should know whether or not his mother's name was on the list. Why has he not written to his aunt? He must surely be aware that the Goodes are sick with worry."

"Do you think her visit might have been intended as a surprise, and that Ernest had no idea his mother was sailing on the *Titanic*?"

"I doubt it, Bessie. For a woman to travel alone in that way would have taken no small amount of courage, and I don't think she'd have embarked on such a journey without knowing for certain that she'd be met in New York by her son. But it can't be too difficult for *us* to obtain a copy of the American newspaper in which the survivors were named. Leave it with me, Bessie. I'll see if I can request this information from London. I'm sure Ronald will know whom to approach."

"The Goodes may not want to see a list of survivors if it doesn't include Hilda's name, but I suppose it's better for them to know the truth. I'm sure that if Ernest *did* have any news – be it good or bad – he would have sent a telegram. But, as Walter says, the family have received nothing and the tragedy happened over a month ago. Perhaps Ernest is unable to accept that his mother is deceased, and is trying to convince himself that she's still alive."

"Yes, possibly. Poor boy. What did Walter say the lady's name was?"

"Doyle… Mrs Hilda Doyle. She married an Irishman against her family's wishes, or so I was told. But he died almost two years ago, a few months before Blanche's mother, Yvonne Goode, lost her own dear husband. Henry Goode was a close friend of both my brothers, and Walter too, but we didn't have much to do with the

Doyles, who tended to keep themselves to themselves."

"Let me make a note of the name. I'll write to Ronald first thing in the morning. I believe he has some contacts at the American Embassy. You know Ronald, he has connections everywhere. I'm sure he'll have no trouble at all in obtaining an up-to-date list of the survivors."

Ronald Cavendish is Lionel's son-in-law. Ronald and Mathilda – my husband's only child from his first marriage – are happily married and have a beautiful son, Geoffrey, born last year. Only last week, we received the joyous news that Mathilda is again with child. Why is it that good news is often followed by bad, and vice-versa?

"Thank you, Lionel," I say, putting Walter's letter aside. "Let me lay the table now. You must be hungry. I'm a bit behind with everything, I'm afraid. Ever since receiving that letter, I don't seem to have been able to concentrate on anything else."

I always seem to be involving Lionel in my troubles, expecting him to provide a solution or at least some reassurance. Perhaps this is common in married life, but I do sometimes feel ashamed that it's never the other way round. I don't think he's once come to me with a problem, and often I only find out about something that's been troubling him when he's already put it to rights.

After supper, we sit facing the open front window, enjoying the gentle breeze and the natural light of the May evening. I have a book of poems by Alfred Lord Tennyson on my lap – a farewell gift from Mrs Grist – and Lionel has taken up the newspaper, but is not reading it. He knows instinctively that I'm thinking about the sinking of the *Titanic*, so he begins to speak about the tragedy.

"Bessie," he says, "I know you want to believe that Mrs Doyle may have survived, but you must understand that it's unlikely. As Walter has intimated in his letter, those in third class were the least likely to have been able to reach the lifeboats in time. And I read in the newspaper that there weren't enough lifeboats on the ship to begin with. Passengers who managed to get a place in one of them – and Walter is right, women and children *were* given preference – stood a better chance of survival, but it was four hours before the RMS *Carpathia* came to the rescue, and by that time some may have already perished, either from the shock or exposure to the freezing temperatures. As for those who jumped and hoped to swim to safety, it's believed that most died within minutes. Only a handful were able to reach the lifeboats that were already moving away from the ship as it began to go under, posing a danger to the boats staying afloat.

"Two inquiries are taking place, one in America and one in London, which will no doubt reveal that many mistakes were made. Already it's been confirmed that no lifeboat drills had taken place since the *Titanic* set sail. And, despite the knowledge of icebergs in the vicinity, the ship was travelling at almost maximum speed. It's rumoured that the chairman of the White Star Line – Mr Bruce Ismay – was intent on reaching New York in record time, and he put pressure on the captain to increase the ship's speed. Sheer madness, if you ask me. At least the captain did the honourable thing and went down with his ship, but Ismay took a place in one of the last lifeboats. This is a catastrophe, Bessie, that could have been avoided."

"Oh, Lionel," I say, wiping away a tear. "I know you only want to make me face up to reality, but I can't bear to think of Blanche's aunt perishing in the freezing waters of the Atlantic. Even though her death itself may have been an immediate one, she must have been absolutely terrified in the hours or minutes beforehand, knowing that the ship was sinking and that she would be unable to save herself. And if she did perish, then her death will surely haunt her family for the rest of their lives."

"You're a churchgoer, Bessie. You know that God will give them the strength to bear it. And we should seek solace in the knowledge that He would have been with the poor lady when she needed Him the most. If she *is* no longer among us, then we must try to be comforted by the fact that she is at peace, with her Father in Heaven."

It's not often that Lionel talks about religion, as he doesn't attend church himself and is often sceptical of the Bible's teachings, so it's clear that he's trying to console me and make the woeful news less painful to endure. I thank him for his thoughtful words and tell him that I'm going to retire early. In my prayers, I shall ask the good Lord to bless the Doyle and Goode families and give them succour in the knowledge that His ways, while we cannot always understand them, are infinitely higher than ours.

2

I pass a sleepless night thinking about Walter's letter and its worrying news. For once, I'm anxious to get up in the morning and start my chores. When Lionel comes downstairs for his breakfast at half past seven, he finds me on my knees scrubbing the kitchen floor.

"Bessie," he says, "this must be at least the fifth time this week you've cleaned that floor. There are only the two of us. How can it possibly get so dirty?"

"Probably because I'm in and out of the back garden most days," I say. "If I'm not planting seeds, then I'm digging up vegetables. Besides, you can never have a floor that's too clean. I learnt that at Farringdale House."

"I'm sure that the floors in Farringdale House are not nearly as spotless as ours, my dear. Would it please you if I took my meals off the kitchen floor? No germs could possibly be lurking there."

Lionel loves to make fun of me, but – try as I might – I can never be a lady of leisure like my former employer, Mrs Grist, or the Radcliffe ladies at Farringdale House. To be fair to Lady Marguerite Radcliffe, though, she does undertake a lot of charitable works and uses her influence to advantage in a number of social campaigns. The last one that she was passionate about – or so I've heard from village friends – was the introduction of a minimum wage for the coal miners. There was a national strike earlier this year, which caused a lot of distress before the government finally gave in to the miners' demands after thirty-seven days of unrest. Mind you, not everyone was as sympathetic to the plight of the miners as Lady Radcliffe, who was tireless in drawing attention to the dangers they faced each and every working day, and in insisting that they had a God-given right to a decent wage. And that wasn't her first involvement with the mining industry. She also gave her support and campaigned endlessly for the introduction of the 1900 Act that prevented boys under the age of thirteen from going down the mines.

I sometimes wish I had a good cause that I could become involved in now that I no longer have to earn my own living. In the meantime, I do need to keep myself occupied, even if my daily activities tend to resemble those of a chambermaid rather than the wife of the town pharmacist. The transition from domestic employee to lady's companion was hard enough; I found it hard not to confuse my role with that of the housekeeper and was frequently treading on her toes, for which Mrs Grist reprimanded me on more than one occasion. Now that I'm a housewife, answerable only to my husband, the least I can do is keep the house clean and tidy, and make sure our meals are ready on time. But I don't think Lionel would notice if I didn't clean for a week, and he never complains if food isn't on the table when he arrives home in the evening.

"You make work for yourself, Bessie," he tells me. "As I've said to you before, there's really no need. But I do understand the way you feel. You want to keep busy. That's one of the things I admire about you. You've worked all your life and you're not used to being without an occupation."

"Well, I certainly wouldn't choose to go back to any of my past jobs," I say, giving him his bowl of porridge. "But it's true, Lionel, I don't like being lazy. The devil makes work for idle hands, as Father used to say."

"I hardly think the devil would look upon you as a likely candidate, my dear. But I have an idea. I was going to tell you about it last night, but you were understandably upset by Walter's news, and so was I. So let me tell you now. You've seen what a large storeroom I have at the pharmacy. I only need a quarter of that space for my provisions. I was thinking that you might consider tutoring one or two of the local children in reading, like you did with Michael Turnbull in London. I hate to see you spending all your time cooking and doing housework. You have a brain and it pleases me to see you use it."

"Oh, Lionel, I really don't need to be doing anything outside the house. I don't mind doing housework – in fact, I enjoy it. I feel so proud of the fact that it's *our* house I'm keeping spick and span, and happy that my toil is for *us*, not for the pleasure of others. Besides, Michael was a special case. He'd only recently lost his mother, and he missed his sister terribly and worried for her wellbeing. He was also being teased and bullied at school, at least to start with, and had few friends. Michael is different from most boys his age – he was more than content to sit with me, talk about his troubles and read *David Copperfield*, with whom he felt a kinship. But these local children... I don't think there's much I could do to help them. I doubt that they'd be interested in reading books with me or with anyone else."

"I think you're wrong, Bessie, but I don't want to force you. Just think about it. The children themselves may not want to be tutored, but if their parents think it will be good for them, then they won't have a say in the matter. If they *do* resist the lessons, it may be harder for you than it was with Michael, but that will make it more of a challenge. I think it will do you good. I remember how bored you were as Fanny Grist's companion, and how much you looked forward to those bi-weekly sessions with Michael on Sunday afternoons. I'm sure that, once you start, you'll enjoy helping the local children with their reading, and the lessons will give you a much-needed sense of satisfaction."

"I don't know about that, Lionel. It was Patty's husband Robert who introduced me to Michael. He understood that the boy needed some guidance. But we don't know anything about the children here. If they're not keen on learning and are difficult to manage, I don't think I could cope."

"Well, as I said, give it some thought. No need to rush into anything."

Now that *has* given me something to think about. Lionel is right though; I did enjoy the reading sessions with young Michael, especially since all he really needed was empathy and encouragement. Robert, who works as a groundsman at Michael's boarding school, was concerned about the boy, as he'd heard that he was falling behind in his lessons. He knew from Patty that I was a keen reader and had long ago dreamed of becoming a teacher, so suggested that I sit with Michael every other week and, with the aid of a good book, try to take his mind off his troubles.

I know only too well that few children are as amenable to reading novels as Michael was. Unless the story can capture their imaginations, they're going to look upon their time with me as an imposition, especially when they could be out playing with their friends after school. But I suppose that would be part of the challenge – to help them regard reading as an enjoyable occupation rather than a chore. And if I *had* become a teacher, then I would have had to handle children with a whole range of different abilities and behavioural issues.

My hopes of becoming a teacher had ended at the age of fourteen, when Father died and Mother persuaded Farringdale House, where she herself had worked before marriage, to give me a job as a chambermaid. So, within a month, I had left both my school and my family home. I did understand that, by leaving home, I would be one less mouth for Mother to feed, and I raised no objections at the time. But, in my heart of hearts, I've always resented being forced to abandon my childhood dream.

Punctual as ever, Lionel returns home at half past five. I'm in the back garden gathering some stalks of rhubarb for a crumble I plan to make tomorrow morning. Lionel hangs up his hat, takes off his jacket, waistcoat and tie, and puts on the sleeveless Fair Isle pullover that I knitted for his last birthday.

"Ah, that's better," he says, coming out into the garden. "Can I help you at all, Bessie?"

"No, thank you, Lionel," I say. "I'm just picking this rhubarb while it's still young and fresh. Give me ten minutes and I'll have our meal on the table."

"Don't fret yourself, Bessie. There's no hurry. Come and sit with me for a few minutes here on the bench. It's still warm in the sun. If this good weather continues, we can go for a walk on the beach at the weekend."

The beach is about half an hour's walk from our house. Before we moved to Devon, I had never before set eyes on the sea. The first time Lionel took me to the seashore, I was lost for words. No seascape painting, picture postcard or storybook illustration could have prepared me for its magnificence. I never once imagined that I would one day look upon such a vast and powerful body of water in real life, and it was truly an experience I'll never forget.

"Oh, that will be lovely, Lionel," I say, sitting down next to him. "We can take some sandwiches and have a picnic. And I can look for shells to send to Michael and to Richard, brother Harold's youngest."

"Then that's settled. By the way, have you given any thought to my suggestion this morning, Bessie?"

"Yes, Lionel, I have. I'm prepared to give it a try, though to be honest, I still have my doubts as to whether any parent will agree to their child being tutored by someone as unskilled as myself. But one thing I must insist upon is that the lessons should be free of charge. I won't accept payment, as I can't guarantee that any progress will be made."

"The problem with that, Bessie, is that the lessons might be looked upon as charity. The locals are a proud bunch of people and will be hesitant to accept something for nothing. But we'll tell them that it's a free service that's sanctioned by the school, and see how they react. I'll have a word with the local schoolteacher, just to be sure he has no objections. I *am* glad you're in agreement, my dear – it'll be good for you to have an interesting occupation that will take you out of the house. You need to stop underestimating your talents. I've told you that many times."

"You have indeed. But I've been wondering how we'll *find* those who need help. I'll wager that many of the parents have no idea as to whether or not their children are reading fluently. I'm not sure that it's any different here than it is in Ferndell. Some of the parents may not even be literate themselves."

"Well, I was thinking of putting an advertisement on the pharmacy door. But you're right, only those who are literate will be able to read it. Still, news travels fast in a small town and word of mouth may work better than any advertisement."

"Very well. We'll just have to wait and see if there's any interest. Now, tell me Lionel, did you manage to write to Ronald about the list of *Titanic* survivors?"

"Yes, I did. I told him that we only needed to know whether or not Mrs Hilda Doyle's name was on the list, so suggested that he either send a message or pay a visit to his contact in the American Embassy. I'm sure he'll act on it right away."

"How soon do you think you might hear from him?"

"Probably by next week, one way or the other. But don't raise your hopes, Bessie. As I told you, I think it's highly improbable that she's still alive, given the absence of any communication from Hilda herself, or from her son."

"Well, if Walter and the Goode family have not yet given up home, then I shan't either. But thank you, Lionel. I know you're only trying to prepare me for the worst. Shall we go inside for our supper now? It's only sausages and mashed potato with chives, but I cut some young spring cabbage from the garden to go with it. And your favourite, apple tart and fresh cream for pudding."

Lionel's prediction was right; Hilda's name was not on the list of survivors. He broke it to me gently; he knows how quickly I can dissolve into tears. It was, indeed, disappointing news, but I still could not abandon all hope.

"But Lionel," I say after reading Ronald's letter, "how can we be sure the survivors' list is complete? Did they request the names of every single person who disembarked the rescue ship? Hilda might have seen Ernest waiting for her at the harbour and rushed into his arms before anyone had time to ask for her name."

"That's a beautiful thought, Bessie," Lionel says, "but it's hardly likely to have been the case. The survivors' names would have been taken aboard the RMS *Carpathia* long before it reached New York. And have you any idea how big the port of New York is? By all accounts, the *Carpathia* docked at a different pier from the one where the *Titanic* was expected, so I can't imagine that Hilda's son would have been there. I apologise for sounding so pessimistic, my dear. I'm just trying to be realistic. I told you not to get your hopes up."

"I know, Lionel. But I'm wondering what to do now. Am I to be the bearer of bad news? Do I write to Walter and tell him that Hilda is not a survivor? Is it my place to do so? I don't want to interfere in the private grief of the Goode family. And what if, by some miracle, she *has* survived? How will they ever forgive me for giving them false information?"

"Well, since Walter wrote to you about the tragedy, I think you do owe it to him to tell him what you know. Then it's for him to decide whether or not to tell Blanche and her family. He may prefer not to, but it really is *his* decision. If the Goodes want to go on hoping and praying that Hilda is still alive, then that's up to them. And who knows, they might have heard from Ernest by now and be aware of her fate."

"Yes, perhaps. Very well, I'll write to Walter tonight and post the letter tomorrow morning. Thank you, Lionel, for your good advice. I don't know how I'd ever manage without you."

"You managed without me for more than half a lifetime, my dear. Besides, I wouldn't call it advice – I'm just giving you my *views* on the matter. In a case such as this, it's hard to know what to do for the best. But I'm sure Walter will make the right decision once he receives your letter."

Later that evening, I begin a letter to Walter, struggling to find the right words.

My dear Walter, I write, after much procrastination, *I was so very saddened by the news that Blanche's Aunt Hilda may have lost her life on the* Titanic. *I can well imagine the pain that the Goode family is suffering at this time. I'm sure you'll agree that not knowing the fate of a loved one is sometimes worse than receiving the news we all dread. But until one receives such news, it would be wrong to give up hope. When he read your letter, Lionel decided to write to Ronald, Mathilda's husband, who has an acquaintance in the American Embassy in London. He asked him to find out if Hilda's name was on the list of* Titanic *survivors. Ronald's response was received today. It grieves me to tell you, dearest Walter, that there was no mention of Mrs Hilda Doyle. I hope you're not upset with Lionel and myself for interfering in this way, but we felt that it could do no harm. If, however, you think it best to keep this information to yourself, then we completely understand. As I said to Lionel, the fact that Hilda's name does not appear on the list doesn't necessarily mean that she was not rescued – there must surely be some survivors who weren't identified, and they may, at this very moment, be alive and well in America. Needless to say, I do hope that Mrs Goode's nephew will write soon and put all our minds at rest. In the meantime, I send all my love to you and Blanche, and will continue to pray for the Goode and Doyle families. Your ever-loving aunt, Bessie.*

I hope Walter can read my messy handwriting. I should have waited until the morning, as I'm too tired at this hour to write in a neat script. And it's clear that my pen needs a new nib – it's almost scratched a hole in my precious writing paper, a present from my dear friends Patty and Robert for my last birthday. Patty, knowing that I'm an avid letter-writer and am often running out of stationery, could not have sent me a more thoughtful and useful gift.

That reminds me – I owe Patty a letter. We grew up together in Ferndell and she has long been my closest friend. Patty was reconciled to being a lifelong spinster, but then – as chance would have it – she met Robert, a Londoner, on a train journey. Now they are happily married and live close to the boys' boarding school where Robert works. Celia Harris, Patty's widowed mother, lives with them and has adapted much more easily to city life than Patty, who misses the countryside as much as I did when I lived in London. Bearing a child of her own had never seemed possible for Patty; she'd been a victim of polio as a child and was convinced she would be unable to conceive. But the good Lord had other ideas in mind. Patty gave birth to a healthy daughter last September, and this little miracle continues to delight and astound her doting parents and grandmother.

I'll write to Patty in the next day or two. First, I need

to finish the little jacket I'm knitting for baby Agnes, so that I can send it with the letter. Patty and Robert decided to name their daughter after the late mother of Michael Turnbull and his older sister Harriet. Robert and I first met Harriet at the orphanage where she'd been sent after Mr and Mrs Turnbull died in a housefire. That terrible inferno may well have been started deliberately by Mr Turnbull, who was angry and intoxicated at the time, but the true cause of the tragic incident may never be known. Although an uncle assumed the role of Michael's guardian, he wanted nothing to do with Harriet and, to the children's great dismay, they were separated. But, thankfully, Harriet's time at the orphanage was short; she's been living with Patty and Robert for more than a year now, and is a great help to Patty in caring for the baby, while at the same time learning dressmaking from Celia, a skilled seamstress. In fact, when Agnes was born, Harriet's presence became invaluable, as Patty was an invalid for several weeks, hardly able to get up from the bed, let alone look after an infant.

It seems to me that I have more than enough to keep me busy, so I'm surprised that Lionel thinks I need greater activity in my life. Well, he might be right, at least in terms of scholarly pursuits. Perhaps the tutoring will give me something more interesting to talk to him about in the evenings. Even after a year of marriage, I'm still concerned that he might find my company tedious, as he's so much more intelligent than I am. To be fair, though, he's never once given me the slightest indication that he is tired of my mundane chatter. Quite the opposite, in fact – he actually seems to enjoy it. But I do need to widen my interests and, for me, there is no better way to do that than by helping children learn to read.

I remember Father used to tell me that one should always endeavour to improve oneself, no matter how slightly. So, I will take his advice, which is the same as Lionel's. Oh Father! I do so wish you and Mother could see just how much I've improved myself since Lionel Fielding came into my life and gave it the meaning it had been lacking for so long. And, believe me, in all the long years that have elapsed since I lost you and Mother, our darling Ethel and my beloved fiancé Arthur, never have I felt so cherished.

3

Lionel has placed an advertisement on the door of the pharmacy. It reads: 'Reading help available for children ages six to eleven. Apply directly to the pharmacist'. Now I'm on tenterhooks, half hoping that no one applies, though I know I'll be disappointed if that turns out to be the case.

A week passes without any enquiries. But Lionel tells me he's seen several customers read the advertisement and that I just need to be patient. He's confident that some concerned parent may eventually decide to take up the offer.

If the reading sessions do come to pass, I hope that they may lead to my making one or two friends in Brampton-on-Sea. I have no complaints about my life here – being married to Lionel is wonderful in every way – but I sometimes miss having a close female friend, like Patty for instance, with whom I can talk about matters that wouldn't interest a man. Our house here is quite isolated – we have no immediate neighbours – so there's no opportunity to chat over the garden fence, as folk used to do in the village where I grew up.

Just as I was beginning to give up hope of ever hearing from an interested parent, Lionel tells me that a Mrs Rose Frost has made an enquiry on behalf of her nine-year-old son, Andrew.

"Apparently," Lionel says, "The poor boy is being teased at school for being *backward* because he can't read as fluently as some of his classmates, and this has resulted in his falling behind even more. Mrs Frost says her husband is away a lot of the time and she has five other children, so she has no time to help him, even if he'd let her, which he won't. When she asked, rather hesitantly, what your fee was, I told her not to worry about payment, that you'll be happy to teach Andrew free of charge. She seemed rather surprised and said she found it odd that you'd do it voluntarily. I said it was something you'd done before, that you enjoyed it and found it rewarding in more ways than one. Is that all right with you, Bessie?"

"Yes, of course. We'd already agreed that I wouldn't charge for the lessons. What is she like, this Mrs Frost? Is she a regular customer? Have you met her son?"

"She strikes me as rather sharp-tongued, though polite. Certainly not the type to linger and waste time chatting. I think she has her hands full most of the time. She's usually in a hurry and visits the pharmacy for some kind of pick-me-up for herself. My tonics usually do the trick. I've not met the boy yet."

"I see," I say, thinking that such a person is unlikely to become my friend. "So, when will *I* meet the boy, Lionel?"

"Well, first we have to make my back room more habitable than it is at the moment. There's a fireplace in there, but it looks like it hasn't been used for years and the chimney probably needs sweeping. But we don't need to worry about that at the moment. We can just rearrange the furniture – there's already a table and some chairs – and perhaps I can buy a second-hand bookcase. You can select any books you think you might need from the local bookshop, Bessie. The owner's name is Mr Franklin and he sells used books as well as new ones."

"Do I really need to buy books for the tutoring, Lionel? I have one or two I can use to begin with."

"You mean your old copy of *David Copperfield*? I know how much you love that book, and rightly so, but it's not the only book that will fit the purpose. No, my dear. Go into town and browse the shelves of Mr Franklin's shop. You'll like him – he's knowledgeable *and* friendly. Feel free to buy as many books as you like. The ones you don't use with Andrew may come in useful later on. And choose a book for yourself too. I don't see you reading as much as you used to. Is it because my collection is not as extensive as Mrs Grist's? Admittedly, many of the volumes are scientific or technical, and only of interest to boring people like myself."

"Oh, Lionel, I'm the one who's boring, not you. And I love looking at your books, even if I don't understand them very well. I just feel that I shouldn't be sitting down to read when chores still need to be done. It's kind of you to tell me to buy something for myself, but it's not necessary. I'm reading Miss Austen's *Mansfield Park* at the moment."

"You've been reading that for weeks, Bessie. I insist that you finish it within the next month. I'm sorry for being such a hard taskmaster, but I don't want you to lose your interest in reading."

"You're quite the opposite of a hard taskmaster, Lionel. You're suggesting that I neglect my household chores and spend my time reading books. I can't do that! Rest assured, I'll always be passionate about books, but I find it difficult to read when something is troubling me. My mind keeps wandering and nothing sinks in. I instantly forget what I've just read. You see, I'm still thinking about Hilda Doyle and whether or not Walter has told the Goode family that she wasn't on the *Titanic* survivors' list. I'm sorry I keep bringing this up, but I don't seem to be able to think about anything else."

"You don't need to apologise, Bessie," Lionel says, taking my hand. "It's normal that you should be upset. It's a terrible state of affairs. You've known the Goodes all your life and now Walter is soon to join their family. Didn't you tell me that your other nephew is engaged to Blanche's sister?"

"Yes, Joseph is engaged to Daisy, the eldest of the three girls. You met him at Harold's house, remember? He's the same age as Walter. He and Daisy plan to tie the knot at the end of the summer, and I daresay we'll be invited to the wedding."

"Then we'll make sure we're free to attend."

After our wedding in London last year, Lionel and I visited Ferndell and he met some members of my family. He was much more enthusiastic about the visit than I was. Don't get me wrong, I love my family, but I wasn't sure how they would react to someone as educated and cultured as Lionel. But, in his usual fashion, he put everyone at ease, except perhaps brother Edward, who never has much to say at the best of times and regards all city dwellers with suspicion. Thankfully, Walter was there to smooth over any awkward moments caused by my eldest brother.

Walter attended our nuptials – in fact, he walked me down the aisle – but other family members felt they couldn't afford or spare the time to travel to London. And they might not have wanted to come anyway. I suppose it was generally felt that we should have chosen to be married in Ferndell, but Lionel and I didn't want a big wedding and, in opting for London as our venue, we were able to be married quietly, with only a few guests present.

Besides, I was afraid that some of the villagers might think I was becoming too 'high and mighty', although even in London, our nuptials were on a modest scale. Lionel scoffed at my qualms and said it didn't matter what other people thought, and he was right. It was our happiness as a couple that counted most on that occasion.

I think Lionel enjoyed the afternoon we spent with my younger brother Harold's family. He and Dorothy have three children; besides Joseph, there is Margaret who is seventeen and Richard who has just turned thirteen. Dorothy is quite entertaining, and she'd really made an effort with the teatime spread. Everything was delicious, especially the chocolate cake, which young Margaret had baked. I was amazed at how grown-up Margaret had become, quite a beauty in fact. Dorothy says she's stepping out with the son of the local greengrocer and, although it's still early days, they appear to be inseparable. After tea, Margaret played the piano for us and showed as much talent in her playing as in her baking. Their piano was just an old upright and needed tuning, but even Lionel said she played faultlessly.

I began a correspondence with Margaret when we moved to Devon and suggested that, if she has time, she might like to come and stay with us during the summer. She was thrilled by the invitation and told me that she is longing to see the sea for the first time. I must remember to write and suggest dates, since we're already approaching the end of May and the days are becoming both warmer and longer.

I decide to postpone visiting the local bookshop until I have some knowledge of Andrew's reading ability. Once I've met him and we've talked for a bit, I'll have a better idea of how to proceed. It was easy with Michael because he was a couple of years older, and it soon became clear to me that he could read fluently and didn't need tuition at all. We read only one book – *David Copperfield* – and because we spent such a lot of time talking, we didn't even manage to finish that. But I later bought him a second-hand copy that he could share with his sister. I read that novel with Walter when he was a child, and it's become one of my all-time favourites. It turned out to be a good choice for Michael, as there were some similarities between David's life – aspects of which were drawn from Mr Dickens' personal experiences – and his own. But I don't believe this particular book will be suitable for a nine-year old. I was taking a chance on it with Michael and it paid off, but I think I need to put my well-thumbed copy to one side for now.

A book that I already own and which I think might be suitable is *The Wind in the Willows*, by Kenneth Grahame. It's a children's book, but one that grown-ups can enjoy equally – in my opinion at least. It was published just a few years ago, but I managed to obtain a used copy – although it looked brand new to me – from the bookshop in Wandsworth. I'd been shopping for Christmas presents and happened to see it lying on the shelf in the children's section. I couldn't resist picking it up and having a quick browse, though I had no intention of buying it, since my resources were limited. The shopkeeper, however, sensed my interest and offered to sell it to me at a bargain price. I am so pleased I ended up owning a copy, as the story has brought me many hours of pleasure. Lionel laughs when he sees me reading it – for about the fourth or fifth time – but I make no apologies. I think if he were to read it too, he'd love it just as much.

In the evening, I tell him that I intend to use my copy

of *The Wind in the Willows* for the reading session with Andrew, so had no need to go to the bookshop.

"Why is it so difficult for you to spend my money?" he asks with a chuckle. "I tell you to buy a new dress and you say the ones Fanny Grist gave you will be good for years to come. I suggest that we replace this old settee and worn leather armchair, and you say, no, they are so comfortable and you've grown attached them. And now, I propose that you buy some books, both for yourself and your young pupil, and you don't want to do that either. But I'm not complaining, Bessie. I just never thought I'd end up marrying someone who was so intent on making me a rich man."

"Oh, Lionel," I say, "you should have known before you married me that I'm not a spendthrift at all. For myself, I can make do with the bare minimum of material things, but perhaps *you* would like something more stylish. I'm talking mainly about the furniture. It's true that I've become attached to your old possessions, but if you really want to replace any item, I shan't stop you. As for dresses, I don't see the point of buying more, when I have all the ones I need. Unless, of course, you're tired of seeing me in the same old frocks, hard-wearing though they are. I've read that women should make an effort always to appear attractive before their husbands, but since I've never thought of myself as attractive, I don't know where to begin."

"Honestly, Bessie, how can you say such a thing? You *are* attractive and I shall never tire of looking at you, whatever you're wearing. Anyway, where on earth are you reading such nonsense? I don't see you flicking through popular women's magazines. I know what Mathilda would say if she heard a remark like that. She'd argue, 'And what about the husband? Should *he* not make an effort to appear pleasing before his wife?' Fortunately for Ronald, she has no reason to accuse *him* of being slovenly, as he always looks immaculate. I'm not so sure that *I* measure up, though! You will tell me if I fall short, won't you, my dear?"

"Now it's *you* who's talking nonsense, Lionel. I've never seen you look anything but well-groomed, even on your days off. As for the magazines, Mrs Grist occasionally had certain ones delivered, or she borrowed copies from her sister-in-law, and sometimes I'd skim through them when she wasn't around. But I never took the contents seriously, as I knew I wasn't the right audience for such topics."

Lionel gives another chuckle. "It's true," he says, "you're *not* the right audience, but not for the reasons you think. You're too intelligent, Bessie, to take such frivolities seriously. Anyway, back to the subject of new clothes – and now *I'm* the one who's being frivolous – I've heard it said that new dresses make women happy, but perhaps I'm wrong about that. I seem to have been misled on many matters that concern the opposite sex."

"Well, they might make *some* women happy, Lionel, but I'm not one of them. To be honest, I can't remember the last time I went into a shop to be measured for a new dress. I've always received most of my clothes as hand-me-downs either from Lady Sophia Radcliffe or, more lately, from Mrs Grist. And, as you might expect, they're of good quality and taste, and will last me for a long time. But if I ever find myself longing for something new and fashionable, then I won't hesitate to let you know. And thank you, Lionel, for being the most generous man I've ever met."

"And how many men have you met that you can compare me with, my dear?"

"It's true, I haven't met many. But I'm sure that most men aren't anywhere near as generous as you are."

"We could continue to pay each other compliments all evening, Bessie. But let's return to the subject of books. What makes you think *The Wind in the Willows* is a good choice for a boy of nine? Isn't it about wild animals wearing clothes, talking to each other, messing about in boats and frolicking on the riverbank? But wait, let me guess, it reminds you of Walter's childhood when you used to read to him in the shade of a willow tree on the banks of the River Frome in Ferndell."

"The way you describe it does make it sound quite juvenile and silly. But it's really not such a childish tale. It's about friendship, embracing new experiences, having adventures and, oh, so many other things. I think adults can learn a lot from it. I started rereading it last night, just to refresh my memory, and I came across the sentence, 'After all, the best part of a holiday is perhaps not so much to be resting yourself, as to see all the other fellows busy working'. That's so true, isn't it, Lionel? But it's a very grown-up remark. Would a child ever say that? No, of course not. You really must read the book yourself, but I know you won't. And yes, it does remind me of my afternoons with Walter, but I don't need to read a book to remember those precious times. I think of them every single day."

"I know you do, my dear. And if you insist, I *will* read the book, or better still, you can read it to me. Sometimes my eyes are tired in the evening and I struggle to read the small print in the newspaper. Closing my eyes and listening to your melodious voice will be so much more relaxing."

"Melodious voice, indeed! I don't mind reading to you, but whether you'd actually listen to me is another question. If you're going to be closing your eyes, then most likely you'll drop off to sleep. Honestly, I never know whether or not you're making fun of me, Lionel. But it's all right, I have a better idea. We'll wait until Geoffrey's a little bit older and then you can read the story to him at bedtime when Mathilda and Ronald come to visit, or when we go to London. That way, you'll both be able to enjoy it."

"That's a good idea, though it'll be a while before our grandson is old enough to appreciate the tale. But whether or not he's able to understand it, reading him a story at bedtime will help him in learning to read later on and, hopefully, will ensure an interest in books for the rest of his life. Mathilda is an avid reader, but I have to admit that it's not thanks to me. Annette used to read to her every night, no matter how tired she was. I suppose, at the time, I thought it was a woman's job, but now I know better. Parents should share the task. I promise to make up for my past failings by reading to little Geoffrey as often as I can."

I always feel a bit awkward when Lionel mentions his former wife, Annette. She died from tuberculosis when Mathilda was just fourteen, the age I was when Father was taken from us. He doesn't talk about her often, and I feel I should encourage him to do so, rather than remain silent when her name is mentioned. It's just that I don't know what to say. He has a portrait photograph of her under a pile of papers in his desk drawer – I'm ashamed to admit that I found it when searching for a pair of scissors one afternoon – but the image is quite faded and

I couldn't really make out her features. I think I'll always remember Mrs Grist's remark; she said that Lionel's former wife was 'a quiet, mouse-like creature, but she understood the rules of social class and treated people accordingly'. She was making the point that, in contrast, Lionel and Mathilda treat everyone – rich and poor – equally, and it was clear from her tone and the frown on her face that she disapproved of that policy.

It hasn't escaped my notice that Lionel has just referred to Geoffrey as *our grandson*. I felt embarrassed when he handed me the baby the last time we were in London, saying, "Go to your grandmama, little Geoffrey Lionel." Mathilda was present and, thankfully, behaved as if it was quite normal that I should be considered his grandmother. I'm happy to accept the role, but feel sad that his true grandmother, Annette, will never have the joy of holding the bonny baby in her arms and kissing his rosy, chubby cheeks.

Mr Wright, the postman, has another letter for me this morning. I see him arriving on his bicycle and go to meet him at the front gate to save him from having to dismount. He's such a friendly young man and has told me more than once to call him 'Wrighty', as many of the locals do, but I can't bring myself to be so familiar. It also seems a little discourteous when he always makes a point of calling me Mrs Fielding, even though he knows my Christian name is Bessie.

As I expected, the letter is from Walter. Although I fear what he has to tell me, I tear the envelope open right away and hastily read its contents. He writes:

Dearest Aunt Bessie,

Thank you for your kind letter and please convey my thanks to Uncle Lionel for asking his son-in-law to find out whether or not Blanche's Aunt Hilda was on the list of Titanic survivors. I was sorry to hear that there was no mention of her name, but it was what I expected. I have told only Blanche about this because, as you know, the rest of her family are still holding out hope that Hilda has somehow managed to survive. I suspect that Hilda's son Ernest is also waiting impatiently for some news, one way or the other, which is why he has not communicated with us. This constant thirst for news is painful for the family. The postman's arrival is awaited each day with great anticipation, but when there is no letter from America, it's hard for the family to disguise their feelings of despair.

Aunt Bessie, you'll be sorry to hear that Joseph and Daisy have postponed their wedding due to the tragedy. As you know, they were planning to marry at the end of the summer, but no one is in the mood for celebration at the moment, as I'm sure you will appreciate. I do so wish that Ernest would write to his aunt, telling her whatever little news he has – even if it's nothing at all – and let her know how he is coping and whether he too has postponed his wedding. No doubt it's painful for him to put pen to paper, but it would give Mrs Goode great relief to hear something from New York, be it good tidings or bad.

Rest assured, dear Aunt, if we receive any news at all, I will not hesitate to write to you again.

Your loving nephew,
Walter.

It doesn't surprise me that Walter has told only Blanche that Hilda's name is absent from the list of survivors. I felt from the start that it wasn't really our place to interfere, even though Lionel thought it would be better for them to know the facts rather than place their trust in wishful thinking. I'm not so sure I agree with him. How can anyone begin to grieve the loss of a loved one when there is no lifeless body to confirm that person's demise? Of course, the Goodes will continue to live with the anguish of not knowing Hilda's fate, but it seems wrong to behave as though she is no longer with us when that irrevocable fact has not been established. Perhaps if Ernest were to write and say that *he* has accepted his mother's death, then the family would likewise acknowledge it, but until then they are all resigned to hoping and praying for her safe return.

I am saddened by the news that Joseph and Daisy have decided to postpone their wedding. Joseph isn't much of a letter writer, but I hear from Walter that he is now living in a little cottage on the farm where he works, and that Daisy will move in with him once they are wed. Old Farmer Townsend has no living sons and would be lost without Joseph, who is able to put his hand to any number of tasks, both on the land and in caring for the livestock. Daisy has been busy making the cottage habitable and is so looking forward to beginning married life on the farm. But until her family's troubles begin to ease and their lives return to some degree of normality, it does make more sense for her, as the eldest daughter, to remain at home with her mother and sisters.

4

Mrs Rose Frost is to bring her son Andrew to the pharmacy after school today for a one-hour reading lesson. I shouldn't be nervous – after all, my sessions with Michael were a success and led to a lasting friendship – but I'm still lacking confidence in my ability to tackle new situations. Having grown up in a village, I know only too well how tongues love to wag, and the anonymity of London was the one thing about life there that I welcomed. But in this small town, I would hate it if rumours were to circulate that the pharmacist's wife – of humble background and with no formal academic skills – is promoting herself as a tutor.

"Why do you entertain such thoughts?" Lionel asks me. "Only a handful of the townsfolk will care about what you're doing, and what does it matter if others do find out? You'll probably be admired for taking such an initiative, especially as you're giving your time voluntarily."

"I'm not sure if I agree with you," I say. "But I can't back out now. The boy is coming for his lesson this afternoon."

"Well, as long as *you're* happy with tutoring the boy and feel that it's a worthy cause, then that's all that counts. Besides, I'll be here to protect you from the angry mob if it should arrive to make trouble!"

The back room of the pharmacy has been transformed. Lionel's boxes of provisions have been moved to one corner, a bookcase installed and the table cleared of its clutter. The window is open so I can feel the warm breeze and relish the fragrance of the climbing jasmine just outside the back door. I've brought along a bag of sweets, as I used to do with Michael. Since Andrew will probably resent having to come for a reading lesson straight after school, I suspect he'll need a bit of sweetening up.

Foolishly, I arrived early, so I'm sitting here alone becoming more and more nervous by the minute. Finally, I hear the bell on the pharmacy door ring and Lionel welcoming Mrs Frost and Andrew. When he brings them in to meet me, I notice right away that Mrs Frost looks as nervous as I feel, making me want to reassure *her*, rather than the other way around. Lionel makes the introductions and goes back to his work, giving me a comforting smile before he closes the door.

"Mrs Frost," I say, "you're welcome to stay if you want to, though I think Andrew might do better if you leave him alone with me for the next hour. But it's up to you entirely."

"Oh no, I can't stay," she says quickly. "I've got to get home and make a start on the tea. And I've left my other children on their own. I've six, you see. My eldest, Josephine, is fifteen, and the twins are the youngest – they're four, going on five. Andrew here is in the middle. I don't know if that's good or bad. He's nothing like his brothers and sisters, who are all keen to learn, even the twins. My second daughter, Violet, is two years younger than Andrew and can already read so much better than he can. So, I'll leave you to it, Mrs Fielding, and send his older brother Cyril – he turned twelve last week – to pick him up in an hour, if that's all right with you."

It's obvious that Mrs Frost disguises her nervousness by talking nineteen to the dozen. I'm quite the opposite; I tend to stay silent.

"That's perfectly fine," I say. "It'll give Andrew and myself time to get to know one another and for me to assess his reading level. If I have any message for you, I'll send a note home with him."

"Oh no, please give it to Cyril. I can't trust this one not to lose it."

Mrs Frost turns to her son and says sharply, "Now just you do as Mrs Fielding tells you. No nonsense, all right?"

The boy looks at the floor and says nothing. I know he's nervous by the way he's fiddling with a loose thread on his jersey, and is no doubt embarrassed that I'm a witness to his mother's harsh words. Mrs Frost gives a sigh and, after dutifully thanking me, leaves the room.

I don't really know where to start with Andrew. I do feel sorry for him. He looks so woebegone and reminds me of Michael when I first met him, with his thin, pale face and untidy brown hair. It was unkind of his mother to point out his weaknesses in his presence, and compare his reading ability with that of his younger sister.

"Now then, Andrew," I begin. "Let me first say that I've been really looking forward to meeting you and helping you with your reading. I hope that we'll both benefit from our time together."

The boy looks at me shyly, but says nothing.

"To start with," I continue, "I need to know how well you're able to read. Then we can decide on a book that we can read together. This isn't anything like school, so there's no need to worry. No one's going to force you to do anything you don't want to do. For today, we'll just sit together and talk about the books we've enjoyed reading. You can tell me the types of stories that take your fancy, and I'll see if I can find the right book for our next session. I've brought along this one to show you. Have you heard of *The Wind in the Willows*? It's a book that I've enjoyed enormously. Is this the type of book you think *you* might also enjoy?"

"I'm sorry," Andrew says, shaking his head, "but there's something you need to know. I will *never be able to read*. No one seems to understand that."

"Oh, I'm sure that's not true. You probably just need more practice. If need be, I can find an easier book for our next lesson. Don't worry, you'll be reading as well as your classmates in no time at all."

"It *is* true. I can't read a single word."

"Then we'll just have to start from the very beginning, won't we? Tell me, Andrew, do you know your alphabet?"

"Yes, but it doesn't help. When the letters are put together to make words, they mean nothing to me. I'm *backward* when it comes to reading."

"I don't think you're backward at all. If you're able to explain to me what your problem is, as you've just done, then half the problem is solved already. I'll find another book for next week and we'll take it one step at a time."

"It will never work."

"Never say never, as Mr Charles Dickens wrote in his first novel, *The Pickwick Papers*. Once you are able to read, then the fascinating world of books will be open to you, and you'll be amazed at what you can learn. You do *want* to read, don't you?"

"I don't care. I'm good at other things, like arithmetic. But no one praises me when I get my sums right. Violet can read, but she can't do sums. No one thinks *she's* a dunce. Why is reading more important than arithmetic?"

"Both are important. One skill complements the other.

If you're good at arithmetic, then there's no reason why you shouldn't also be good at reading and writing. Don't let me hear you say the words *backward* or *dunce* again. You need to have confidence in your ability to learn to read and write."

He remains silent. I can tell he thinks that the sessions with me are going to be a waste of time and, to be honest, I'm beginning to think the same myself. But I mustn't reveal that to the boy. It's quite ironic, really, that *I'm* the one telling *him* to have confidence when I've been brooding over my own lack of it for most of the day.

"For today," I continue, "I'll read out loud to you. I'll go slowly and point to the words I'm reading and you can follow along. The more you look at the words, the more they will eventually make sense to you. *The Wind in the Willows* is a story about animals that live on the riverbank and in nearby woodland. Rat, Mole, Toad and Badger are the main characters, and they have such a lot of adventures. I think you'll enjoy it."

"You mean it's about animals that talk, wear clothes and act like human beings?" Andrew says, looking at the book's cover. "Isn't that a bit silly?"

I'm beginning to wonder whether Andrew and Lionel have been communicating telepathically. I'm sure Mr Graeme wrote his book for boys and girls of all ages – and adults as well – to enjoy, but clearly only those with lively imaginations are able to appreciate a story about animals behaving like humans.

"It may *seem* childish," I say, "but the characters' conversations are convincing and amusing at times. And their friendships are wholesome and heart-warming. Let's give it a try, since it's the only book I've brought with me. While I'm reading you can help yourself to sweets –

I hope you like liquorice allsorts."

"Yes, thank you," Andrew mumbles.

I begin reading as slowly as I'm able. Fortunately, the book has some pictures, so every now and again I read a word and then point to the corresponding illustration. I do this a few times in the hope that Andrew will memorise the spelling of the word, but that seems unlikely as he's hardly looking at the words at all. He's evidently bored by the story and is beginning to look as disconsolate as I'm starting to feel. I'm glad when Lionel comes in with Cyril, a tall, sullen-looking boy, who clearly resents having to pick up his younger brother.

"Come on, you," he says to Andrew. "I hope I don't have to come here every week. I have better things to do."

"You're helping your mother, Cyril," I say. "What could be better than that? Andrew and I will meet at the same time next Wednesday. You'll pass that message on, won't you?"

"I suppose so," he says with a grimace.

I give Andrew the rest of the sweets, telling him to share them with his siblings. Cyril brightens up at the prospect of a treat and obliges me with a farewell nod before pushing his brother through the door and slamming it.

"Oh dear, that didn't go very well," I say, joining Lionel in the pharmacy. "Andrew's not able to read at all, and is adamant that he can't be taught. I really don't know what to do. He's nine years old – I thought he'd at least be able to read at a beginner's level, even if he still needed help in gaining fluency. But he can't read a single word, or so he says. I'll need to start from the very beginning. He says he knows his alphabet, but isn't able to understand how letters form words. I'm beginning to doubt that I can help him, Lionel."

"Perhaps he's not telling the truth, Bessie," Lionel says. "It might be that he doesn't want to come here for his lesson, so is claiming that it's a lost cause in the hope that you'll agree and give up on him."

"No, I don't think so. He doesn't seem to be lying. He was embarrassed to admit his inability to read and at one point seemed close to tears, claiming that no one understands his problem. He insists he's backward – he's obviously been told that many times – but he doesn't seem to be backward in any other way. He says he's good at arithmetic – much better than his younger sister, who can read well but often gets her sums wrong. He thinks it's unfair that he gets no praise at all for being good at arithmetic. Why do you think it is that he can do sums but can't read?"

"Hmm, I wonder... I was reading in *The Lancet* about children with learning difficulties, in particular those who find reading hard. It used to be known as 'word blindness', but now they've given the condition a proper name and called it 'dyslexia'. Children with this disability – if you want to call it that – tend to learn to read and write much more slowly than their classmates. They have trouble recognising letters – for example, they might confuse *b* with *d* or *p* – and struggle in learning to spell. Doctors and educators used to think that it was because of an injury to the brain and that nothing could be done to help them. But research has discovered that they are often quite normal in other ways."

"Do you really think Andrew has this disability? How would I ever be able to teach him if that's the case?"

"Well, current thinking is that if dyslexia is recognised early enough, the child may be helped, with patience and a good teacher. I'm not saying that Andrew definitely has dyslexia, Bessie, because if he confuses letters then, presumably, he would confuse numbers as well, and he clearly isn't doing that if he's good at arithmetic. Besides, it would take a doctor to confirm such a diagnosis. Since no one has done anything to help the boy, he's just given up, convinced that he'll never be able to read. I do think you can help him, Bessie, but it'll be a long, slow process and, yes, you'll have to start from the beginning."

"If he *does* have this condition, I very much doubt that *I'm* the one who can teach him. Why has no one helped him at school? Or at home?"

"Most likely no one so far has had the time or the inclination to help him. How can a teacher with so many pupils pay attention to just one boy? In small towns like Brampton-on-Sea, the teacher has a class of up to fifty students, ranging in age from five to fourteen, and is required to teach only the basics of reading, writing and arithmetic. Besides, a good number of the children probably miss class regularly if they're required to work at home. In rural areas such as this, as I'm sure you're aware, they're often needed to help out with farm work at certain times of the year. I'd hazard a guess that Andrew isn't the only child who's unable to read at the age of nine. Much of the learning in class is done by repetition and memorisation. The teacher is not going to spot a boy with learning difficulties, especially if that boy is quiet and doesn't cause disruption.

"And at home… Well, as you know, the Frosts have six children. Even if Andrew's parents are able to read and write themselves, which we can't take for granted, they don't have time to sit with the boy and help him with his reading. At least his mother has noticed that there's a problem – probably because of his siblings' teasing – and has brought him here. That's a start. As to whether or not he *does* suffer from dyslexia, I think that might become clearer after a couple of lessons. You'll soon notice whether or not he's confusing his letters. There's no cure as such, but I'm pretty sure he can be taught to read at an elementary level. It'll take patience, though. Are you prepared to give it a try, Bessie?"

"I can hardly say no, after what you've just told me. I'll do my best, but whether or not I'll succeed is another question. I might do more harm than good. I have no teaching qualifications, as you know. How common is this, dys... whatever you call it?"

"Dyslexia. I think it's much more common than doctors realise. In the past, reading and writing weren't required for many professions, certainly not for outdoor ones, and school attendance wasn't compulsory until 1880 and, even then, only up until the age of ten. I'm sure many children left school unable to read or write, and no one batted an eyelid. Now that education is both compulsory and necessary, children with this disability are being recognised, even though there's still no easy way of helping them."

"But what books am I supposed to use, Lionel? *The Wind in the Willows* is much too advanced for poor Andrew. When I say advanced, I mean in terms of his reading ability. When I started reading it to him, he found the story silly – just like you did."

"And I'm sure you explained to him that it isn't silly at all, as you did with me. But since that book clearly won't work in Andrew's case, I must insist that you go to the bookshop in town and select something more appropriate. Why are you so reluctant to set foot inside that shop? As I've told you, Mr Franklin is a pleasant, friendly man and will be only too happy to assist you in choosing something that will help – and please – the boy."

"Very well, I'll visit the bookshop. But I always feel people are judging me when I go to the shops in town. Everyone seems to be looking at me and whispering, 'There goes the pharmacist's wife'. And goodness knows what they then go on to say."

"Bessie, dear Bessie," Lionel says, smiling. "I can't believe that we've been living here for almost a year and you still feel that way. I'm sure what they say is complimentary – how could it be otherwise? You don't go around with your nose in the air, do you? If they greet you, you greet them back. Try to pluck up enough courage to exchange a few words with the womenfolk now and again. The weather is always a good topic to start with and, once you know them a bit better, you'll find that they can talk about their ailments until the cows come home. I'm sure you'll discover that the local people are harmless enough and you might even make a couple of friends. How many times have you told me what a likeable young man the postman is? Believe me, he's not the only friendly soul in Brampton-on-Sea."

"I'm sure you're right, Lionel, but a lasting friendship doesn't happen overnight. Still, I'll go to the bookshop tomorrow and try to find one or two elementary reading books, though they're probably going to be too childish for a boy of nine. But I suppose we have to start somewhere."

"Yes, indeed. I have every confidence that you'll help

young Andrew Frost get the better of his word blindness, or whatever his problem happens to be. A little patience and encouragement are likely all that he needs. Those are attributes that are sadly lacking in the school classroom. Unfortunately, it'll be some time before advances in education, which are beginning to be made in London, reach small towns like Brampton-on-Sea."

5

It's a glorious Sunday morning and Lionel and I are finally going to the beach. We were unable to do so last week because scattered showers kept us inside for most of the day. A visit to the seashore is a good reason for my missing church today. I started attending the Sunday morning service at the local Anglican church when we first arrived here, but Lionel refuses to come with me. I hate going alone and being stared at simply because I'm the newest member of the congregation. I do feel guilty about my frequent absences, especially since the Reverend Sidney Pratt was welcoming and kind. But he always asks me why I don't bring my husband along, and I no longer know what to tell him.

I haven't given up trying to persuade Lionel to accompany me, but he maintains that his faith is not strong enough to allow him to attend church regularly. I still find it odd that Lionel, who has every virtue that a true Christian is supposed to possess, claims not to have a strong faith. And if his religious belief is as weak as he insists it is, how can it possibly become stronger if he doesn't go to church? I keep asking him that question, but he just laughs and says that's between him and the Lord, and church attendance doesn't come into it. In fact, that's just what Mrs Grist told me when I had the audacity to question why *she* didn't go to church. But as far as Lionel is concerned, it's clearly his scientific training that makes him doubt some aspects of the Christian faith. He once told me that, as a man of science, he often finds himself in conflict with the teachings of the Bible, and he doesn't want to feel a hypocrite by going to church. But he's adamant that *I* don't lose my faith as a consequence of *his* doubts, and encourages me to attend the Sunday service, even when I'd rather give it a miss.

Since we plan to have our midday meal on the dunes, we set off before noon. I've filled a wicker basket with cheese and tomato sandwiches – the tomatoes are the first ones we've picked from the vine in our back garden – two Scotch eggs, a few slices of ginger cake, a couple of apples and some elderflower cordial. I don't want to weigh the basket down with plates, but glasses are a must and I've wrapped them carefully in two large linen napkins.

Lionel carries the basket, to which he's added his latest medical journal, and my novel *Mansfield Park*, which he's urging me to finish. To be honest, though, I'd rather just lie on the sand and doze, especially since I haven't been sleeping well for the last week or so due to my concern about Blanche's Aunt Hilda.

For my part, I'm carrying a tartan blanket for us to sit on and a towel in case we feel like paddling a bit later on. Lionel suggested that we take our bathing suits with us, but I resisted, pointing out that this early in the year, the water will be much too cold for us to immerse ourselves completely, as we did once or twice towards the end of the summer last year.

There's a shortcut through the fields that takes us directly to the seashore. I'm not sure whether we're allowed to cross fields that are not common land, but Lionel says not to worry, we're doing no harm. When we reach the dunes, I take off my shoes – I'm wearing no stockings today – and Lionel does the same. It's a pleasure to feel the warm, fine grains of sand beneath our bare feet, though we do need to look out for sea holly and other types of thistle that might prick our toes, not to mention the pretty amber snails that we would hate to crush accidentally while invading their natural habitat.

We find a secluded spot, spread out the blanket and sit down next to each other. Facing us is an unbroken view of blue-green sea, the sight of which still fills me with awe. Lionel finds it hard to believe that he was the one who first showed me the sea; that I had never once visited a coastal town or resort until he brought me here. But that's not so unusual, I tell him. Many folk in my village, my mother included, go to their graves without ever having caught even a passing glimpse of any of our Maker's wondrous seas or oceans.

The beach just beyond the dunes is not at all crowded – just one or two dog walkers and a few children splashing each other at the water's edge. That's what I like about this particular section of the beach; it's never swarming with folk, even on a warm day like today. Because of the shortcut that only Lionel and myself and one or two others seem to know about, we are able to enjoy the least populated part of the mile-long stretch of sand.

Lionel pours us both a glass of elderflower cordial and hands me my book.

"Can't I just lie down for a few minutes and enjoy the warmth of the sun?" I ask him.

"My dear," he says, "you don't need to ask my permission. I've brought your book in case you become bored. I want to finish this journal before the next one arrives in the post and, as you know only too well, I'm not much of a conversationalist at the best of times, and especially not when I have my nose in a medical journal."

It's not true what Lionel has just said. He *is* a conversationalist. It's me who isn't. When I first met him, I was so fearful that he'd find me uninteresting and inarticulate that I became even more tongue-tied. Every day he met ladies who could strike up a lively conversation within seconds of entering the pharmacy, whereas I was the complete opposite. To this day, I've never understood what he sees in me, but I've learnt better than to keep questioning it.

"Bessie, be careful," he cautions, as I lie down on the blanket, using my towel as a pillow. "The sun's rays are strong today. It may not feel like it because of the slight breeze, but you'll burn your face and neck if you don't take care. That's right, cover your face with your hat. I don't mind at all if your freckles start to multiply, but I don't want you to burn."

It's true about my freckles increasing if I face the sun directly. Unfortunately, I didn't inherit my mother's silky golden-red hair, but she gave me her fair, freckle-prone complexion. Lionel is always reminding me about the damaging effect of the sun's rays on bare skin. That's probably something he's learnt from reading his medical journals, and is the reason why all the fashionable ladies in London carry a parasol – they want to retain their lily-white complexions. As for me, I'm not so fussy. I think I look healthier when I've been out in the garden for a while without my hat, and even Lionel notices it and says he likes my *country girl look*. He sometimes talks as if I'm a lass of twenty, rather than a mature woman of forty-one, and tactfully overlooks the fine wrinkles around my eyes and mouth, and the increasing number of grey strands in my chestnut brown hair. I should add that I have never before referred to my hair as 'chestnut brown', but Lionel insists it is that shade and no other. I plan to make the most of such a description before I turn completely grey.

The balmy weather and the relaxing sound of the waves make me feel even more drowsy than before, and I soon begin to doze. But I sit up with a start when Lionel pats me on the shoulder. For a moment I think it's Walter who's woken me up – as he occasionally used to do when I dozed off on the riverbank – and I look at Lionel in surprise. I don't tell him that I feel a twinge of disappointment that it's not my nephew sitting next to me; it's been so long since I last saw him, and I miss him every single day. Lionel tells me it's time for lunch – that he's hungry and can't wait a minute longer. He's already opened the wicker basket and unwrapped the sandwiches and Scotch eggs. The fresh air has given us both an appetite and we marvel at the fact that even simple food tastes so much better out of doors. Before we set out, I felt that we'd packed far too much for the two of us, but we manage to finish every last morsel.

Lionel suggests we go for a paddle, insisting that we need some exercise. I don't object, though truth be told, I would prefer another nap.

The beach is a combination of fine white sand and pebbles of all different shapes and sizes. We carefully cross the strip of pebbles at the base of the dunes and stroll, hand in hand, towards the sea, which looks so inviting on a fine day like today. The tide is receding and the wet sand feels warm and squelchy beneath our feet. I have tucked my skirt up into my drawers and, as a result, feel a bit embarrassed, but there is no one to see me besides my husband. He makes a playful comment about my shapely legs, which I tell him is nonsense – they're not shapely at all. Why else would I stick to full-length skirts and dresses, when other ladies are beginning to show their ankles?

The further we walk into the water, the colder it becomes, and I make a quick retreat before it reaches my shins. Lionel, with his trousers rolled up as far as his thighs, stays in the shallows, knee-deep, until the tail end of a more forceful wave splashes him unexpectedly. I laugh at his startled face.

"You may be laughing now, Bessie Fielding," he says, joining me at the shoreline, "but just you wait. The next time we go for a paddle, I'm going to make sure that *you're* the one who gets wet!"

On our way back to the dunes, we find that we no longer have the beach to ourselves. A small, dark-haired boy is sitting with his back to us. He seems intent on picking up pebbles, one at a time, and examining them carefully. A canvas bag at his side looks as if it's already full of the ones that have passed his scrutiny.

"I may be wrong, Lionel," I say, "but isn't that Andrew over there? I'm sure it is. What on earth is he doing? It looks like he's collecting pebbles."

"Yes, I think you're right – it *is* Andrew," Lionel says. "Let's go and ask him what he's searching for."

Andrew looks up in alarm when he hears us call his name.

"Why, Andrew," Lionel says. "What are you doing here all by yourself on a Sunday afternoon?"

"Nothing much," Andrew says, a little defensively. "Just finding some more pebbles."

"Do you collect them?" I ask. "Some are so pretty – perfectly smooth and round. I especially like the pink speckled ones, and the grey and black ones are just as nice."

"Each one is different. No two pebbles are alike. Yes, I collect the unusual ones, but please don't tell anyone."

"Why do you want to keep it a secret, Andrew?"

"Because Cyril and Violet would just make fun of me. And Mother would say I was wasting time."

"That sounds a bit unfair. What do you do with the ones you collect?"

"We have a large back garden. It's mostly overgrown, but I've cleared a patch and it's my secret place. I keep my pebbles there and other stuff that I find when I go beachcombing. I sometimes make pictures with the treasures I collect."

Andrew is a boy after my own heart. He reminds me of both Walter and Michael; Walter in the sense that he also sees beauty in pebbles and stones, and is aware of what can be created with them, and Michael because he too has an artistic streak that he used to be at pains to hide in case he was made fun of.

"I would love to see your artwork, Andrew," I say. "Would you care to show me something that you've made? Only if you can easily carry it, of course."

Andrew doesn't respond. He seems to be contemplating my request and considering whether or not it will invade his privacy.

"Aren't you a long way from home, son?" Lionel asks finally. "Do your parents know where you are?"

"I know a way through the fields and woods. I can be home in half an hour. No, my parents don't know where I am, but I don't think they'll have missed me. They're used to me doing things on my own after church on Sundays."

"All right, Andrew. We won't keep you from your pastime any longer. We'll see you after school on Wednesday."

Walking home across the fields, I reflect on Lionel's easy familiarity with young Andrew and wonder – not for the first time – whether he would have liked to have had a son of his own. His daughter Mathilda is a credit to him, caring and kind, and now his pride and joy is his little grandson, Geoffrey. But a son of his own, to carry forward the name of Fielding into the next generation, must surely be something he would have wished for if circumstances had been different. He told me that his former wife had always been weak and that, after the birth of Mathilda, it would have been risky, if not fatal, for her to carry another child to full term. But he also said that Mathilda was everything he could have desired, and that he's never regretted not having had more children. Still, sometimes I wonder why he didn't marry again sooner; after Annette died, he was still young enough to start another family and might have had the chance to father a son.

"Lionel," I say, pursuing this train of thought. "Do you sometimes wish you'd had a son, if only to carry on your family name?"

He laughs, as he often does when I ask a question completely out of the blue.

"Bessie," he says, "whatever makes you ask such a question? If I'd have wanted a son, it certainly wouldn't have been for the family name. I have two brothers who have five sons between them, so the family name – for what it's worth – is surely going to survive for generations to come. No, my dear, I'm more than happy with just a daughter. But tell me, Bessie, would *you* like a child of your own? We've never really had this conversation – I accept the blame for that – and perhaps I'm being selfish. You're still young enough to bear a child, though I admit that I'm rather old to father one."

"Oh no, Lionel! That's not why I asked. I'm happy with the way we are and, besides, I'm forty-one years old. I don't want to be a mother when I'm old enough to be a grandmother."

"That's not a good reason, Bessie. Look at your friend Patty. She gave birth for the first time last year and she's the same age as you. She doesn't regret becoming a mother, does she?"

"No, of course not. But she did have a difficult time both during the birth and afterwards. Of course, Patty's health has never been strong, but I don't think having a baby over the age of forty is risk-free, even for the healthiest of women. Baby Agnes, although not planned, has been the most wonderful blessing for Patty and Robert, but there were certainly moments when I thought neither mother nor daughter would survive."

"You're right, childbirth *is* a risk for older women, although many continue to give birth well into their forties. Those are usually the families that can ill afford to have more children and, as a result, sink deeper into poverty. By the time the mother reaches her menopause – if, indeed, she lives that long – she's worn out and is often at the end of her tether. But how did we get onto this topic? Was it because we met Andrew on the beach? I saw you looking at him wistfully – were you feeling broody, my dear?"

"I'm sure I didn't look at Andrew in any such way, Lionel. If I did, I was probably just thinking what an unusually sweet boy he is, but so misunderstood. The thought of having a child of my own never entered my head. But then, when you called him 'son', I thought about how you've been such a good father to Mathilda, and it crossed my mind that perhaps you'd have been an equally good parent to a boy as well."

"Probably not. Boys are normally rowdy, if my brothers are anything to go by. I'm not sure I could tolerate so much disturbance at home."

"Are you saying you were the exception, Lionel? That you weren't the least bit rowdy when you were a boy?"

"Well, I was certainly less trouble to my parents than my brothers. But really, believe me, I'm also happy the way things are – just the two of us. Besides, we have a grandson, don't we? And another grandchild on the way. We need to plan our next trip to London or, better still, Mathilda and Geoffrey – and Marie-Thérèse too – can come here. I'm not sure how easy it is for Ronald to take time off work, but there's no reason why the others can't come on the train for a few days."

Marie-Thérèse is Geoffrey's young nanny; she used to be a sister in the Roman Catholic orphanage, run by the Sisters of Gethsemane, where Harriet, Michael's sister, was sent after her parents died. When Harriet managed to abscond from the forbidding Hammersmith institution, Marie-Thérèse, who was getting ready – against her wishes – to take her vows, soon followed suit. She and Harriet had become close friends at the orphanage, where they both suffered – mentally and physically – from the harsh rules and methods of discipline imposed on them by those in charge. It's a comfort to know that the two girls – or young ladies, I should say – have now found safe and meaningful employment with caring families that are personally connected to Lionel and myself.

This last conversation with Lionel has left me feeling quite embarrassed. I didn't realise he would think I was hinting at our having a child together. I have certainly never entertained the idea. I was joyous and fearful in equal measure when Patty announced last year that she was expecting, and the thought of having to go through such an ordeal myself is not something I would ever wish for. If I were ten years younger, it might be different, but now that I'm in my forties, I'm resigned to remaining childless. And Lionel is fifty-seven years old – far too old in my opinion to become a father again. He always takes care during our marital relations, which I have learnt to enjoy, although – never having engaged in such intimacy with a man before – I did struggle at first. Before we tied the knot, I told him of my inexperience and, thankfully, he was kind and understanding, saying there was nothing to worry about, that we'd take it one step at a time. Even now, he is gentle and patient, and never forces me to do anything I don't want to do. That said, oftentimes we are both too tired to do much more than hug and kiss before closing our eyes and falling asleep. That seems to suit us both most of the time.

To listen to me, anyone would think I didn't love Lionel, but I do. Admittedly, it's not the same sort of love I felt for Arthur, who was my first sweetheart and who tragically died at the age of twenty-two in a freak accident. That was something much more heightened and passionate, as was natural at our young age. Arthur and I had agreed that we would wait until we were married before engaging in the *ultimate* act of love, though oftentimes we came close to forgetting that pledge. And I have to admit that there were many times in the lonely years that followed his death when I wished I *had* given myself to him. Still, I speak the truth when I say that my feelings for Lionel are not the least bit diminished by my earlier love for Arthur. And I know he loves me too, as he treats me so affectionately and has never once raised his voice or uttered an unkind word, even during our most impassioned arguments, which only occur on the rarest of occasions.

We have had such a lovely afternoon that my concern about Blanche and her family has not once crossed my mind. But as soon as we arrive home, I start thinking again about poor Hilda. Why is there still no news from Ernest, her son? Walter told me that he went to America with the intention of eventually travelling west and working on the land until he had saved enough money to buy his own small farmstead. A close friend of his had done the same thing and had apparently met with some success.

Daisy, the eldest of the Goode daughters, was a little bit put out when Hilda told the family that Ernest intended to marry the young lady he'd met in New York and had thus put his plans to travel west on hold. He *had* stated in an earlier letter to Daisy that he was still in New York and was stepping out with a girl he'd met in the famous park there – Central Park, I think Walter said it was called – but had made no mention of a forthcoming wedding. She wondered why he had not confided in her, given that they had always been close and used to share secrets with each other when they were growing up.

Poor Ernest! How will he ever forgive himself for being the cause of his mother setting out on such a perilous journey – one that must have been embarked upon with such joy at the thought of a dear son's impending marriage? Clearly, Hilda's probable death serves as a grim reminder to us all that we can never take the good times for granted; tragedy can strike at any moment, even when our lives appear to be at their brightest and most hopeful.

6

The bookshop is in the centre of town, at the end of a pretty cobbled street where window boxes and hanging baskets, filled with lobelia, begonia, petunia and many other perennials that I cannot name, add a splash of colour to the shop fronts. I walk past the bookshop several times before plucking up enough courage to go inside. I don't know why I am always so fearful and self-conscious in situations such as this. Lionel says there must have been some incident in my youth that has rendered me scared to enter certain establishments for the first time, but I can't think of anything that would have affected me in that way. There was nothing frightening or disturbing in my West Country childhood, apart from the usual economic difficulties and, of course, the loss of loved ones, but those were misfortunes that afflicted every family.

Finally, I count to ten and step inside the shop. It's much larger inside than it appears from the outside, and customers are so intent on their browsing that no one looks up to see who has just entered. Their disinterest makes me feel better; part of my fear is being the only customer and having to converse with an unknown shopkeeper. I make a beeline for the children's section, which is instantly recognisable thanks to colourful pictures on the wall. To be honest, I have no idea what I'm looking for. I've met Andrew only once, but it's clear to me that he's not an imaginative sort of child. If he could not conceive of woodland animals having fun and conversing with each other, then stories that are unrealistic and fanciful are out of the question. Yet most early reading books are designed for very young children, who love such whimsical tales.

"May I help you, madam?"

I turn around in surprise. A stocky, bald, middle-aged man is holding a pile of books that he's about to arrange on a table by the window. This must be the proprietor, Mr Franklin, whom I was at pains to avoid until I was ready to purchase a book.

"Thank you," I say, "but I'm not entirely sure what I'm looking for."

I realise now that I was foolish to believe I could enter a shop without having to talk to anyone. I must pull myself together and behave in a manner that befits the wife of the town's pharmacist.

"Well, it's clear that you have a child in mind," he says, putting down the books he's carrying and smiling. "May I ask his or her age?"

"Yes, it's a young boy. Andrew is nine years old, but hasn't yet learnt to read. I've been tasked with trying to help him. He says he knows his alphabet, but doesn't seem to understand how letters form words. Does that make any sense?"

"It does indeed. It's not the first time I've heard of such a problem. I daresay his teacher at school has ignored his plight. That's usually the case."

"Yes, that's what my husband thinks. But, whatever the cause, it's clear that he's never going to catch up with his classmates unless he's given some sort of help outside of school."

"Are you a relative of his, madam? A concerned aunt perhaps?"

"No, we're not related. I helped another boy with his

reading last year and my husband thinks that perhaps I can help this young lad. But it's going to be hard. He's already convinced himself that he doesn't need to learn to read."

"Everyone needs to learn to read to get on in life, especially these days. Those who think otherwise are fooling themselves. But he's still young, and I'm sure he can be helped. May I introduce myself? My name is Bertrand Franklin. I'm the owner of this establishment, modest though it is."

"I'm pleased to meet you, Mr Franklin. I'm Bessie Fielding. My husband is Lionel Fielding, who runs the local pharmacy."

"Ah, Lionel, our excellent pharmacist. I've run into him on several occasions. It's a pleasure to meet you, Mrs Fielding. Now, let's see what we can find for your young charge."

"Thank you. I should add that he's not a boy who would appreciate anything too childish or fanciful. I started reading aloud to him the first chapter of *The Wind in the Willows*, a book that's dear to my heart, but he thought it was silly. That's my problem, really. Most books for teaching children to read are quite babyish."

"I see your problem. But I think I may have one book that might interest the boy and educate him at the same time. Let me see now, where is it? Ah, here we are. It's called *The Navy Alphabet* and is in verse. Each page is dedicated to a letter of the alphabet, and all the verses relate in some way to seafaring activities. I think the drawings are impressive and will no doubt arrest the boy's interest. It's not childish at all – in fact, quite the opposite. Listen to the verse dedicated to the letter *A for Admiral*.

"Here is the Admiral, gallant and true,
Lord of the Navy, in peace, or in war;
Warrior, sailor and diplomat too;
Winning our battles in countries afar.
Grand is the Admiral, great is his fame,
Favors and riches are his to command.
Ev'ry American honors his name –
Victor at sea and a hero on land!

"As you can tell, Mrs Fielding, it's by an American author – perhaps that will put you off, as certain words are spelt in the American way, and some are abbreviated. Poetic licence is, of course, an excuse for the abbreviations, but we don't want your young pupil spelling words incorrectly, do we now?"

"No, but I don't think that's a problem. It will be a while before my pupil, Andrew, can recognise incorrect spellings and, besides, I can explain them to him. I think it's a good choice. All boys dream about joining the navy, after all, just as all girls dream of marrying a sailor."

"Indeed. There's a similar book for the army as well, but I think that one is based on America's wars with the Indians, and is perhaps not appropriate for that reason alone. I should confess to being American myself, though I've lived in this country for many years now. But I still follow what's popular among readers over there and have a number of books shipped every few months. And I go back to the home country at least once a year for business purposes. The author of this particular book – Mr L Frank Baum – wrote *The Wonderful Wizard of Oz*. Perhaps you've heard of it?"

"Oh yes, I have. In fact, I'd love to read it myself! But I'm sure Andrew won't like it. He doesn't have much of an imagination, and I suspect he'd have no interest in the magical land of Oz."

"What a pity. I feel sorry for those who lack imagination, don't you? So much is denied them. Where are you from originally, Mrs Fielding? I recognise your accent but can't quite place it."

"I'm from Somerset, a small village called Ferndell. But I did spend a year in London, which is where I met my husband."

"Ferndell, really? What a coincidence! I spent some time living close to your village a few years ago. I was writing a book, which – I should add – is not yet finished, and felt the need to be in a place of peace and quiet, far from the turmoil of town or city. Living in the heart of the charming Somerset countryside was perfect for me at that time."

"Yes, it is lovely, isn't it? Although when you grow up in a place, you don't always appreciate its beauty or its peacefulness – until you move away, that is."

"Very true. In fact, while I was there, I got to know a young man who was about to leave the village for the mayhem of New York City. Coming from that urban jungle myself, I was able to provide him with some useful tips. His ambition was to buy land and start a farm in the American West. He had such wild dreams and had no idea how to prepare for such a life-changing prospect. His father is from Ireland and he'd tell him stories of countrymen who'd left the homeland during the potato famine and started a new life in America. He was a sensitive young man and felt a kinship with those poor souls. I thought I should give him a few words of advice – though I feared it might dampen his expectations – but whether or not he was able to benefit from my counsel, I have no idea. Sadly, we appear to have lost touch with each other. I know that he survived the crossing, as he wrote to me from New York to tell me he'd arrived safely and had found lodgings in Brooklyn. I must admit I was relieved to hear that he'd suffered no ills on the journey. Travelling in steerage on a steamship is usually seen as a last resort for the poor and destitute. He didn't really fall into that category, but I suppose his means were limited. I do hope he's managing to fulfil his dream, as leaving his family must have been a difficult decision for him to make."

"I'm sure it was. What was the name of this lad, if you don't mind me asking?"

"Doyle. His father is Declan Doyle. The boy is called Ernest."

I stare at Mr Franklin, quite lost for words. Of all the families in the West Country, he is acquainted with the Doyles! He clearly has no knowledge of Declan Doyle's passing, or that Hilda Doyle has most likely perished at sea. It seems that it will be up to me to apprise him of both misfortunes.

"Are you all right, Mrs Fielding?" Mr Franklin says. "You've turned rather pale. Would you like to sit down?"

"No, it's all right. I'm just a bit shocked. You see, Mr Declan Doyle's wife, Hilda, is actually known to my family. I've not met her personally, but she's the aunt of my nephew's fiancée. And I hate to be the bearer of bad news, but I'm sorry to tell you that Mr Doyle passed away almost two years ago."

"Oh no! I had no idea. That *is* a shock. What on earth was the cause of death? He always appeared healthy and full of life. And he was surely only in his early forties."

"I'm not sure how he died, but I know it was sudden.

A heart attack, perhaps. But there's more bad news, I'm afraid. His wife Hilda was on her way to America to visit Ernest in New York – he's still living there, apparently. She was going to attend his wedding. The news came as rather a surprise to the family, but perhaps his plan was to forgo a long engagement and marry his sweetheart in New York before heading west to start a farm, like you said. But... Hilda was travelling on the *Titanic* and we're almost certain that she didn't survive the sinking. She was also travelling steerage and, apparently, those passengers were the last to access the boat deck from which the lifeboats were launched. Lionel's son-in-law in London was able to obtain a list of survivors and, unfortunately, Hilda Doyle's name was not mentioned. The family has heard nothing at all from Ernest or anyone else and, although they're clinging to the hope that Hilda has somehow managed to survive, that outcome is becoming less and less likely."

"My dear Mrs Fielding, I am so sorry to hear this news. The poor woman! How very unfortunate that she chose to sail on the *Titanic*. Its sinking is a tragedy, that's for sure – the ship was making its maiden voyage and was supposed to be unsinkable. Ernest must be devastated. You say there's been no word from him?"

"No, nothing. If only he would write to his aunt and let her know whatever news he has, it would be such a relief for her and her three daughters. I think that if the family knew for certain that Mrs Doyle had perished, they could begin to grieve her passing. That sounds heartless, but I'm sure you know what I mean. Not knowing is such a terrible thing. They've written Ernest several letters, but he hasn't responded to any of them."

"I know from experience that letters from overseas

have a habit of getting lost en route. That may have been the case with Ernest's responses. But perhaps I can help. It just so happens that I'm leaving for New York next week. I expect the crossing will take about five days to a week, depending on the weather, but as soon as I arrive, I can pay Ernest a visit. I have his address in Brooklyn from the time he wrote to me soon after his arrival. It was some time ago but it's possible he's still there. I'd like to know how he's getting on, especially now you've told me that his father died two years ago. So I'll be more than happy to try to locate him."

"Oh, that's very kind of you, Mr Franklin. Yes, the family say they've been writing to him at an address in Brooklyn. But are you sure it won't put you to any inconvenience? How long are you planning to stay in New York?"

"No inconvenience at all. I'll be there about a month. I'll be doing some more research for the book that I'm writing – it's on the American Civil War, about which there's so much conflicting information – and plan also to visit a number of bookshops to see what's selling successfully across the pond. But as soon as I have any news from Ernest, I'll write to you care of the pharmacy straight away. Or, better still, if I can find an acquaintance who's travelling to England sooner than I am, I'll have him carry a letter and post it upon arrival. That way, there'll be less likelihood of it getting lost."

"Are you sure, Mr Franklin? You're going to have a thousand and one things to do in New York, and I don't want this to take up too much of your time."

"Believe me, it'll be no trouble at all. Besides, I'm now as concerned as you are about Ernest and want to know that he's all right. It must have been such a terrible shock for him to hear about the *Titanic*'s sinking, knowing that his mother was on board. And if he also knows that her name is not on the list of survivors, then he must be stuck in a state of solitary bereavement, so far away from family members. Poor boy. I assume he was expecting her? Or was her visit planned as a surprise?"

"I wondered that myself. But Lionel thinks she wouldn't have made that journey on her own without telling her son first. So, I imagine he knew about it, but I can't really say for sure."

"Well, I'll find out when I visit. Thank you for telling me all of this, Mrs Fielding. As I said, I had no idea that Declan had died – I really should have made more effort to keep in touch with the family. Now that you've told me about their troubles, I feel terribly guilty that I failed to do so. It's a strange coincidence, but just recently I was reading a book by another American author, Morgan Robertson, entitled *Futility*. It's a collection of short stories, but the first one is about the sinking of a huge passenger ship, the SS *Titan* – described as unsinkable – after hitting an iceberg in the North Atlantic. This book was written in the late 1890s – more than ten years ago – but it really does seem as if the author was foretelling this real-life tragedy. When I first heard about the sinking of the *Titanic*, I felt chilled to the bone, as though someone had just walked over my grave."

"Goodness me. I had no idea such a book existed. Perhaps if the *Titanic*'s passengers, or even the captain himself, had read it beforehand, they might have been dissuaded from embarking on such a voyage."

"Indeed. Though I daresay some – and almost certainly the captain – would have scoffed at such superstition and set sail without a second thought."

"You're probably right. If you don't mind me asking, Mr Franklin, what was Mr Declan Doyle like? According to my nephew, the family were not happy about Hilda marrying an Irishman. I've never met anyone from Ireland, so I'm curious to know why they were so much against the union."

"Ah, Declan was a fine fellow. Like many of his countrymen, he loved to tell a joke and could burst into song at the drop of a hat. But he was an educated man, very well read, and could quote great chunks of William Butler Yeats' work. He might have been guilty of having one drink too many upon occasion, but that just seemed to heighten his intellect. Believe me, Mrs Fielding, I'm deeply saddened to hear of his passing and shall say a prayer for his soul tonight."

"I think that many of us are now praying for the Doyles and wishing we'd been better neighbours. You see, Hilda's twin sister's husband, Henry Goode, died not long after Mr Doyle. He was a particular friend of my family – my brothers went to school with him – so I'm afraid we may have inadvertently overlooked Hilda's bereavement. We didn't know the Doyle family so well, partly because of the estrangement between the sisters, though I think estrangement is probably too strong a word. They are twins, after all, and I'm sure that in their heart of hearts they're still exceedingly close."

"I know what you mean. Life is so fleeting – we should never fall out with those close to us. And we should never take the gift of life for granted. That family seems to have had more than its fair share of sadness in the recent past."

"They have indeed. I hope, Mr Franklin, that the next time I come into your shop, it'll be with better tidings. I mustn't take up any more of your time. I'll be happy to buy this book about the navy that you've kindly recommended, and will see how Andrew gets on with it. If I could pay for it now, I'll leave you free to attend to your other customers."

"Of course. Let me ring it up for you right away."

"Thank you. I hope your crossing to America is a smooth one, and I look forward to hearing from you if you're able to contact Ernest. But please don't think of it as an obligation."

"I already feel obliged to locate him so as to lessen my own guilt at not keeping in touch with him or his father. I'll certainly let you know if I'm able to reach him. It's been a pleasure talking to you, Mrs Fielding. Do give my regards to your husband and tell him I've discovered a new book on naturopathic medicine that I'm sure will interest him."

I'm in a much better mood when I leave the bookshop than I was when I set out this morning. I was dreading going into that shop for the same reason that deters me from doing lots of things – lack of self-confidence. In a short space of time, Lionel gained the respect and trust of his customers here in Brampton-on-Sea, and I would be mortified if my foolish inhibitions were to tarnish his good name. Of course, I'm happy and proud to be his wife, but I'm terrified of letting him down in any small way. It's ridiculous, I know, but I can't seem to overcome this feeling of inadequacy, however much Lionel chides me for it. Still, Mr Franklin couldn't have been nicer, which just goes to show how unreasonable my fears usually are.

And I can't get over the fact that he knows the Doyle

family – at least the late Declan Doyle and his son Ernest. What a small world we live in! I must write to Walter and tell him this latest news. If Ernest can be found and spoken to, it might help the Goode family come to terms with what now seems to be an inevitable outcome.

My walk home is a delightful one; it's a warm, cloudless day and, as I approach Hawthorn Lane, I am able to glimpse the sparkling blue sea in the distance. Had I more time, and if Lionel were with me, it would be so pleasant to cross the fields and sit for a while among the dunes, like we did last Sunday. But Lionel will be home in an hour and I need to begin preparing our meal. Not that he would mind if I'd not even made a start on it; he'd just smile and suggest going out for fish and chips. We've done that a few times and it's a real treat; the fresh plaice or cod is coated in a golden batter and the chips are delicious, crispy on the outside and soft in the middle. My mouth is watering just thinking about it!

Lionel arrives home to the smell of liver, bacon and onions – a tasty enough meal, but certainly not a treat like fish and chips. He never complains about the food I serve him, but today he suggests that we eat more cold meals, like salad, when the weather is so hot.

"Well, we have a cold pudding," I say, placing a bowl of fresh strawberries on the table, along with a jug of cream. "I was going to make a treacle tart, but didn't have time in the end, as I went into town and visited the bookshop."

"Ah, how did that go?" he asks me.

"It went well. You'll be pleased to know that I've made a friend of Mr Franklin. He was so kind, just like you said he would be."

"Is that so? Do I have reason to be jealous? I believe

he's closer to your age than I am."

"Of course not, Lionel! And, if you ask me, I'd say that he's older than you are. He's certainly not as sprightly. Besides, I told him I was married to you and he wasn't the least bit improper. We chatted for some time and – you'll never guess – he knows the Doyle family! At least he used to know the late Declan Doyle and he's met his son. Apparently, shortly before Ernest left for America, he gave him some useful tips, since he himself hails from New York."

"Goodness me, how did he come to reveal all that information? And how on earth does he know the Doyle family? They're from your village, aren't they?"

"Yes, they are. Mr Franklin asked me where I was from originally, as he recognised my accent, and when I told him, he said he was familiar with that part of the country. He said he'd lived close to Ferndell for a while – he wanted some peace and quiet while writing a book, which he's yet to finish. Apparently, while staying there, he became friendly with an Irishman and his son. There couldn't have been many Irish folk living in Ferndell at that time, so it wasn't hard to guess that he was referring to the Doyles.

"He said that Declan Doyle was his good friend and a 'fine fellow'. But, having lost touch with the family, he had no idea that he'd passed away, and it saddened him to hear this news. And, as if that wasn't bad enough, I then had to tell him that Hilda Doyle was travelling on the *Titanic* and is presumed dead. He was most sympathetic and is concerned about Ernest, especially when I told him that no one had heard from him. He says he's going to New York on business next week and will try to locate him."

"That's excellent news. But how on earth does he plan to find him?"

"Well, he says he still has the address Ernest wrote to him from when he first arrived in America, though he's not heard anything since then. If he *is* able to find him, he promises to let us know. He thinks it's quite possible that Ernest *has* written to the Goode family, but that his letter or letters may have become lost in the post. That often happens, apparently. But perhaps he just said that to make me feel better."

"I'm not altogether surprised that he's willing to take the time to track Ernest down. I've always sensed that he's a good man. But what was the likelihood of him knowing Declan Doyle and Ernest? We do live in a small world, don't we?"

"Yes, those were my thoughts exactly. I also have a good feeling about Mr Franklin, Lionel. I think he'll be true to his word."

"When you have a good feeling about someone, Bessie, you're rarely mistaken. You seem to be able to assess someone's character just from a brief conversation."

"I don't know about that. I think I'm often wrong about folk. Remember how I always thought Mrs Grist was unkind and uncaring? You were the one who convinced me that she *did* have a heart, and that her bark was worse than her bite."

"Fanny Grist is a special case. She deliberately puts up a front to hide her true feelings. I wonder how she is, and Phillip too. Didn't you say you wrote to her a few weeks ago?"

"Yes, I sent her a postcard, but she hasn't responded yet. She probably thinks there's no need to reply, since it was just a card. I suppose I should write her a letter. I did hear from Edie though, and she told me that she and Phillip went for a walk in Hyde Park earlier this month on a day that started out warm and sunny, but then turned cold and wet. She said they both got drenched, and she was worried that Phillip might have caught a cold. Still, she said he was in good spirits – no longer melancholic – and happy that his mother is enjoying the company of her cousin-in-law Bertha, who now lives with her."

"I did wonder whether Phillip was still afflicted with melancholia. I know that Fanny also worries in case he suffers a relapse. But it seems that Edie's company is doing him good, at least as far as his mental health is concerned."

"Edie's company would do anyone good, Lionel. I do miss her."

I'm glad that Edie continues to write to me. She and Walter were sweethearts for about two years; their courtship ended when Edie moved to London to train to be a paediatric nurse at the Great Ormond Street Hospital. I believe that Phillip, Mrs Grist's youngest son, influenced her decision, but she claims it was a career move, nothing more than that. Edie and Phillip are not formally courting, but it appears they meet regularly for afternoon tea or a walk in the park. I don't know if Mrs Grist knows about her son's friendship with Edie; she might not approve of his walking out with a village girl, well brought up and intelligent though she is. In my opinion, Edie would be an enviable catch for any man – she's well educated and considerate, and a beauty by anyone's standards. I was devastated when she and Walter split up, but it wasn't too long before my nephew began stepping out with Blanche Goode. As much as I love Edie, I have to admit that Blanche is a far better match for my dear Walter.

"So did you buy anything from the bookshop, Bessie?" Lionel asks. "Or did you spend all your time making a good impression on Bertrand Franklin?"

"Of course I bought something," I say. "He was so helpful that it would have been discourteous of me not to have bought a book. I actually came away with the one he recommended. I told him about Andrew – the fact that he can't read and how he dislikes fairy tales and the like, making it difficult to find a book for beginners that would suit him. He suggested a book by the American author who wrote *The Wonderful Wizard of Oz*. You look surprised, Lionel. I was too. This book is all about the navy and it's in verse. Each page is dedicated to a letter of alphabet. There's one about the army too, but I'll see how Andrew gets on with the navy one first. Believe me, these books couldn't be more different from Mr Baum's bestseller, which I'd love to read if given the chance. But not with Andrew, obviously."

"You could have bought that as well, if he had it in stock. I'm sure there'll come a time when you'll find yourself tutoring a child who loves make-believe. But you're right, if Andrew doesn't care for a book like *The Wind in the Willows*, I don't think he would appreciate one about a girl named Dorothy, who's swept away by a tornado to a magical land called Oz."

"You seem to know a lot about the story, Lionel. Don't tell me *you've* read it!"

"Ha, that would surprise you, wouldn't it? But no, I can't say I have. I overheard a light-hearted conversation in a London bookshop and considered buying a copy for my niece Mary, who was about ten at the time. But on second thoughts, I thought it would be too American for her extremely English tastes."

"Well, I think this book about the navy is very American too, and the army one even more so. But we'll see if it helps Andrew. The goal is to get him to read phonetically; the story doesn't really matter that much, but obviously it'll be better if it sparks his interest. Oh, and striking pictures accompany each verse, which I'm sure will please him."

"That sounds like an excellent choice. Can you show it to me? Your description has certainly piqued *my* interest."

7

I arrive a couple of minutes late for my next session with Andrew and find him waiting for me, along with his sister Violet. Lionel tells me that Mrs Frost has asked if Violet can sit quietly in the corner of the room during the lesson; she promises that the little girl won't cause a disturbance.

"We're not a baby-sitting service," Lionel whispers to me, "but I told her it would be all right just this once. I hope she doesn't make a habit of it, though."

"It's fine with me," I say, "but it's Andrew I'm worried about. Mrs Frost says Violet is a fluent reader. I don't want to hear her sniggering every time the boy struggles with a word. But we'll see how it goes."

I'm glad that my copy of *The Wind in the Willows* is still in my bag from last week. It's perfect reading material for Violet, and she seems happy to sit in the corner and make a start on it. In appearance, she couldn't be more different from Andrew. Although two years younger, she's almost as tall as he is, and is plump with fair curly hair and bright blue eyes. Whereas Andrew appears serious and thoughtful, she looks as though she's bursting with energy and enthusiasm. She certainly seems thrilled at the prospect of reading about woodland and riverbank animals, and spends some time looking at the pictures before starting on the first chapter.

"So, Andrew," I say, once Violet has quietened down, "look what I've found for us to read today. It's called *The Navy Alphabet* and is written in verse, with one page for each letter of the alphabet. The verses are all related to different aspects of the navy, so I think you'll enjoy it.

I'm beginning to suspect that you have a keen interest in all things nautical."

Andrew looks doubtful as he turns the pages of the book.

"We don't need to read the verses in any particular order," I continue. "Why don't you have a quick look and choose the one you want to make a start on. You can tell by the pictures what each verse is about."

The boy takes his time looking at the illustrations, examining each one carefully, and finally chooses the verse that has a picture of a lighthouse below it.

"Can we read this one?" he asks. "Is it about lighthouses?"

"Yes, that's right" I say. "Lighthouse begins with the letter *L*. Let's read the verse out loud a couple of times."

I point to each word as I read the verse.

"The Lighthouse throws its piercing ray
Across the sea for miles away,
Warning all ships upon the deep
From treach'rous shoals and reefs to keep.
It guides them into harbor fair
By reason of its steady glare,
And so the Lighthouse proves a friend
Our ships and sailors to defend."

"I love lighthouses," Andrew says. "In fact, I want to be a lighthouse keeper when I grow up. Father took me and Cyril to see the lighthouse on Eddystone Rocks last year. It's a tower lighthouse and was first built more than two hundred years ago, but had to be rebuilt three times since then. The first one was destroyed in the worst storm ever to hit the south-west coast."

"I don't know why *I* wasn't allowed to go," says a voice from the corner.

"Because you're a girl, silly," Andrew retorts. "Besides, Mam took you and Josephine out for tea that day."

"Yes, with the twins, who cried all the time. It wasn't fun at all."

"That's enough," I say. "Violet, you carry on reading *The Wind in the Willows* while Andrew and I continue with our lesson."

Violet, who hasn't lifted her eyes from my book throughout this exchange, doesn't respond. Is she reading, I wonder, or simply listening to my conversation with her brother?

"That's an interesting piece of information, Andrew. I had no idea of that lighthouse's history. And becoming a lighthouse keeper is a noble ambition. But a bit lonely perhaps. You really have to love the sea, but I know already that you do."

"I won't find it lonely. I'll be glad to be on my own."

"You might not be entirely alone. I'm told there's often more than one keeper and the duties are shared."

"We'd probably get along all right if we like the same things. No one at home cares about what interests *me*."

I decide to ignore that remark. It's becoming clear to me that the teasing Andrew receives because of his solitary nature and his inability to read has given him a chip on his shoulder. I need to make him understand that everyone's personality is different – some people are born to be loners – and that everyone has strengths and weaknesses He shouldn't feel inferior just because he finds reading difficult.

"Do you think you can learn to recognise the spelling

of *lighthouse*, Andrew? It's not an easy word to spell, as the *g* and *h* are silent – that means you don't pronounce them. You can split it into two words, *light* and *house*, and they will always be spelt the same way."

Andrew looks puzzled. "If you take out the *g* and *h* in *light*," he says, "you're left with *l-i-t*," he says, pronouncing each letter separately. "Why isn't that the spelling for *light*?"

"I agree that it should be, but *l-i-t* is pronounced *lit*, as in *he lit the fire*. The *i* vowel sound can be pronounced in two ways. *Light* uses a long *i* as in *sight* or *right*. *Sight* and *right* are also spelt with a silent *g-h*. But oftentimes, just adding an *e* to the end of a word causes it to be pronounced with the long *i* vowel sound, as in *bite, b-i-t-e,* or *kite, k-i-t-e*. Words like *lit*, *hit* or *sit* use what is called a short *i* vowel sound."

"I don't think I'll ever be able to understand that. I'm sorry, but it's no good – it's too difficult."

"I know, it is complicated, especially when words are spelt with silent letters. But it'll get easier, I promise. I've brought along a notebook for you. Let's make two columns, one for words with the long *i* and one for those with the short *i*. We'll read the verse once more, and then look for words that are pronounced with either of the two *i* vowel sounds. You follow along, while I read."

As I read the verse again, pointing to each word with my forefinger, I try to quell the unhelpful thought that teaching Andrew the basics of reading is going to be a long, slow process. I *must* persevere and not even think about giving up. I need to gain his confidence, like I did with Michael. Then, hopefully, it'll become easier.

"Now, Andrew," I say, "show me a word that you think has one of the *i* vowel sounds. Don't be afraid of making a mistake. Everyone makes them. When I was at school, I used to make lots of mistakes and was once made to stand in the corner of the classroom for an entire lesson."

Reluctantly, Andrew looks at the verse. He wasn't looking at the words when I pointed to them; so far, he's just been staring at the picture. It's as if he has some kind of aversion to the printed word. He finally points to the word *miles*.

"Very good," I say. "Can you read that word?"

He shakes his head.

"Never mind. The word is *miles*. You know your alphabet so you can see it starts with an *m*. The word is pronounced with the long *i* vowel sound. Take away the *s* and you can see it has an *e* at the end. An *s* at the end of a word usually means it's written in plural form, that is, there's more than one – in this case, more than one mile. The line reads, 'Across the sea for miles away'. Let's write the word *miles* under the long *i* column. Can you spot any others?"

He points to *ships* in the next line.

"Excellent. That word is *ships* – *s* and *h* together make a *sh* sound. *Ships* has a short *i*. Again, it ends with an *s*, so it's in the plural. Now we have both a long *i* and a short *i* in our lists. You do see the difference, don't you Andrew?"

"I think so," he says, though I'm not really sure that he understands.

"There's another word with the long *i* vowel sound in the verse, but it's a difficult one. It's *guides*. See this line? It reads *It guides them into harbor fair*. In this case, the *u* is silent. If you look at the word without the *u*, you'll see that it's similar to *miles*, which also has the long *i* vowel sound. Sometimes, in written English, you have to know when to ignore the letters that are silent."

Andrew is looking more baffled than ever, and I'm not surprised. Whoever came up with all these different spellings for words that sound similar when spoken aloud? I add a few more words to the lists and ask him to try to memorise their meanings and spellings before our next session. We'll start on another vowel sound then, as I think we've done enough on the subject for today. We read the verse one more time and I point out and write down the prepositions, which are essential for being able to read any sentence. Then I ask him to copy the whole verse into his notebook so he can practise reading it at home. But I make sure that the words 'harbour' and 'treacherous' are spelt correctly, explaining to him that the book is written by an American, hence some unusual spellings, and that in poetry it's sometimes necessary to truncate a word or two so that the verse flows smoothly.

Copying out the verse is a laborious task for Andrew. He writes each letter as it appears on the page; he doesn't seem to have learnt cursive, which is the way I was taught to write in school. I decide to let him do it in his own way; once he learns to read, fluency in writing may follow automatically.

When the lesson comes to an end, Violet asks me if she can borrow my precious copy of *The Wind in the Willows*. I feel I have to say yes, though I hate to part with it.

"All right, as long as you take good care of it," I say. "Do you promise that you will?"

"Yes, I promise," she says, sneaking a look at *The Navy Alphabet*. "So easy," she says. "Alphabet books are for babies."

"That's not true," I say. "Especially not this one. It has a lot of difficult words. Do you want me to test you on some of them?"

"Test her on her times tables," Andrew says. "She doesn't even know her five times table, which is the easiest."

"Everyone has different strengths, Andrew. Violet finds reading easy, but perhaps she struggles with arithmetic. You struggle with reading, but not arithmetic. We need to be understanding of each other's difficulties and realise that we're not all the same. Then we can give each other help when it's needed."

At this point, thankfully, the door opens and Cyril enters the room. He looks just as dour as he did last week, but Violet jumps up and gives him a big hug.

"Stop it, Violet," he says, disentangling himself from her arms. "Don't be so annoying. Come on, let's get home. I'm starving."

"Me too," Violet says. "Do you know what's for tea?"

"Bread and dripping, I think. Mam didn't have time to cook. But she said there's some leek and potato soup left over from yesterday."

I give each child a toffee to offset any disappointment they might feel about their prospective meal. Before he leaves, I remind Andrew to study the words we've listed and learn them off by heart before our next lesson. He gives me a nod, throws his satchel over his shoulder, and follows his siblings out of the door.

"How did it go today?" Lionel asks me, as I sit reflecting upon the last hour. "Any progress?"

"A little bit," I say. "Andrew seems to be able to recognise consonants and doesn't get them mixed up. It's just forming them into words that he still finds difficult. He has no idea about vowel sounds. So we're starting with vowels and adding consonants to them, which often changes the sound of the vowel. There's a lot for him to learn. I've made lists of words and asked him to memorise them for next week's lesson. I have no idea whether or not this is a good method for teaching a child to read. I fear it's going to be a long, slow process."

"I'm impressed, Bessie. How did you learn this? I mean, I know you're a keen reader yourself, but to be able to help the boy understand vowels and how their sounds change according to the consonants they're added to… that's not something many people would know how to teach."

"Well, I'm not sure that I know how to teach it either. As I've told you many times, I always wanted to be a teacher, but had to go to work at Farringdale House after Father died, so had no opportunity for any training. But out of curiosity, I would sometimes stand outside the schoolroom and listen to the governess teaching the children to read, and that was the method she used. The girls learnt quickly, but little Alexander was always naughty and wouldn't pay attention – he's was an intelligent boy but hated to study – so she had to go over and over the same lesson with him. I suppose it stuck in my mind. I don't know if that's the way children are taught to read in school these days, but it seemed to work with the Radcliffe children."

"It sounds like a good method to me, though I'll wager that there's more than one way of teaching reading. But if Andrew's not confusing letters of the alphabet – and, from what you've told me, it doesn't seem that he is – then I don't think he has dyslexia or, if you like, word blindness. You would notice right away if he were muddling up consonants. That will make it a lot easier for you, Bessie. I think he probably just fell behind early on in school – at least in reading, which didn't interest him as much as arithmetic – and then was unable to catch up. He seems to be something of an introvert, not keen on drawing attention to himself, and this is the result. What a pity no one helped him earlier on.

"And what about the girl? Was she a nuisance?"

"No, not really. I gave her *The Wind in the Willows* to read, and that mostly kept her quiet. Unlike you and Andrew, she was delighted with the book. She asked to take it home and I reluctantly agreed. I hope I get it back eventually. At the end of the lesson, she tried to embarrass Andrew by saying alphabet books were for babies, but he gave as good as he got. He said she's hopeless at arithmetic and doesn't even know her five times table."

"Sibling rivalry. Now that sounds familiar."

"Hmm, I can't say I was a victim of that. Learning wasn't highly valued in my family, so it never became a cause for argument. Father always praised me for my schoolwork, but the others didn't see *that* as something to be envious about. Thankfully, I wasn't teased for being studious, although Mother was never very impressed when I had my nose in a book and found chores for me to do instead."

"My brothers and I were always at odds with each other over who was the best in various subjects. But we all had different strengths. I was good at science and ciphering, Lawrence excelled in Latin and French, and Stuart was the bookworm of the family."

"And your sisters, Lionel?"

"Ah Bessie, you know I'm a man of a certain age. Female education was extremely limited at the time I went to school. For the average girl, sewing, cookery and learning to run a household were considered more important than academic subjects. The luckier ones were taught the basics of the three *Rs*, reading, writing and arithmetic. In middle to upper class families, playing the piano and a pleasant singing voice were looked upon as desirable talents and thought to be necessary for finding a good husband."

"I don't think much has changed, at least not outside of the big cities. But women are beginning to make their voices heard, as we both know, so there is cause for hope. Thankfully, young ladies like Mathilda and Edie are ready to fight for equality in education."

"Indeed, and about time too. It's been forty years since education became compulsory for both boys and girls, but attitudes about girls' education still seem to be stuck in the 19th century. Well, enough of that. Are you ready to go home now, my dear?"

"Yes, I'm beginning to feel hungry. I've prepared a stew that just needs heating up. We should consider ourselves fortunate – the Frost children are having to make do with bread and dripping for their supper."

"Ah, my favourite. If you don't feel like cooking, Bessie, you can give me that any day of the week. In my opinion, bread and dripping, with a chunk of cheese and a pickled onion, is a feast fit for a king."

8

A letter from Walter arrives in this morning's post. I wasn't expecting to hear from him so soon, as it's my turn to write. I tear open the envelope right away, hoping there's some news about the Goode family, but it's another troubling matter that my nephew is writing about. He's concerned for his uncle, my brother Edward, who is ill with a bout of influenza and too weak even to get out of bed. This comes as a shock to me, as Edward is hardly ever sick – he has a strong constitution and has always kept himself in reasonably good shape. Walter says he needs to work away from home for a few days – he's been asked to assist with a restoration job at Gloucester Cathedral – and he wonders if I can possibly stay with Edward while he's away.

I normally wouldn't ask you, Aunt, Walter writes, *as Blanche would happily take care of Uncle Edward while I'm gone, but her mother needs her at home. There's still no news about her aunt, and Mrs Goode isn't at all well at the moment. The absence of any communication from Ernest is especially painful. She continues to believe her sister is still alive – she says that, being her twin, she'd know instinctively if she had perished – but she can't rest or concentrate on anything else until we know the truth. Daisy and Blanche are doing everything at home, in addition to their nightly cleaning jobs at the woollen mill. Millie is of little help – she's highly strung, as you know, and still hasn't recovered from her latest stomach upset. It you do agree to come, Aunt, it wouldn't be for more than five or six days, and the doctor will visit every morning until Uncle Edward shows some signs of improvement. Already I can see cause for hope – he's not as delirious as he was last week – but he shouldn't be left alone just yet.*

Of course I shall go and stay with Edward. It's the least I can do. I feel so guilty about not being there more often, especially when Walter has to work away. And even if he were working locally, he could hardly be expected to care for his uncle on top of eight or more hours of hard physical labour each day. As for Mrs Goode being poorly, it doesn't surprise me at all. I should think losing a twin is like losing half of oneself. I'll reply to Walter right away and tell him I'll be there by tomorrow evening. If I can catch today's post, my letter is certain to reach Ferndell in the morning. I don't need to ask Lionel; I know he'll agree with me that I shouldn't waste any time. It's Edward's health that's the priority now.

I quickly respond to Walter's letter. I have an ample supply of penny stamps, so there's no need for me to go to the post office in town. Luckily, I am just in time to catch Mr Wright emptying the post box at the end of the road, so I hand him my letter.

"You've been running, Mrs Fielding," he says, as I stop to catch my breath. "It must be something urgent."

"Yes, it is," I say. "My nephew's written to tell me that my brother is ill and has asked if I'll go and look after him for a few days. Naturally, I cannot refuse. I'm planning to travel by train to my home village in Somerset in the morning and will arrive by the evening, so I need to let him know I'm coming."

"Oh, I'm sorry to hear about your brother. I hope it's not too serious an illness."

"Well, it's the flu, but my nephew thinks he may be over the worst of it. It's keeping him in bed that's going to be the most difficult task."

"I do hope he recovers quickly, Mrs Fielding. I'm sure he will, with your excellent care."

"You don't know my brother, Mr Wright. I'm the last person in the world he'll want caring for him, but thank you for your kind words."

I rush back home and pull my shabby suitcase out from under the bed. I throw in two old, plain dresses – I certainly don't want folk thinking that I've become too stylish for village life – and just one smart blouse and skirt in case I decide to pay a visit to Farringdale House. The suitcase is standing next to the front door when Lionel comes home from work.

"What's this, Bessie?" he asks. "Are you leaving me already?"

"Oh, Lionel," I say, giving him a hug. "I'm so glad you're home. Walter has written to say that Edward is ill with a bad bout of flu. He asked if I would stay with him for a few days, as he has to travel to Gloucester for work. He says Edward's still too poorly to stay alone in the house, and Blanche and Daisy have their work cut out for them at the moment. I wrote back immediately, saying I'd come right away. You won't object to my leaving tomorrow morning, will you?"

"No, of course not, Bessie. I'm sorry to hear about Edward. I take it the doctor is attending to him regularly? Walter's right, he shouldn't stay alone. But are you sure you'll be all right travelling on your own, my dear? I'd be happy to come with you, but I can't really close the pharmacy at such short notice."

"Don't worry, Lionel. Travelling alone will do me good. I've become too reliant on you this last year – though happily so, I might add. Besides, I have taken the train on my own once before – when I travelled to London to begin work at Mrs Grist's. But do you think you could check the times for me? As long as I know the stations where I need to change trains, and how long I'll have to wait for the next one, I'll have nothing to worry about."

"Yes, of course. I have an up-to-date timetable in my desk drawer. I'll write down the times and the stops for you, and of course I'll see you off at the station in the morning. I think it'll be just two changes – the local train will take you as far as Exeter, then you can take the Great Western Railway to Taunton, and from there another local train. You'll need to take a horse-drawn carriage to Ferndell – it's too far to walk with your suitcase – so it might be evening by the time you arrive. It does sound like quite a long journey, Bessie."

"That's all right. At least the evenings are light now, so I won't have to travel in the dark. And if Walter receives my letter in time, he's sure to check the times of the trains from Taunton and meet me at the local station. You know how considerate he is. Oh, Lionel, I do hope Edward gets better quickly. I can't believe he's caught the flu in June, of all months."

"It's not uncommon in the spring and early summer, especially after a bout of cold weather. If the house is damp – as you've said it is – then mould becomes a problem and its spores can weaken one's immune system, leading to bacterial illness. Walter needs to be careful as well."

"I know that Walter usually keeps a fire going, even in summer, and does his best to dry out the house when constant rain causes leakages and rising damp. It's such an old house that it's almost impossible to keep it warm and dry throughout the whole year. And when Walter travels and Edward's on his own, I don't think he bothers to light a fire, even in winter. He's out in his workshop all hours of the day and night, and I dread to think how cold and damp it gets in *there*."

"Well, you go and try to make him as comfortable as possible and talk some sense into him. If the doctor's managed to ease his fever, he probably just needs bed rest until he's strong again. That's going to be the most difficult part for you, Bessie – keeping him in bed."

"I know, that's what I'm worried about. And I'm not the one who can talk sense into him. He never listens to me. He can be quite stubborn at times and, if he's feeling better, he's going to be anxious to get back to his workshop. He hardly ever takes a day's rest. It's really a wonder he's not fallen sick before now."

Edward works as a carpenter and is never short of work. He is skilled in his trade and takes pride in it. Most houses in Ferndell possess some item of furniture that he's made from scratch, and he does a lot of repair work as well. But since the death of his wife Mabel, some six years ago, my brother has become quite the recluse, mixing with folk only when he absolutely has to, and keeping contact with family members to a bare minimum.

Clearly, my stay with Edward is not going to be an easy one. He'll be upset that I've been asked to come and care for him, and it will be a fight to keep him in bed. But I'll do my best, as he has provided a home for Walter since he was five years old and, while it wasn't exactly one filled with love and affection, it was more than I was able to offer him at the time.

The suitcase I hurriedly packed is the old cardboard one that I used for my first train journey almost two years ago. Admittedly, it has seen better days. Lionel insists that I transfer its contents into his leather one, which is much sturdier, though quite a bit heavier. Fortunately, I'm not taking much with me. Lionel's suitcase has his initials *LHF* – Lionel Hugh Fielding – engraved in the leather; he calls this inscription his personal monogram.

"Call it what you like," I say. "Those aren't *my* initials. I hope I don't accidentally leave the suitcase on the train, or I'll never be able to claim it."

"They *could* be your initials," Lionel says, smiling. "Lizzie Hardwicke Fielding. How about that? You were christened Elizabeth, after all, and Hardwicke is your maiden name."

"Lizzie! No one has ever called me that in my life. And whoever uses their maiden name once they're married?"

"It's certainly unusual, but it wouldn't surprise me if it becomes more common in the future. That wouldn't be a bad thing. I feel sorry for ladies who have to give up their family name when they marry. Didn't Mathilda suggest that Blanche keep her maiden name of Goode when she marries Walter, rather than becoming Mrs Blanche Blanch? I think she said it was an American suffragette who first introduced the notion of women declining to take their husbands' surnames."

"Well, I'm sure Mathilda was only joking, despite her sympathies for the suffragette movement. In any case, Blanche would never consider it. She's looking forward to becoming Mrs *Walter* Blanch."

"Poor Blanche. She'll have to put up with no end of ridicule. The things we do for love, eh Bessie? Oh, before I forget – take this tonic for Edward. It's not a medicine, as you know from the many bottles you used to buy for Fanny Grist, but it's a healthy pick-me-up for when he's on the road to recovery, but still feels weak and tired."

"Oh, thank you, Lionel. Your tonic used to make Mrs Grist feel better in an instant, so I'm sure it'll work for Edward too."

I would never tell Lionel, but I'm not at all sure that Edward will be willing to take the tonic without checking with the doctor first, and I can hardly tell the doctor that it's a pharmacist's concoction. Lionel is trusted in his profession and would never deceive any customer, but he tells me that not all pharmacists are as principled as he is. And, although it pains me to admit it, Edward would love to have a reason to belittle Lionel, as he knows that would hurt *me* most of all.

Lionel and I walk together in silence to the station the next morning. It's about a mile from our cottage as the crow flies. We cut across a couple of fields to save time. It's another beautiful day, with just a few fluffy white clouds in an otherwise clear blue sky. The seagulls are making their usual racket, but it's a sound that I've come to enjoy, reminding me always that I live near the sea.

We arrive at the station about fifteen minutes before the train is due and sit down on the platform bench to wait.

"You will write to let me know about Edward's recovery and when you plan to return, won't you, my dear?" Lionel says, taking my hand.

"Yes, of course, Lionel. I'll send you a letter in a day or two and give you all the news. Walter won't leave for Gloucester until I arrive, so Edward won't be alone even for a day. He'll only be away for a short time, five or six days at the most, but I think I should stay until the doctor says Edward is out of danger, don't you?"

"Definitely, Bessie. You stay as long as you need to. And don't you worry about me. You know I'm quite capable of looking after myself."

"I know that. I'm certain you won't miss me at all."

"Now, you know that's not true. I'll be counting the days until you return. I just don't want you to come back too early and then be worried about Edward. Stay until he's completely well. And talk to Walter about the dampness and mould in the house. As I've said, it's not good for his health either."

"Yes, I will, but I don't know what he'll be able to do about it. Their moving house is out of the question."

"Well, during this fine weather, he can at least keep the windows open and allow fresh air to circulate, especially in Edward's bedroom. Hark, I think the train is coming – that was its whistle, if I'm not mistaken. Don't forget to give the family my regards, and you will take care of yourself, won't you, Bessie?"

"Yes, I will, Lionel. I promise. Will you let Mrs Frost know that I won't be here to give Andrew his lesson this week? Tell her I'm sorry. It's a pity – we were just beginning to make a bit of progress."

"Of course, I'll let her know. And don't worry. There'll be plenty of time over the summer for you to work with Andrew."

The train grinds to a halt and Lionel opens the carriage door for me. He gives me a peck on the cheek and hands me the suitcase. I climb in, suddenly feeling fearful. I do so wish Lionel were coming with me! But I mustn't let him see that I'm nervous, or he'll be worried about me. I find an empty compartment, sit down next to the window, and blow him a farewell kiss. With an ear-piercing chugging sound, the train moves away from the platform and, after one last wave, Lionel is out of sight.

I'm alone in the compartment for the first leg of my journey. I've brought a book with me, but am unable to read; my mind is too preoccupied. I haven't been to Ferndell since I went with Lionel in the days that followed our London wedding. As I've said before, Edward wasn't exactly welcoming on that occasion. I think Lionel's presence made him feel uncomfortable, although there was no reason at all for him to feel that way, since Lionel was his usual good-humoured self. My younger brother Harold is always easier company; he talked at length with Lionel on a range of different topics, and his wife Dorothy is a chatterbox – she finds conversation easy, even with a stranger. Edward, as head of the family, should have been the one to make Lionel feel at home, but he resents any intrusion by outsiders, and I'm sure my husband will always be an outsider in *his* eyes. He won't be happy to see me, that's for sure, but at least I'll be alone this time, so he won't need to make any attempt to be polite.

I am greatly looking forward to seeing Walter, even if it's just for one night before he leaves for Gloucester, and another one when he returns. I haven't yet had a chance to tell him about Mr Franklin, the bookshop owner, and his promise to try to make contact with young Ernest Doyle in New York. I hope Walter will agree with me that it can't do any harm. Whatever the reason for Ernest's silence, the Goode family needs to find out what has become of Hilda; being ignorant of the truth is making everyone feel wretched and in a permanent state of anxiety.

On the second leg of my journey, an energetic-looking woman of about fifty enters my compartment. I noticed her pacing the platform at Exeter; we had alighted from the same train. I can tell just by looking at her that she's a friendly sort of person, so I bid her good morning and ask her how far she's travelling.

"I'm going as far as Bristol," she says. "I'll be staying with my daughter Maud for a week or so to help her pack up her belongings. She and her two children are coming to live with me and my husband for the foreseeable future."

"Oh, that will be enjoyable for all of you, I'm sure."

"Well, yes and no. You see, she's just lost her husband and is in a pretty bad way – in fact, I'd go so far as to say that her heart is in pieces. She doesn't have the will to get up in the morning, let alone see to the children or do any packing. I don't know how she'll ever manage on her own – Colin was so good with William and Wendy and has always been the love of Maud's life. But hopefully, a change of scenery will do her good and, since we live right on the seashore, the children will enjoy playing on the beach. They'll miss a bit of school, but I'm sure they won't complain about that. They're being very brave, but they must be grieving just as much as their mother is."

"I'm sure they are. I'm so sorry to hear about your loss, Mrs…"

"Smith. Winifred Smith. And you are?"

"Bessie, Bessie Fielding. I'm pleased to make your

acquaintance, Mrs Smith. Was your son-in-law's death a sudden one, may I ask, or had he been ill for some time?"

"Sudden, yes. And tragic. He died at sea. He went down with the *Titanic* on his way to America."

"Oh, my goodness! That really is tragic. No wonder your daughter is heartbroken, and the children must be suffering terribly. As it happens, that disaster has been on my mind a lot these last few weeks. You see, the aunt of my nephew's betrothed is missing following the sinking. We are desperately trying to find out whether or not she's still alive. No one seems to know anything. How did you find out that your son-in-law had perished, Mrs Smith, if you don't mind my asking?"

"My daughter received a letter from one of the other passengers..." Mrs Smith pauses, pulls a handkerchief from her cleavage and wipes her eyes. "I'm sorry," she says, "it still pains me to talk about it."

"Please don't feel you have to continue. I would hate to upset you."

"No, it's all right. Sometimes it helps to talk about it. It seems that Colin befriended one of the passengers – Barlow is his name – during the voyage. *He* managed to make it to safety and sent Maud a letter telling her that, sadly, Colin had not been able to reach a lifeboat in time. That was the case for many of the third-class passengers, apparently. The two men must have exchanged addresses at some point. It was good of him to write, even though it wasn't the news we were praying for. But at least it put an end to the futile hope that Colin *might* have survived. It's terrible not knowing one way or the other. I'm sorry to hear you still have no news of the lady you've just mentioned. Was she also travelling third-class?"

"Yes, and she was alone. We're trying to reach her son

in New York, since the purpose of her voyage was to attend his forthcoming wedding. But the family hasn't received any news from him at all, which is strange as he must know that they're all terribly worried. My husband's friend is going to New York on business – he may have already left – and will try to contact him. But, with every day that passes, it becomes more and more doubtful that his mother is still alive."

"I can understand your concern. If you like, I can ask Colin's friend if he knows whether or not the lady is alive. There's always a possibility that they may have become acquainted before the ship went down. Or, if she did survive, he may have met her on the rescue ship."

"It's a kind offer and I thank you for it. But you have your own troubles – I really shouldn't burden you with mine."

"Oh, don't worry. I'll be happy to help. All I need to do is write a letter, which I'll be doing anyway. I'm going to ask Maud to give me Mr Barlow's address as soon as I get to Bristol."

"Well, if you're sure it's no trouble. Her name is Mrs Hilda Doyle. I'll write it down, along with my own name and address. Like I said, we don't expect her to have survived, but until we hear word to the contrary, we can't really stop hoping and praying. Thank you so much for your kindness, Mrs Smith."

People are so considerate when you least expect it, I think to myself. This poor woman, whom I've only just met, has so many cares of her own; her daughter and grandchildren having lost not only a cherished husband and father, but also the family bread-winner, no doubt. Yet she's willing to make enquiries about Hilda on my behalf. Compared to what others are suffering, my own life at present seems idyllic – although, to be fair, it hasn't always been so. I suppose everyone is dealt their fair share of ups and downs during the course of a lifetime, but for some reason we always seem to remember the downs more often than the ups.

Mrs Smith and I share our sandwiches and slices of cake. We both have a flask of tea, although perhaps a cold drink would have been more refreshing, as it's so warm today. We are continuing to move speedily across glorious countryside and the sun is shining directly onto our carriage window, heating up the compartment. We talk for a little while about the fine weather, which surely won't continue for much longer, and then she asks me what my husband does for a living. I tell her he's a pharmacist, that we met in London and have been married for less than two years.

"A pharmacist?" Mrs Smith says, raising her eyebrows. "Then you've made a good catch, if I may say so."

I feel myself blushing.

"I'm sorry," she says. "Sometimes I just blurt things out without thinking. I should really have said that *he's* made a good catch."

"No, you're right, I'm the one who's gained the most from our marriage. To this day, it still surprises me. What about your husband, Mrs Smith? What work does he do?"

"He's a lighthouse keeper. That's why we live on the coast. The lighthouse is onshore, so he's not away for weeks at a time like many others doing the same job. He enjoys the work and wouldn't change it for the world. He was brought up in a coastal town and loves the sea. I don't think he could live anywhere else."

I think of Andrew and his dream of becoming a lighthouse keeper.

"I know a boy who would also love that job," I say. "What does it involve, exactly?"

"Well, I'm not sure that any special skills are needed, apart from dedication to the safety of all ships and sailing vessels, and respect for the changing moods of the sea. There's a lot of cleaning and maintenance work to be done and, of course, they have to keep the light burning at all times. A keeper's sleep is often disrupted, especially during rough weather, though during periods of calm, nothing much happens. If the lighthouse is on an island or a rock, then isolation can be a problem. I think folk have to be of a certain character to take on such work. Since they are on their own a good deal, it helps if they are solitary by nature. Stan and I are complete opposites. I'm happy being with other people, while he enjoys his own company and is always keen to escape to the lighthouse – just to get away from me, I think."

"Oh, I'm sure that's not true. The boy in question is a solitary soul, too, and doesn't have many friends. He's only nine years old, so his future ambitions will almost certainly change. At the moment he's just anxious to avoid the teasing of his siblings, who regard him as a bit of an oddity. He certainly loves the sea, and collects shells and pebbles from the beach to use in his artwork, which he keeps hidden from his family. I can see why becoming a lighthouse keeper appeals to him."

"Perhaps I can ask Stanley to show him around the lighthouse one day and explain what he does. I'm sure there's a lot more to it than he lets on. My grandson William is the same age, so they could go there together. Who knows, they may become friends. Stan and his assistant work in shifts, so we'd need to pick a day when he's not on duty. Why don't you check with the boy's parents to see if they'd agree to such a visit? You could bring him yourself on the train one afternoon. I saw you board this morning at Brampton-on-Sea – we live at Larkin's Cove, some thirty-odd miles along the coast."

"Oh, thank you, Mrs Smith, that sounds like a wonderful idea. If your husband agrees, I can certainly ask Andrew's mother if she'd allow him to come with me."

"Stanley will agree if I'm the one who proposes it. He wouldn't dare to say no! We'll stay in touch, Mrs Fielding. I need to get Maud and the children settled in with us first, and that's going to take a few weeks. But perhaps later in the summer, during the school holidays, we can arrange a visit."

How excited Andrew is going to be when I tell him of this excursion! But I won't mention anything until it's settled. After all, Mrs Smith and her husband are going to have their hands full with their daughter and grandchildren moving in with them, which is likely to be quite an ordeal for the whole family, given their recent bereavement. She's promised to write to me after making enquiries about Hilda, so I'll wait and see if she remembers her suggestion and proposes a date for our visit.

9

Walter is on the platform waiting for me, just as I'd hoped. He received my letter this morning and travelled to the station to meet both late afternoon arrivals. Fortunately, he didn't have long to wait; I arrived on the five o'clock train from Taunton, which was right on time.

It's so good to see him! It's been almost six months since we were last together. Lionel and I went to London shortly before Christmas 1911 to stay with Mathilda and Ronald, while Walter and Blanche stayed with Mrs Grist for two nights. It was Blanche's first time in London and we were able to spend a whole day together, touring the city by motorbus. I was so surprised when I heard that Mrs Grist had invited them to stay with her in Wandsworth, but it seems that she and Walter got to know one another at my wedding reception and have since kept in touch. I'd always told her what a fine young man he was, but I suppose she needed to meet him herself to be convinced. Walter told me he'd slept in my old attic room – the thought of which pleased me a great deal – while Blanche was given Phillip's more spacious bedroom for the night.

Walter and Blanche also met with Edie while in London. Thankfully, they are now the best of friends, though it took a while for Walter to forgive Edie for putting her career before their courtship. But once Blanche had effectively taken away the sting of his heartache, he finally began replying to Edie's letters, some of which he'd not even opened. Blanche was initially a little suspicious of Edie's desire to stay in touch with her former sweetheart, but Walter has assured her that she has nothing at all to worry about; there is no danger of his affections wavering. He said she should rest assured that she is the one with whom he intends to spend the rest of his life, and to shun Edie's obvious wish for friendship would be unwarranted and unkind.

"How was your journey, Aunt?" Walter asks me, freeing himself from the tight embrace that I've been longing to give him for so many months.

"It all went well, thank you, Walter. Your aunt is no longer afraid of travelling alone. Besides, I met a nice lady on the train and we've become friends. I'll tell you about her in the carriage. But first, tell me, how is Edward? Is he any better?"

"He's a little bit better – certainly no worse. The doctor thinks he'll pull through, if only he can be persuaded to stay in bed. He keeps trying to get up and it's not easy telling him not to. You know how stubborn he can be. I hope he'll listen to you more than he listens to me."

"Oh dear. I don't think I'll have any more success than you've had, but I'll do my best. I can stay for as long as you think is necessary, my dear. You have your work to attend to. Don't worry too much about your uncle – I'll make sure he recovers as quickly as possible."

I notice that Walter looks unusually tired as he picks up my suitcase and escorts me to a horse-drawn carriage that's ready and waiting. It's clear that he's been worried about his uncle and has not been sleeping well. It pains me to see him so anxious and drawn and I wish he'd asked me to come sooner. He should not have had to shoulder the burden of caring for Edward alone.

It takes almost an hour to reach the village of Ferndell.

It's a bumpy journey, but compensated – for me at least – by the pleasurable sights and smells of the serene countryside that is so familiar to me.

During the ride, I tell Walter about Mrs Smith and her offer to write to her late son-in-law's friend who managed to survive the sinking of the *Titanic*.

"It's kind of her," I say, "considering her own terrible loss. It's doubtful that this fellow ever made Hilda's acquaintance, or knows of her fate, but there can't be any harm in her asking him. There probably weren't a lot of women travelling alone in third class, so she might have stood out."

"Well, regardless of the outcome, you're right, it's good of her to take the trouble. We can't leave any stone unturned, as I've often heard *you* say, Aunt Bessie."

"Exactly. It's what your grandfather used to say. There's another person I should tell you about, who's also offered to help us. He's an American, by the name of Bertrand Franklin, and he owns the bookshop in Brampton-on-Sea. Believe it or not, he's acquainted with Ernest, and he says he'll try to contact him while in New York on business. He knew his late father too, though he didn't know he was deceased."

"Really? My goodness, what a coincidence!"

"It is indeed. I hope you don't think I was too forward in telling Mr Franklin about Hilda, Walter. It's just that when I told him where I grew up, he said he used to live near Ferndell and knew an Irishman by the name of Doyle, whose son, at that time, was about to leave for America. After hearing that, I couldn't *not* tell him about the misfortunes that have struck the Doyle family. He hadn't been in touch with them for quite some time, so had no idea about Declan's death or Hilda's ill-fated voyage."

"It's quite all right, Aunt. I know that you're only trying to help. But we'll keep what you've told me to ourselves until you hear from this gentleman, or from your new friend. As I've said before, I don't want to raise Mrs Goode's hopes for no good reason. She needs to come to terms with the fact that, most likely, her sister *isn't* coming back, despite her insistence that her heart would have told her if Hilda had perished. She keeps saying that no news is good news and, until she's told by an authority that her sister is deceased, she won't believe anything to the contrary. It's difficult for her to accept the reality of the situation. I think it's only by deceiving herself in this way that she's able to get up in the morning. As it is, she does very little in the daytime apart from moping about the house."

"Poor woman. Mrs Smith's daughter is the same, apparently. And she has two young children to take care of. You will take me to visit the Goodes during my stay, won't you Walter? I feel I should make my sympathies known to Mrs Goode, though obviously not my condolences."

"Yes, of course, Aunt. We can go there the day after my return from Gloucester. Well, here we are at last. The garden's looking a bit of a mess, I'm afraid. Everything is growing so quickly and I haven't had time to attend to it."

"I can do a bit of gardening while I'm here and see what vegetables need harvesting. You probably have fruit that needs picking too. We won't let anything go to waste, Walter."

"Oh, thank you, Aunt Bessie. I'm so glad you're here. I feel like a weight has been lifted from my shoulders."

"Say no more, Walter. I can see how tired you are, and I'm glad to be here to lighten your load. I just wish I could have come sooner. Now, let's go inside and see how that my brother of mine is getting on. I hope we'll find him in bed."

Walter insists on paying the coachman himself, refusing to take my coins, and then leads the way into the cottage where my siblings and I grew up. The dwelling belonged to my father and his father before him, and it remains dear to my heart. When Edward married, he moved away for a few years, as Mabel and Mother would not have been able to live harmoniously under one roof. But Edward knew that the cottage would be his eventually and he didn't have too long to wait. After Mother's death, he and Mabel, two growing sons and five-year old Walter moved back in. I was already working at Farringdale House by then and had no need of a home – at least that was Edward's assumption. My younger brother Harold, however, sensing my overwhelming sadness at this change in domestic circumstances, told me that I would always find a welcome in his family's cottage on the outskirts of the village, modest though it was, and that I should henceforth look upon it as my home away from home.

Although the exterior of the Cotswold stone cottage – covered almost entirely by clinging ivy – looks more or less the same, the interior bears no resemblance to the cosy home in which Mother and Father raised four children, or the rather less comfortable but immaculately clean one that Mabel kept for Edward and the boys. I can see none of the personal touches that make a house a home; all items that might have reminded me of my parents or of Mabel have disappeared. Walter apologises for the lack of domesticity, but I know it's not his fault.

Edward is the one who insists on the bare minimum of homely comforts, and prides himself on being able to live that way. Perhaps once he recovers from his illness, he'll realise that he's not as resilient as he likes to think he is.

"Let me take you up to Uncle Edward's bedroom," Walter says, "though you hardly need to be shown the way. Nothing much has changed."

I have not been in the master bedroom, which is at the back of the house and has the nicest view, since Mother died, and it comes as a bit of a shock to see that Edward is now the sole occupant. I'm pretty sure that the double bed, with its handcrafted headboard, is the same one that witnessed the births of all four Hardwicke children, myself included.

Edward is sitting up in bed, carving a piece of wood. Shavings are scattered all over the counterpane. As we walk in, he tries to speak, but is cut short by a fit of coughing.

"Bessie, why on earth are you here?" he croaks, finally. "I told Walter not to send for you. I can manage perfectly well on my own."

"Of course you can't manage on your own, Edward," I say. "That's a nasty cough you've got. And you look as pale as a sheet."

"I'm all right now. It's just the cough that remains. Tomorrow morning you can go straight back to wherever you came from – Devon, isn't it? I don't need you here, thank you very much."

"Are you going to be difficult all the time I'm staying with you, Edward? I hope not. Whether you like it or not, I'm going to look after you for a few days while Walter is away. And I shall make sure you stay in bed and eat some good, nutritious food. You would never be able to manage on your own. Just look at the mess you've made on that eiderdown. And you're probably making your cough worse, breathing in all that sawdust. Who is going to clear that up?"

"Well, you, now that you're here," he sighs.

This is not a good start to our time together. I need to be more sympathetic, despite his objection to my presence; the poor man has been seriously ill for the first time in his life. He's beginning to look older than his forty-seven years. It shocks me to see that his hair, although still plentiful, is now mostly grey and badly in need of a cut. His pale face is gaunt, with sunken cheeks, and the dark circles beneath his watery blue eyes lay bare a succession of sleepless nights.

"Of course, I'll do whatever you ask of me," I say in a kinder tone, "as long as you do what I ask of you. Walter, could you find some old sheets of newspaper that your uncle can use to cover the eiderdown and catch the wood shavings? And Edward, if you're going to sit up in bed, you should wear something a bit warmer. Your nightshirt is looking quite threadbare."

I spot an old jacket lying on the chair next to the bed and place it around my brother's shoulders, ignoring his protests. I feel like asking him if he still has any of Mabel's handmade shawls – she was an expert in crochet – but I know what the answer will be. Edward got rid of all Mabel's clothes shortly after her death. It was as if he wanted to retain no reminders of their twenty-year marriage, even though it was a solid one as marriages go, and produced two fine sons.

Once I've made Edward comfortable and cleared up the wood shavings on the counterpane, I peer into the small room at the end of the landing where I will be sleeping. Walter has placed my suitcase at the foot of the bed next to the window. This is the room that I shared with my sister Ethel for almost twelve years, and the sight of those two narrow beds brings back so many memories that I am quite overcome with emotion for a few moments. But there will be time to reminisce and reflect on those times when I retire for the night and, if tears begin to flow, no one will be any the wiser. For what remains of this evening, I need to savour every minute of Walter's company.

In the kitchen downstairs, I busy myself making a broth for Edward. Carrots, onions, potatoes and turnips are laid out on a tray, and Walter tells me that there's a freshly skinned chicken in the food safe. The dear lad says that he'll be more than happy to prepare our meal if I'm tired from my journey. I know that he usually cooks for Edward and himself, but I'm not going to let him lift a finger while I'm in the house. I quickly re-familiarise myself with the workings of the ancient kitchen and soon have Edward's broth simmering in a saucepan. Walter and I decide to have eggs for supper. The chicken will keep until the morning when I can roast it. Walter will have left at the crack of dawn on his bicycle – on which he regularly travels great distances – but he assures me that he skinned the chicken for my benefit, not for his own. Tomorrow I will also make chicken soup for Edward, which – according to Lionel – alleviates flu symptoms and helps to fight infection.

"It's a bit of shock for me to see Edward like this," I say to Walter, once we're sitting down to a meal together. "He's always been as strong as a horse and, even when everyone else was poorly with coughs and colds, he stayed well."

"I know," Walter says. "I can't remember him ever being sick. But, as I said, the doctor thinks he's over the worst of it. Not everyone recovers from such a bad case of flu. Do you remember Mrs Pullinger from Avery Farm? The poor woman passed away last week. Her symptoms were the same as Uncle Edward's, but her fever never broke. Farmer Pullinger and their four children are beside themselves with grief."

"Oh, Walter, I am sorry to hear that. Yes, I knew Maggie Pullinger and her sister well. We were at school together, though Maggie was a few years older than me. Her youngest child can't be more than nine or ten. How very sad. Are there others in the village who've been ill?"

"One of the Pullinger boys was also poorly, but he's now recovered. Just between us, Aunt, Uncle Edward was over at Avery Farm earlier this month. He was delivering a footstool he'd made for Mrs Pullinger. He may have caught the flu there. But then again, there must surely be others in the village who've been sick with it too – I've been so busy with work and caring for my uncle that it's been a while since I've heard all the local news."

"What about the Goode family? I sincerely hope they manage to avoid catching it. That would be the straw that breaks the camel's back, as your grandfather used to say. Have you seen much of Mrs Goode and her girls in the last week or so?"

"No, hardly at all. Not even Blanche. I thought I might be contagious, being so close to Uncle Edward, and I certainly didn't want to inflict more suffering on the Goode family. Blanche drops me a letter every couple of days, but she hasn't much to tell me. As you know, they're still trying to convince themselves that Hilda has survived, but as time passes and there's still no word from Ernest, it seems less and less likely."

"Well, let's wait and see if Mr Franklin from the bookshop is able to contact him. If Ernest is still in New York, he must have heard *something* about his mother. The list of survivors that Ronald obtained from the American Embassy may not have been complete, and surely a list of those who *didn't* survive has been drawn up by now. Shocking as it may sound, if Hilda's name appears on the latter list, then the family can at least begin to come to terms with their loss, however difficult that might be."

"That's true. I do feel sorry for Mrs Goode, Aunt. She's not a strong woman and is still grieving for her husband Henry. His passing came as a terrible blow to the whole family. And now her sister – her *twin* sister no less – is missing, presumed dead. Not only that, but her beloved brother John died just before Christmas. That was expected – he'd been ill for a long time – but it still came as a shock. They'd always been so close. She feels as if she's losing all her family, one by one."

"Poor woman. They do say misfortune comes in threes, and that certainly seems to be the case for Mrs Goode. But it must be some consolation to her that Joseph and yourself will soon be joining her family. It's a pity Joseph and Daisy's wedding has been postponed, but let's hope that by the end of the year the nuptials can take place. Do you have any date in mind for your own wedding, Walter dear?"

"No, not yet. We still haven't decided where we're going to live. Blanche would like us to stay with her mother and younger sister, but Uncle Edward assumes we're going to live here. Don't mention this to anyone,

Aunt, but he's told me that he plans to leave the house to me. Cousin Victor has his own place, close to his work, and it's unlikely that Ralph will ever return to Ferndell. The last we heard was that he was in Singapore, walking out with a pretty Chinese girl. The Royal Navy has taken him to so many parts of the world that I'm sure he'd find life stifling in this tight-knit community if he were ever to return. In terms of where he will eventually decide to settle, you could say that the world is his oyster. In a way I envy him, but I don't think I could ever leave the village for good. Anyway, to be honest, I don't feel comfortable about Uncle Edward's plan to leave me the house. I'm only his nephew, after all, and I'm not even a Hardwicke. It should go to one of his sons."

"I can understand the way you feel, Walter. But remember, this was your grandparents' house, so it really belongs to all of us. Your mother grew up here, so it seems to me that you're just as entitled to the house as Victor or Ralph, and if they don't intend to live in it, then why shouldn't you and Blanche make it your home? The important thing is that it remains in the family. Besides, for the best part of your life, you've grown up in this house too, haven't you, my love?"

"Hmm… if you put it that way, then I suppose I do have an equal right to its ownership. But if Victor or Ralph object, then I shan't insist on it. I certainly don't want to fall out with either of them. They're my cousins, but are more like brothers to me. We'll see what happens. Hopefully, Uncle Edward won't be leaving us for many years to come. As for the immediate future, at the moment Blanche isn't ready to leave her mother. Millie is still young and not very sensible, so is no substitute for Daisy or Blanche. And Daisy will be going to live with

Joseph at the farm cottage as soon as they're married. We'll just bide our time and hope that things will fall into place by next year.

"You must be tired from your journey, Aunt, and I don't want to keep you up. I'll need to make an early start in the morning, so you might not see me before I leave. I do hope that Uncle Edward won't be too difficult while I'm away. I should be back by next weekend, depending on how the work goes. But I don't think it'll be a lengthy job and I won't be working alone. You'll be free to leave as soon as I return – I'm sure Uncle Lionel is already feeling your absence. I'm really grateful and relieved that you've come at such short notice. I could never have left my uncle alone, and it would have been hard to give up this particular job."

"I'm only too glad to be of help, Walter. As I've said, coming to look after Edward while you're away is the least I can do. At times like this, I wish I didn't live so far from Ferndell. It should be *me* taking care of your uncle, not you. Anyway, I can stay as long as you need me. Don't worry about Lionel – he's perfectly able to look after himself. In fact, I think he enjoys showing me how independent he is."

"He probably misses you much more than you give him credit for. Remember, this is *your* home too, so you're certainly welcome to stay as long as you like, now or at any other time. I'll say goodnight now, Aunt Bessie, as I'd like to get a full night's sleep before my journey. I haven't been sleeping well, as you've probably guessed, but now that *you're* here to care for Uncle Edward, I know I'll be dead to the world until sunrise. It'll be the first time in I don't know how long."

10

Edward is not an easy patient by any means, but I'm thankful that the doctor thinks he'll make a full recovery. Old Doctor Thornberry arrives mid-morning and says he's pleased with his improved condition. He no longer needs to take the pain reliever phenazone, which had been prescribed earlier.

"All your brother needs now is rest, good hygiene and a healthy, nutritious diet," the doctor tells me on the landing just outside Edward's bedroom. "If his fever returns, which I don't think it will, make sure he drinks plenty of fluids and please insist that he eats. The latest medical thinking – which I agree with – is that one should not starve a fever, as was advised in the old days. Good nutrition promotes good health, whatever the illness may be. I won't call again, now that I know he's being looked after by your good self. You know where to find me should you need me, Miss Hardwicke."

"Thank you, Doctor," I say. "I'm Mrs Fielding now, though having been Miss Hardwicke for so many years, I still answer to that name. Most of the time I don't even remember to correct folk when they use my maiden name."

"Oh, I'm so sorry. I had no idea you were married. I can't think why I didn't hear of it before now. News like that usually travels so quickly in the village."

"Oh, my wedding was a small affair, and it took place in London. That's probably why you heard nothing about it. My husband and I are living in Devon now, in Brampton-on-Sea – we moved there last year – and I must say I was happy to leave the smoke behind me and breathe fresh air once again."

"Well, now that you remind me, I think I did hear that you'd gone to live in London. You're right, the persistent smog in big cities like London isn't at all good for people's health. It's now common knowledge that breathing in the sulphurous fumes from coal combustion leads to respiratory illness and slower growth during childhood. Your nephew Walter might never have reached a height of six foot had he been living in a city. But I suppose not everyone is happy with a quiet country life, and industry does provide job opportunities to those who'd otherwise be unemployed.

"Anyway, please accept my belated congratulations on your marriage, Mrs Fielding. As I recall, you were rarely sick, so I had few reasons to call on you after your dear father passed away. He had a weak heart, if I remember correctly. I knew both your parents well. And of course, I've not forgotten your poor sister who died in childbirth. That was a sad affair, though I must say her firstborn has grown up to be a fine young man."

"Yes, and soon to be married himself. How time does fly."

"Indeed, it does. Now, I'll bid you farewell, as I've few more calls to make this morning. And I'm sure you have plenty to do yourself instead of standing here chatting to an old man like me. It's been a pleasure talking to you again, and I wish you every happiness in your married life."

"Thank you, Doctor. And thank you for calling on my brother. I'll make sure he's taken good care of, at least until Walter returns. And don't worry, I'll insist that he eats properly. My husband also maintains that a nutritious diet is the key to good health."

"Rightly so," the doctor says, as he carefully makes his way down the stairs, one hand on the banister and his Gladstone bag and cane in the other. At the front door, he tips his hat to me before shuffling down the garden path.

It's been years since I've spoken to old Doctor Thornberry. He's been the village doctor for as long as anyone can remember. Certainly, he's of my parents' generation, and is no doubt several years their senior. And yet, he carries on working and never considers retiring. You'd think that after at least fifty years of visiting the sick and the dying, hearing their complaints and tending to their illnesses, he'd be ready for a bit of a rest. But no, Doctor Thornberry is a Ferndell institution and will probably continue with his practice until the day he draws his last breath. I do wish Lionel could meet him; they'd probably have so much to talk about. Lionel could seek his opinions and pick his brain on the ancient homeopathic remedies that he has a preference for. Still, he has to be careful these days, as many folk – physicians included – are beginning to distrust the old cures, tried and tested though they are.

As far as I'm aware, the doctor has never taken a wife, which is probably the reason why he was unaware of my having become a married woman. I'm sure my marriage was a hot topic in the village at the time, but the good doctor wouldn't have heard any of the gossip without a wife to enlighten him. I did once ask Walter what folk were saying about me, but he was his usual discreet self and told me that I should know by now that he never listens to idle chit-chat and, besides, no one would dare to say anything – critical or otherwise – about me in front of him. Of course, the villagers mean no harm. So little happens in their daily lives that when a single woman from a local family moves away from the village, the occurrence naturally provokes a great deal of interest. Even more so if the person in question has been in domestic service for many years, and then – after less than a year – marries a Londoner of a different class from her own. But I'm probably giving myself far more importance than I have a right to expect. Doubtless, once someone is absent for a year or more, they're no longer of interest – 'out of sight, out of mind', as Father used to say.

Once Edward is settled with a cup of tea and a newspaper, I spend the morning cooking and giving the house a good clean. There's a pile of washing to be done, but I'll leave that until tomorrow. The weather looks set to remain fine, so I'll have no difficulty in drying it out in the back garden. Edward and Walter pay a village girl to come once a week to do some housework and take away the laundry, but glancing around the kitchen and parlour, I can see that she's not very thorough. Naturally, being men, they don't notice. They're both so engrossed in their work and, as a rule, spend little time indoors.

I check on Edward every hour or so. In the afternoon he's once again sitting up in bed and whittling away at a wooden horse that he's crafting for his son Victor's eldest boy. My brother is an expert in sculpting and can fashion striking objects from any piece of wood; the mantelpiece in the parlour is lined with his creations. In fact, for a wedding present, he gave Lionel and myself a foot-high statue of a lion; it's a unique piece of work and is always admired by our visitors.

I offer to read to my brother while he works – a few

Walter Scott novels are collecting dust on the bookshelf – but he declines, telling me to get on with whatever I'm doing and not to keep fussing over him.

"Tomorrow I'm getting up," he says. "I'm losing my strength staying in bed all the time. I need to take some exercise. Look how fine the weather is – I've yet to enjoy the early summer sunshine. A walk as far as the river will do me good. Better than being stuck in this bed, day in, day out."

"But Edward," I say, "Walter and Doctor Thornberry have entrusted me to look after you, and they both insist that you stay in bed. It was only a week ago that you had a raging fever and it was touch and go as to whether or not you'd pull through. I don't think you should go out-of-doors just yet. It's warm enough in the sun, but still a little cool in the shade."

"I'll just walk to the river and back. You can come with me if you like, unless you want to avoid seeing anyone you know."

"Naturally, I'll come with you when you do go for a walk. But I still think it's too early, and I'll be the one to decide if you're well enough. I'm certainly not trying to avoid seeing anyone, Edward. Why would you say that?"

"Well, you know how nosy village folk are. If they meet you, they're going to want to know what's going on in your life. My customers often ask me about you, but I tell them I know nothing."

"Really? Why do you say you know nothing? I write to you at least once a month, and to Walter every week or so. He says he always passes on my news. Saying such a thing makes it sound as if I'm estranged from you and Walter. That couldn't be further from the truth."

"I don't know what Walter tells folk if they ask *him*.

Perhaps he says more than I do. I thought you'd be pleased that I don't talk about you. You've always wanted to keep your personal affairs to yourself. Mind you, I can't talk, as I'm the same – we have that in common at least. But the only real friend you had, Bessie, was that Patty Harris – you didn't mix with anyone else. There was no end of gossip when *she* married and moved to London. When you left too, I heard that folk were saying you wanted to follow in her footsteps."

"I don't care if they say that about me, although it isn't true. And if they had any sense, they'd know that Patty's life changed for the better when she married Robert Cartwright. Folk can say unkind things about me if they want to, Edward, but I wish they'd spare Patty that humiliation. She had a difficult start in life because of her disability, but she's thriving now, thanks to Robert and the arrival last year of her beautiful baby, Agnes.

"Besides, there's no comparison between Patty's life and mine. She moved to London as a married woman because that was where Robert lived and worked. I went there as a lady's companion and had no intention of marrying anyone. I don't mind telling you, Edward, you could have knocked me down with a feather when Lionel started paying me attentions. And it was actually Patty who encouraged me to take him seriously and stop putting myself down. I'm glad I took her advice – in fact, it was the exact same advice that I'd given her when she was in a similar situation."

"I didn't say *I* disapproved of either your marriage or Patty's. I just said that you both provoked quite a bit of gossip in the village. People thought the two of you were getting a bit above yourselves. Perhaps they were more sympathetic towards Patty, as Robert Cartwright seems like an ordinary, decent enough fellow, even though he's no oil painting and has such a dreadful accent – but *you*, Bessie! You worked at Farringdale House for more years than I can remember, and then you suddenly announce that you're becoming a 'lady's companion', whatever that's supposed to mean. And then, as if that wasn't enough to excite the gossipmongers, they heard shortly afterwards that you'd married a man many years your senior – and a pharmacist, no less! Folk just couldn't quite get their heads around that. How you wangled it is beyond me – you're no beauty and you hadn't a penny to your name."

Edward's unkind words make me want to weep, but I don't want him to see that he's upset me, and I must make allowance for the fact that he's still unwell.

"I've nothing more to say, Edward. I've already told you that it took me completely by surprise when Lionel began to take an interest in me. But I don't need to make any excuses or explain myself to my own brother, who should be pleased that I've finally settled down and am happy in my marriage. I really don't give a jot what folk say about me, as long as they've a kind word to say about Patty. *She* doesn't deserve their reproaches. Oh, and one final word, Edward. I would kindly ask you never to speak disparagingly about Lionel in *my* presence. He's the kindest, most considerate human being I've ever had the privilege to meet, and I would have married him if he'd been thirty years my senior, instead of a mere sixteen."

I leave Edward to his whittling. I should have guessed we'd end up arguing. Mother always did say that we'd be the death of her with our bickering, although she usually took his side. I never did get along with my elder brother as well as I did with Harold, my younger one. Edward is almost six years older than me and had our parents' undivided attention until I appeared on the scene. Perhaps that's why we never became close, but you'd think he'd be over it by now. He adored Ethel – well, we all did – and was as distraught as the rest of us when she died. But instead of becoming closer to *me* – as I thought might happen – he seemed to grow more distant. Well, nothing is going to change now; I'd better just accept that we rub each other up the wrong way and try not to say anything to aggravate him. At least not until he's well again!

I'm glad I cooked and cleaned yesterday, as I've been busy today with the laundry. Admittedly, it's Tuesday, not Monday – as Edward is at pains to point out – but whoever came up with the idea that only Mondays could be wash day? I'm not sure when Edward's sheets were last washed – not for some time, I'm pretty sure of that – and in the meantime he's been feverish with night and daytime sweats. So, ignoring his complaints, I ask him to sit in a chair while I change the bedding. He moves too quickly while getting out of bed and almost loses his balance, but I catch his arm in time. Thankfully, after that, he makes no mention of going for a walk this afternoon. He would never admit it, but I think he now realises it'll be at least a couple more days before he's strong enough to take a stroll to the river and back.

Laundry is a task that I hate, though I should be used to it by now. It's physically taxing, even for someone as sturdy as myself. I soaked Edward's and Walter's dirty clothes in the tub overnight, and my first task this morning is to transfer them to soapy, boiling water. With the aid of a dolly, I stir the heavy load until my arms ache, and then scrub each garment on a washboard. Then I rinse everything several times in cold water. The whole tedious process is repeated for the sheets. I pass both clothes and sheets through the mangle to drain away as much water as possible before hanging them outside on the washing line. The clothes line prop that aids me in my task is Edward's creation; one of many he's made over the years from fallen branches in nearby woodland.

Now that the washing is drying in the midday sun and gentle breeze, I heat up yesterday's chicken soup and cut two slices of crusty bread for Edward. The loaf is a fresh one, delivered by baker's son with his handcart early this morning. Much to my annoyance, when I give my brother his meal, he asks me what I've been doing all this time. As if he didn't know I was doing the laundry!

"I've been washing your clothes and Walter's," I say, "as well as your sheets, which I don't think have been changed for weeks. Have you forgotten that I stripped the bed this morning, while you sat in the chair and pointed out that Monday is normally wash day, not Tuesday?"

"Well, the girl, Eliza, will be coming next Monday. She always takes our dirty clothes away with her and brings everything back washed and ironed the following week. You could have left the sheets for her."

"It doesn't look as if anything's been taken for a while. There was a pile of clothes in the kitchen waiting to be washed. When did she last come?"

"It must have been before I fell ill. Walter said her mother didn't want her coming to the house in case I was infectious. But it looks like she'll be back next week."

"There's sure to be another pile of washing to be done by then. I can't stand idly by while all those dirty clothes are staring me in the face. And you desperately needed the sheets on your bed changed. The house needed a thorough clean too, so it's good that I'm here. If you want me to come more often, I can do that. You only have to let me know."

"No, it's all right. Walter and I can manage with Eliza's help. And once Walter gets married and Blanche moves in, then our housework and laundry will be taken care of, and Walter will no longer need to do the cooking. I have to say, though, he is rather good at it and doesn't see it as a chore, as Mabel did."

I say no more. Blanche's future as a married woman looks as though it's already mapped out for her – housework, laundry and cooking. But I'm sure she won't complain about being a full-time housewife and, should she wish to continue with her job at the woollen mill, Walter is unlikely to object. Obviously, once babies come along, she'll have to give in her notice. Babies! What a blessing that will be! But I wonder how Edward, who worships peace and quiet, will react to children in the house should Walter and Blanche decide to reside with him, as he seems to think they will. I don't think he's thought of that. Perhaps it would be better if they do choose to live with Mrs Goode and Millie after all. But would Edward be able to cope by himself? Clearly, I'm getting ahead of myself; Walter and Blanche are not even married yet. And as Walter said, things will surely fall into place eventually and – with a bit of luck – all parties will be content.

11

Even though I told Edward that I didn't care what people in Ferndell said about me, that's not strictly true. At one point in London, when I was particularly low and before Lionel's intentions became clear, I was all set to return to the village with the purpose of keeping house for my brother and nephew – if they agreed, of course. But the thought of what local folk might think deterred me from making such a move. Back then, I was afraid of people saying that I tried to rise above my station and failed miserably, but now it's a fear of the villagers believing that I'm no longer one of them, or have become – to use one of Mother's oft-repeated phrases – 'too big for my boots'.

Thankfully, Walter has left enough provisions to last for more than a week, so I've no need to go to the local shops, and a walk as far as the post box is nothing to be afraid of. If I do meet anyone, a friendly greeting should suffice. I did think about going up to Farringdale House to see my old friends, both above and below stairs, but I fear it may sadden me. I'd volunteered to leave my old job, not just because Lord and Lady Radcliffe were laying off a number of domestic staff that they could no longer afford to keep, or had need for, but because I'd been successful in my application to become Mrs Grist's companion. The timing was advantageous, as my leaving meant one less employee would lose his or her position.

Clearly, changes have been made since my departure and, if I return to find that the house is no longer the thriving and bustling place it used to be, and that the Radcliffes are having to economise in ways they are not used to, then that will spoil the good memories I have of the years I worked there. The eldest daughter, Lady Sophia, writes to me regularly from Rome, where she now lives with her husband, Count Massimo Boncompagni, but her letters are usually about her own activities, her love of the Italian way of life and, of course, the antics of her young son Giacomo, rather than the state of affairs at her former home.

But while I can easily put off a social call at the big house, I cannot avoid – nor do I want to – going to see Mrs Goode and her daughters before I leave. It will be a difficult visit, as she probably doesn't want to talk to anyone at the moment, but it's only right that I should call on her, so as to express my sympathy for her present suffering. After all, the Goodes will soon be family, once Joseph marries Daisy, and Walter marries Blanche.

I've finally finished my chores for the day, so I sit down and write a letter to Lionel. I should have written to him yesterday, or at least first thing this morning in order to catch the early post, but there was so much to do and I couldn't rest until the house was in some sort of order. My letter is brief; I begin by telling him about Edward; that he's on the mend, thankfully, but is back to his irritating ways. Then I tell him about Mrs Smith, whom I met on the train and whose son-in-law perished in the sinking of the *Titanic*. I also mention the fact that she lives a short train ride away from us and has invited me to pay a visit later in the summer. Other details can wait until I return home. I close by telling him how much I miss him and trust that he's managing to cope – though I don't doubt that he is – in my absence.

It's still light at nine o'clock, so after checking on

Edward who, surprisingly, has fallen asleep, I take a stroll to the post box, hoping not to bump into any former acquaintance on my way there. The village is so peaceful at this time of day. My old family home is situated at the end of a lane where leafy horse chestnut trees on either side form a canopy during the summer and provide a treasure trove of conkers in the autumn. It's just a few minutes' walk to the main road that leads to the shops, which are less than half a mile away.

The post box is situated opposite the old coach house, close to the village square. I pass by a row of cottages, all with flower gardens in the front and vegetable patches at the back. The familiar scent of roses in full bloom tempts me to slow down and inhale deeply. Patty and her mother used to reside in one of these cottages before they moved to London to live with Robert. I cannot help but compare the idyllic situation of their old home with the one that they now occupy where the front doorstep meets the dusty pavement. I know that Patty continues to yearn for the countryside and worries about raising Agnes in a big city, even though they are much better off now than they were following the untimely death of Mr Harris. Her mother Celia, in contrast, is happy living in London. When not busy with her needle, she loves to watch the world go by from her chair next to the window. Ignoring Patty's protests, she provides a running commentary on the city folk she observes from behind the net curtains. Having worked all her life as a seamstress, she is fascinated by the latest fashions sported by London ladies, in particular the extravagance of their hats, which are enormous and lavishly decorated. Certainly, the fancy styles of dress in London – at least for those with adequate means – are vastly different from the practical garments worn by most women in the countryside.

On my return to the house, I meet just one fellow walker – an elderly man with his dog on a long lead.

"Nice evening, madam," he says, lifting his cap.

"It is, indeed," I say, "and it'll be light for a good while longer."

"Ah, yes, that it will. I do enjoy my evening walks at this time of year. And so does this one 'ere. He keeps me on my feet, come rain or shine. Three walks a day. But it helps me stay fit, and he's the best companion. Give me a dog any day over a wife who natters all day long, like my missus used to do, may God rest her soul."

"Dogs are most certainly loving companions. They ask for so little, yet give so much."

The dog – a cocker spaniel, also quite advanced in years – allows me to give him a stroke. I compliment his owner on his silky coat and friendly nature.

"Are you from these parts?" the old fellow asks me. "I haven't seen you around before, though I must admit my eyes are beginning to fail me."

"Yes, but I no longer live here. I'm back for a few days, visiting my brother who's been ill."

"Is that so? Not too serious, I hope?"

"Well, he's had the flu, but is on the mend now, thankfully. In fact, I must be getting back to him before he starts calling for me. He doesn't know that I left the house to post a letter, and it's already taken me longer than I expected. So, I'll bid you and your dog goodnight, sir. May you enjoy the rest of your walk."

Before he can ask me any more questions, I turn and walk away, hoping that I didn't appear rude. I know only too well that such conversations with village residents usually last many more minutes. My excuse, however, was a valid one; as soon as I enter the house, I hear Edward calling my name.

"Where on earth have you been?" he asks, rubbing his eyes. "You need to tell me if you're going out. I've been worried sick about you."

"Oh, don't exaggerate, Edward," I say. "Since when have you ever been worried sick about *me*? I only went as far as the post box to drop off a letter to Lionel. I've barely been gone twenty minutes. You were fast asleep when I left and, by the looks of it, you've only just woken up. What is it that you need?"

"I could do with a cup of tea. My throat is so dry."

"All right, I'll make you one right away. Take a few sips of water in the meantime."

"Water doesn't help. I need a *hot* drink."

Lionel is always telling me that folk don't drink enough water, which he says is good for our general health. Of course, clean, running water has not long been available to much of the population, so it's understandable that people of a certain age are hesitant to drink it straight from the tap. Even I prefer to boil the water and let it cool before drinking it as a thirst-quencher, though Lionel says that's not necessary where we live. Edward rarely drinks plain water, but consumes many cups of tea throughout the day. I suppose that is better for his health than beer, which is the most popular beverage among most men of his age. He stopped drinking that particular tipple after the scandal, some twelve years ago, concerning arsenic-tainted beer that caused many cases of poisoning and more than a few deaths.

Before retiring for the night, I make a cup of tea for myself and sit at the kitchen table with the back door open, enjoying the late-night quietude. Now that it's dark outside, the only sounds I can hear are the distinctive hoots of a tawny owl and the night song of a little robin, who's been a frequent visitor to the garden for the last couple of days. It is so peaceful sitting here! I haven't actually lived in this house since I was fourteen years old, and I'm sure I didn't appreciate the tranquillity at that young age. But I suppose it wasn't so peaceful then with six of us under one roof. Of course, our cottage in Devon is just as secluded and quiet, but for some reason I don't notice it as much. Perhaps it's because of the ever-present seagulls whose noisy squawks begin early in the morning and continue throughout the day. I don't mind their hullaballoo, but it does drown out the sweet sounds of those birds that are not native to the seashore. I woke up early this morning and it was a real treat to lie in bed with the window open and listen to the dawn chorus, uninterrupted by the ear-piecing cries of gulls.

By Thursday, Edward is much stronger and insists on getting up in the afternoon. I finished a pile of ironing this morning, so am able to give him a clean shirt and undergarments. I managed to find a pair of flat irons in the cupboard under the sink, which I think date back to Mother's time and clearly haven't been used since Mabel died. Heating the irons on top of the range made the kitchen so hot that I took off my frock and did the ironing in my chemise and petticoat. Thankfully, there was no one around to see me in such a shameful state of undress!

Edward proposes that we walk as far as the river. He says we'll take it slowly and, if he feels tired, we can rest before returning to the house. I agree, but insist that he dresses warmly, despite the fine weather. He pushes me away when I take his arm upon leaving the house, as I knew he would. But I tell him that if he doesn't accept my support, then I'll go back and bring him Father's old walking stick, which I've noticed is still in the hallway. I know only too well that he will never allow himself to be seen walking with a cane.

"You're worse than Mabel," he says. "Even she didn't fuss the way you do. I don't know how Lionel Fielding is able to put up with you."

"You were never sick in Mabel's time," I say. "But you're right, Mabel wasn't the type to fuss. Even when *Walter* felt poorly, she'd say there was nothing wrong with him and insist that he go to school without further ado. As for Lionel, he's the one who fusses over me, and I have to admit that I rather enjoy it."

Edward gives a grunt in response. He hates me talking about Lionel, though why this should be so, I really don't know. Still, so as not to annoy him, I try not to mention my husband's name too often.

When we finally reach the river, memories of Walter as a boy come flooding back to me. Every Sunday when it was dry, we'd come here and I'd read to him, or we'd play some little game. Then we'd have a picnic of tasty left-overs from the Farringdale kitchen and I'd make up stories to amuse him. I hated having to take him back to Edward and Mabel and then return alone to the big house, knowing that I'd be unable to see him for another week.

"Shall we rest here, Edward?" I ask, as we approach the slight incline where Walter and I always used to sit. "The grass is quite dry, and it'll do you good to lie down for a while in the sunshine."

My brother nods. He lowers himself slowly and then lies back. I place my shawl under his head and he closes his eyes. If I close *my* eyes, I'll picture Walter and myself sitting here reading *David Copperfield*. The memory is a good one, but I dwell on it far too often, always wishing we'd had more time together.

Instead, I sit and gaze at the winding river; the water is as clear today as it was when I was a child. Since little rain has fallen in the past few weeks, it's at its shallowest, but an abundance of life can still be spotted beneath the surface. I can see quite clearly a shoal of minnows and more than a few brown trout. Father used to love to come here fishing when he needed some peace and quiet, and he'd let me accompany him if I promised to stay silent. I would bring a book and lie on the grass and read; it was so peaceful that I sometimes nodded off. Father would occasionally catch a trout for supper, though we children rarely got a taste of it.

On the opposite bank, the branches of the weeping willow sway gently in the breeze and create a myriad of ripples as they caress the flowing water. The last verse of 'The Willow-Tree', a poem by Lewis Carroll, pops into my head. I first read it in an anthology belonging to Mrs Grist, and I memorised it because it reminded me of this exact spot.

But when I die, oh let me lie
Beneath thy loving shade,
That he may loiter careless by,
Where I am lowly laid.
And let the white white marble tell,
If he should stoop to see,
'Here lies a maid that loved thee well,
Beneath the Willow-Tree.

It seems to me that to be laid to rest underneath a willow tree, alongside a river such as this one, would be a fitting end to one's earthly life. I suppose I had Arthur in mind when I read and reread, and finally memorised this poem, even though he had long been in his final resting place in the village churchyard. Of course, the willow tree has always been a symbol of grief and sorrow. Lovers would 'wear the green willow' to make it known that they had been thwarted in love. And our great poet and playwright, William Shakespeare, prepared his audience for Desdemona's slaying at the hands of Othello by her plaintive singing of 'The Willow Song'.

I remind myself that, before leaving Ferndell, I should place some flowers on Arthur's grave and those of my parents. And, of course, that of my sister Ethel, who was buried with her stillborn daughter, Catherine. Walter has told me that he regularly visits the family graves, as well as Arthur's, and tries to ensure that they're kept tidy and adorned with fresh flowers in the spring and summer.

My solemn thoughts are interrupted by the sight of a young lady walking in our direction along the footpath. I shade my eyes to see who is approaching and am pleasantly surprised to recognise Blanche Goode, Walter's betrothed.

"Blanche!" I call out, waking Edward from his nap. "How lovely to see you!"

"Oh, Aunt Bessie, and Uncle Edward too," Blanche says in surprise. "Walter told me you were coming to stay for a few days, Aunt, but I didn't expect to see you here. Uncle Edward, how are you? You must be feeling better if you've walked as far as the river and are enjoying this fine weather."

"Blanche, my dear," Edward says, sitting up and looking embarrassed. "Yes, I'm much better, thank you kindly. Walter and Bessie here have been taking good care of me."

"I'm so pleased to hear it. We were all worried about you, especially Walter. I wish I could have done more to help, but Mother... well, you know how it is."

"Sit down next to me for a few minutes, Blanche," I say. "How *is* your mother? I take it you've still not heard word from New York?"

"No, we've heard nothing," Blanche says, her eyes filling with tears. "If only we could hear *something* from Ernest, I think it would help Mother a lot. We've tried to reach him, but have had no response at all, as Walter will have told you. It's so strange. You'd think he'd be in touch with family here to let us know what has happened to his mother, even if it's not the news we want to hear."

"I do understand your concern, my dear. But let me tell you what I told Walter before he left. An American fellow, an acquaintance of Lionel's who runs our local bookshop, is going to try to contact Ernest in New York. He's travelling there for business and has only just left, so it might be a couple of weeks before we hear anything, but I'll let you know as soon as we receive any news. Walter doesn't think you should tell your mother just yet. We don't want to get her hopes up, or down, as the case may be."

"Oh, thank you, Aunt Bessie. It would be wonderful if he does manage to contact Ernest. But how on earth does he plan to do that? New York is a huge city, or so I've been told."

"Yes, let me explain..."

"You've not told *me* this story about an American,

Bessie," Edward says, cutting me short. "Who is this person?"

"Well, I've only met him once, but Lionel knows him well. His name is Bertrand Franklin. He told me he used to live close to Ferndell and – believe it or not – was friendly with the late Declan Doyle, Blanche's uncle."

"Really?" Blanche exclaims. "How extraordinary!"

"Yes, I know. He said that he'd also met Ernest prior to his leaving for New York, and had given him some helpful advice – information about the job market, how to find affordable lodging, things like that. Listening to Mr Franklin talk about the Doyles, I soon realised that he had no idea about Declan's death, or the fact that Hilda was missing. I had the unenviable task of apprising him of both misfortunes. He was genuinely sorry to hear such sad news and is anxious to do what he can to reach Ernest and, hopefully, put the family's minds at rest."

"In my opinion, you're far too trusting, Bessie," Edward says. "You know how I feel about Americans. You shouldn't have been so open with the man. This is a family affair and is none of his business."

"That's the reason why I didn't tell you earlier, Edward. I knew you'd react in this way. Mr Franklin is not a stranger – he's Lionel's friend and is well acquainted with the Doyle family. If he can help, well and good. If not, there's no harm done."

"I'm sure he means well," Blanche says. "And if he's a friend of Mr Fielding, then I think we can trust him. But thank you for your concern, Uncle Edward. And I'm so glad you're feeling better. I need to be running along now, Aunt Bessie. Mother is on her own, as Millie's out buying groceries with Daisy. I won't mention anything about what you've just told me, but I'll keep my fingers crossed. You will come and see us before you leave, won't you?"

"Yes, I intend to, Blanche. As soon as Walter returns, we'll visit together. In the meantime, please tell your mother that she's in my thoughts and prayers."

"Thank you, Aunt, I will. Would you like to walk with me as far as the old stile, while Uncle Edward rests a bit more?"

"Of course, Blanche. Just lie back down again, Edward. I'll be back in a few minutes."

"I didn't want to say anything in front of Uncle Edward," Blanche says, as we walk towards the stile. "And I haven't said anything to Walter either, or he'll start to wonder what sort of shameless family he's planning to marry into, but I know you'll keep this to yourself. Mother had a terrible row with Aunt Hilda before she left for America, and some awful things were said. You see, Uncle Declan has a brother, Fergus, who now lives in New York, and Mother believes that he was the one who invited her. My aunt has always had a soft spot for her brother-in-law, who's the youngest of the Doyle brothers and has never married, and Mother accused her of trying to find a new husband before Uncle Declan is cold in his grave. Aunt Hilda denied it, of course, but Mother, who insists that she knows when her twin sister is telling a lie, said some unforgivable things about the entire Doyle family and was particularly scathing about Fergus. Well, you can understand how guilty she now feels, having had such a dreadful argument with her sister just before she set sail on the *Titanic*. If Aunt Hilda *has* perished, then Mother will never have a chance to say she's sorry and take back her bitter words."

"Oh, Blanche, I'm so sorry. No wonder your poor mother is in such a bad way. But what about Ernest's wedding? Surely that would have been the main reason for her voyage?"

"News of Ernest's wedding came as a surprise to all of us – we had no idea he'd become engaged. And I have to admit that we were all a bit suspicious when Aunt Hilda mentioned it. Daisy, especially, was unconvinced. You see, as Walter may have told you, Ernest writes to her quite regularly – they've always been close, as their birthdays are on the same day. Strange, isn't it, that Mother and Aunt Hilda, who are twins, each had their firstborn within hours of each other? Well, even though Ernest did sometimes mention a sweetheart in his letters, we had no idea it was serious, and he never once spoke of plans to wed this young lady. Daisy says she's sure he wouldn't consider getting married until he'd earned enough money to buy a farmstead in one of the western states, like his friend had done. After all, that was his main reason for going to America.

"Personally, I think Aunt Hilda just felt terribly lonely after Uncle Declan died. Ernest is her only child – her daughter May died in infancy – and he'd already left for America. Our family has had its own set of problems since Father died, and we didn't visit her as often as we should have done. She did say that she'd be back after a few weeks, but she may have thought that perhaps she could make a new life for herself in New York, or wherever Ernest ended up. And the fact that Fergus is now living in America too is obviously an added incentive for her to stay, if she's able to. Of course, Mother didn't see it like that. I think she was afraid she might never see her sister again. And now it looks as if she was right."

"I feel for your mother, Blanche, I really do. It's terrible when the last words spoken to a loved one are accusatory and unkind. It happens so many times. We never know when a conversation is going to be the last one that we have with someone dear to our hearts. But Hilda will have known her sister loved her deeply, despite her harsh words. Your mother needs to forgive herself or the guilt – if your Aunt Hilda *has* perished – will become unbearable. You and Daisy must persuade her to stop being so hard on herself. And please, do confide in Walter, Blanche. He needs to know everything that's going on in your life – you shouldn't have secrets. Besides, Walter is the last person in the world who would ever pass judgement on your family. Believe me, he'll always be *at* your side and *on* your side, and will do his level best to put things right, whatever the problem may be."

"Yes, I know. I'll tell him as soon as he comes back. It's just that I haven't seen much of him for the last few weeks, and I didn't want to speak about it in a letter. As for Mother, I'll keep trying to convince her that she's not at fault, and so will Daisy. But it's not easy. Anyway, I just wanted to let you know how things stand. I must get back now – as I said, Mother is on her own. Thank you for listening to me, Aunt Bessie. I look forward to seeing you again very soon. Goodbye for now."

I shed a few tears after hugging Blanche farewell. Surely Hilda's fondness for her brother-in-law can be forgiven? Loneliness can be hard to bear for someone who has, for many years, been embraced by the steadfast love of a husband and son. And I can well understand Mrs Goode's remorse at the memory of how unkindly she spoke to her sister before they parted company, perhaps for the last time. But I mustn't let Edward see my tears or he may become suspicious as to what Blanche and I have been talking about. He would not be sympathetic to the notion that Hilda might have been sweet on Fergus Doyle, even though the poor woman may have paid the ultimate price for her surreptitious love.

Blanche mounts the stile and disappears from my sight. She's wearing a floral cotton dress, simple yet flattering, and a straw hat decorated with a blue ribbon and a bunch of forget-me-nots. Her long, wavy red hair is loose under her hat and almost reaches her waist. She is tall and slim – the word willowy comes to mind, perhaps because of my recent thoughts about willows – with green eyes and freckles, and when she smiles her whole face lights up. Blanche has a natural way about her; she is without airs and graces, and will never stray far from her family home. She's an honest, down-to-earth village girl, rooted to the countryside and desiring no other lifestyle – so different from Edie, Walter's former sweetheart, who was modern and ambitious, and found village life suffocating.

I pull myself together and return to Edward, who's now sitting up again, and beginning to cough.

"Let's go home now, Edward," I say. "You've been outside long enough and will be needing to rest after your exercise. And I must start preparing our supper. If you feel up to it, we'll go for another walk tomorrow."

12

In the late evening of my fifth full day in the village, Walter returns. He's cycled all the way from Gloucester – some sixty miles – and is quite exhausted when he stumbles into the kitchen. I tell him to sit himself down while I make a pot of tea, after which I'll boil some potatoes and heat up the remains of the hotpot that Edward and I had for supper.

"Tell me, how has it been, Aunt?" Walter says, sitting down at the table and stretching out his long legs. "How is my uncle?"

"I think it's gone well," I say. "Edward is much better and is taking short daily walks. But he still tires easily, though he doesn't want to admit it. He's sleeping a lot better – in fact, he's been fast asleep for the last hour or so. It's been difficult keeping him away from his precious workshop, but I've managed it, goodness knows how. You know what he's like. Once he goes into that shed, he never wants to come out, no matter how poorly or tired he is."

"That's very true. Sometimes I don't see him from one day to the next. I'm glad he's up and about, though. Perhaps next week he can start working again. What do you think?"

"Yes, I think with a couple more days of rest, he'll be as right as rain. But he does need to understand that he's not as young as he used to be, and should start taking better care of himself. By the way, we met Blanche on the first of our walks to the river and she asked me if I'd visit her mother before leaving. I told her that I intended to, but planned to wait until you were back. Do you think we could go tomorrow? I can post a letter to Lionel in the morning telling him I'll be returning the following day, and then he can meet the train that evening. Unless, of course, you want me to stay for a few more days, Walter?"

"No, Aunt. You've done enough already and, if Uncle Edward is better, there's no need for us to keep you here. Not that I wouldn't love it if you were to stay longer, but I'm sure Uncle Lionel is missing you a great deal. And yes, we can visit the Goodes tomorrow, in the afternoon perhaps, before Blanche and Daisy go to the mill for their night shifts."

"That sounds perfect. Now, tell me about your trip, Walter. Did you find somewhere to stay in Gloucester? And what's the cathedral like? Impressive, I've no doubt."

"All went well, thank you. I found a place to lodge not far from the cathedral. It was with a Mrs Arbuthnot, who's originally from Scotland. She said she used to live on the banks of the Firth of Forth and, from the way she described it, it sounded wonderful. I was extremely well fed, you'll be pleased to hear. She gave me a cooked breakfast every morning and insisted that I try her homemade haggis, which was tasty but took a bit of getting used to. As for the work, it wasn't too complicated, and my fellow masons were easy to get along with. You're right, the cathedral *is* impressive. It's one of the finest in England, or so I've been told, and is a wonderful example of Gothic architecture. The vaulted ceilings in the cloisters are really beautiful. I wish you could see them for yourself. But, Aunt Bessie, what I think will interest you most is the fact that the setting for Miss Beatrix Potter's story, *The Tailor of Gloucester*, was just yards from where I was working. Her fictional tailor lived in a house in College Court, next to the ancient St Michael's Gate. Now, what do you think of that?"

"Why, Walter, of course! *The Tailor of Gloucester*. How could I have not made the connection? Yes, I remember now, he lived in College Court with his cat Simpkin, but was so poor that he rented only the kitchen. You're so lucky, Walter, to have passed through the streets that Miss Potter immortalised in her account of a tailor whose work on a waistcoat for the mayor's wedding is finished by his secret helpers, the mice he'd rescued from Simpkin. You see, I'm such a Beatrix Potter fan, I know almost the entire story off by heart. Apparently, it's one of her personal favourites, and it's one of mine too."

"Well, the next time I go to Gloucester, I'll travel by train and I promise to take you with me. Ah, this supper is just what I need, as I've not eaten since breakfast. It wasn't a bad cycle home, but I shouldn't have stopped for a pint of beer at the Hunters Arms. It's made me feel so sleepy. As soon as I've finished my meal, I'll go straight to bed, if you don't mind. I know I'll feel much fresher in the morning, and you can tell me more about what's been happening here."

"After all your hard work, you surely deserved that pint, Walter. Yes, you'll feel much better once you've eaten and had a good night's rest. I remember well your grandfather's words when he was tired of our chatter and wanted your mother and me to get ready for bed. 'There is a time for many words, and there is also a time for sleep', he would say, pointing to the stairs. I believe he was quoting an ancient Greek poet. He was a well-read man, your grandfather. I do wish you could have known him, my dear."

Early the next morning, before either Walter or Edward are awake, I write a letter to Lionel telling him I'll be back the next day in the evening. If I manage to catch the first post box collection, my letter will arrive tomorrow before he leaves for work. I know he'll check the times of the trains and calculate the hour I should be arriving, so as to meet me at the station – just as Walter did earlier in the week.

It's another beautiful morning and I enjoy my brisk walk to the post box. There's no one around, not even the old fellow with his dog, and all I can hear are the birds chirping in the trees and the leaves rustling in the gentle breeze.

I lit the range before setting out, so upon my return, I busy myself cooking a breakfast of bacon, sausages, mushrooms and eggs for Walter and Edward. I know the smell of bacon frying will wake Walter up and he'll be downstairs within minutes. And it'll probably awaken Edward too. I haven't given him any fried food during Walter's absence, much to his disappointment, so this will be a welcome treat. At least today I won't have to suffer his complaints about lumpy porridge.

I was right; five minutes later, Walter walks into the kitchen.

"Hmm, that smells good," he says. "Shall I take Uncle Edward's tray up to him? He'll be surprised to see me back, though it might not be a welcome surprise, as it means you'll soon be leaving us."

"Oh, my leaving will make Edward happy," I say. "He's not going to miss me one little bit. All we've done is bicker since you've been away, so he'll be glad to see the back of me. We always did get on each other's nerves."

"I'm sure he *will* miss you, Aunt. I think he enjoys having a woman around the house, even if he doesn't show it."

"Well, if that's true, he should have remarried when he had the chance. I'm sure I've told you this before, or perhaps you've heard it from others, but there was a certain widow in the village, who had her eye on him. Her name was Marigold. She was about his age and had a pleasant personality. Not bad looking, either. But he showed no interest in her whatsoever and she eventually married an aging bachelor, who wasn't half as good a catch. When I asked him why he'd ignored her obvious attentions, he said he never could abide marigolds, so why would he want to live with one. Now isn't that just typical of your uncle?"

"Yes, it does sound like something he would say," Walter says, chuckling. "But perhaps it was too soon after Aunt Mabel's death. He's never been one to show much emotion, but I think her passing came as quite a shock, especially since it was entirely unexpected."

"You may be right. They never *appeared* to care a great deal for each other, but I expect they did, in their own way. Yes, Walter, you can take Edward's tray up to him. He's probably awake by now, though he's been sleeping late these last few days, which is a good thing. Let me just pour him a cup of strong tea and butter a couple of slices of this fresh bread. Hopefully, he'll have nothing to grumble about this morning."

Walter and I spend the morning in the garden, pulling up weeds and harvesting broad beans, peas, radishes and spring onions. The garden is certainly different from how I remember it during Mother and Father's time, when it was completely weed-free and every square foot was filled with seeds or plants. Edward never really had much interest in the garden; it was Mabel who took care of it, and now it's up to Walter, whose free time is scarce. He's tried to maintain the vegetable patch and make sure that it's adequately nourished, but it could do with a bit more care and attention.

Edward, at my insistence, reluctantly took a bath after breakfast. He complained relentlessly the whole time I was filling the tub with hot water, but I'm sure he feels better for it now. Afterwards, he comes outside and sits in the sunshine while Walter and I work. We refuse to let him return to his workshop at the bottom of the garden, even though he's aching to do so and is looking mournfully in its direction.

"Don't look so downcast, Uncle," Walter says. "Another couple of days of inactivity won't do you any harm."

In the afternoon, while Edward takes a rest, Walter and I walk the mile or so to the Goodes' family home. I haven't been there since well before Mr Henry Goode passed away. He was such a kind man, always ready and willing to do others a good turn. I remember him helping Walter during his apprenticeship years, teaching him accounting and other skills that have been invaluable to him since he began working independently. It was a sad day for everyone when he died after a brief illness. I was in London at the time and, unfortunately, was unable to attend his funeral. I do wish he had lived long enough to see two of his beautiful daughters engaged to be married to my two handsome nephews. He would have been so proud and happy.

We knock at the open front door, inhaling with pleasure the fragrant honeysuckle that frames the porch. Blanche comes to greet us and beckons us inside. She and Walter have not seen each other for at least two weeks and exchange meaningful looks, but it is not the moment for hugs or kisses. Mrs Goode is sitting in a chair next to the window, but stands up to greet us, pulling a crocheted shawl tightly around her shoulders as if she is chilled to the bone, despite the warm weather. I can't help noticing how much she has aged and how much weight she has lost since I last saw her, which was at the village fête the year before I left for London. She was arm in arm with her devoted husband and the whole family looked happy and carefree. Daisy and Blanche, deep in conversation, were strolling along behind their parents, while Millie was skipping happily at their side. All three girls were identical in their long flowery frocks, their shining red tresses tied back with colourful ribbons.

"I'm so pleased to see you again, Mrs Goode," I say, "and I *am* sorry for all your troubles. I've been praying every night that the Lord will bless you with his mercy and compassion. He sometimes works in ways we cannot understand, but we should always put our trust in Him, however much heartache He sees fit to bestow upon us. I know you don't need me to tell you that, as it's what the Church teaches us, and you have always been one of its most devout attendees."

"Thank you, Mrs… I'm sorry, I don't remember your married name."

"Oh, it's Fielding, but please call me Bessie, as your dear husband used to do."

"Then you must call me Yvonne. I appreciate your

prayers. I've been doing nothing else for the past few weeks, though at times it's hard to believe that anyone is listening. But tell me your news, Bessie. Blanche says you're living in Devon now. Do you like it there?"

"Yes, very much. To live so close to the sea is like a dream come true for me. I hated living in London, I don't mind telling you. Devon is much more to my liking, but I still miss Ferndell and good friends like yourself."

Mrs Goode is silent for a few moments before telling Blanche to put the kettle on and fetch some seed cake from the pantry. I realise, with mortification, that my mention of the sea was not tactful. No doubt she's envisioning her sister Hilda lost somewhere in its depths. I quickly change the subject.

"My brother Edward sends his best regards and says he's also thinking of you. He's much better now and plans to return to his workshop next week. He's anxious to finish working on the bench you ordered for your garden, and is ashamed that he's kept you waiting for so long."

"Oh, I've hardly given it a second thought. Tell him there's no hurry. I'm glad he's better though. That flu has kept a number of people in bed these last few weeks. You'd expect it in the winter, but not the summer."

"Indeed, that's what I said to my husband. But he said it's not uncommon for flu to strike in the spring or summer, when we least expect it. I still can't believe that Edward has been a victim, though. He's hardly ever ill."

We continue making polite conversation and drinking tea for half an hour or more. But I must admit that I'm finding it a bit of a struggle. Mrs Goode's mind seems to be elsewhere most of the time and the long silences are hard to interrupt. She doesn't mention her twin sister by name, and neither do I. When I comment on the absence of Daisy and Millie, she tells me they are both down at the farm, busy decorating Joseph's cottage.

"Though I daresay Millie is just in the way," she says. "They'll be sorry they've missed you. We get so few visitors these days."

"I'm sorry to have missed them too. I'd have liked to congratulate Daisy on her engagement, even though it's been a while since the happy news was announced. You'll pass on my best wishes, won't you?"

"Of course. Joseph is a fine lad, as is Walter, and I'm pleased my two daughters are their chosen sweethearts. Daisy and Blanche deserve no less – they're both good girls and will make their husbands proud."

"I'm sure they will. I think it's wonderful that our families are uniting in this way. Your dear husband would also have been delighted at the prospect of his two girls making such excellent matches."

Meanwhile, Walter has been busy rehanging a coat rail that's come away from the wall. He tells Mrs Goode that he'll be back later in the week to dig up some potatoes in the back garden and cut the grass on the front lawn. I'm proud of both my nephews and the way they are assisting their fiancées' family, and I'm glad that Yvonne Goode, for all her present misfortune, appreciates the virtues of her future sons-in-law.

Walter, Edward and I eat a last supper together in the kitchen. We've almost finished our meal of braised liver, mashed potato and onions when Joseph appears carrying a plucked pheasant.

"A gift from Farmer Townsend," he says. "What a pity I didn't bring it earlier. Mrs Goode says you're leaving tomorrow, Aunt Bessie. Would you like to take it with you?"

"Oh, Joseph, thank you, that's a kind offer. But I'd rather leave it here for Edward and Walter to enjoy. I can get up early tomorrow and roast it before leaving, as Walter has a job to go to and Edward still needs to rest. Not that your uncle here would know the first thing about roasting a pheasant. But please thank Farmer Townsend for his thoughtfulness."

"Are you sure you want to do that first thing in the morning, Aunt?" Walter says. "I don't mind cooking it when I finish work."

"I know you're a good cook, Walter. Better than me, in fact. But I'll be more than happy to do it for you. Tell me, Joseph, how are you? You're looking a picture of health if I may say so."

"Thank you, Aunt. Working on the farm and being outdoors most of the day agrees with me. I've turned quite brown, as you've noticed. I'm not sure if this good weather's going to last though. Farmer Townsend says we're in for a lot of rain later on this summer, especially in August. You've no doubt heard how he's always been able to predict the weather weeks in advance. I don't know exactly how he does it, but I often see him consulting his *Old Farmer's Almanac* and studying the behaviour of the livestock and wildlife, not to mention his constant observation of the sky."

"Farmer Townsend is a remarkable man. He's one of the true country types and has no time or patience for new-fangled ideas. I'm sure he's already taught you a great deal about the old ways of farming, which are probably still the best. And you're right, Joseph, he's rarely wrong in his weather predictions. I remember when I was a girl – it was late November and we children were playing outside, marvelling at how warm it was, yet Farmer Townsend said we'd have snow by nighttime. Do you remember, Edward? We all laughed – it seemed impossible – but he was right. The temperature dropped late in the evening, and the next morning we awoke to a dazzling white blanket of snow. Of course, we were happy – it meant we could go sledging and build a snowman. So I don't doubt the good farmer for one moment, though I hope we're not in for a wet late summer. It's been perfect so far. I suppose we should make the most of it while it lasts."

"Yes, but I wish it would rain *now* and we could get it over with. A wet August means the harvest will be ruined. It's quite worrying for us farm labourers, but there's nothing we can do except pray to the weather gods and keep our fingers crossed."

"Of course, you're right. Without a good harvest, many folk will go hungry this winter."

"Well, you don't have to worry about that, Bessie," Edward says. "You've chosen to live far away from the concerns of the countryside."

"That's not true, Edward, and you know it. My heart is still here in Ferndell. And, in case you've forgotten, I'm no longer living in London. There's as much countryside in Devon as in Somerset. Besides, you know as well as I do, that town and country people are dependent on each other for their livelihoods."

"How are the family, Joseph?" I say, turning away from Edward's cynical face. "I'm sorry I haven't had time to come to see you all. But next time I'm here – which I hope won't be to nurse the sick – I'll be sure to visit."

"They're all well, as far as I know. Even I haven't seen them for a couple of weeks. Now that I'm living in the cottage and have only Sundays free, I try to spend that day with Daisy and her family. But we do write to each other often, and I told them you were staying with Uncle Edward. Mother and Father send their love, as do Margaret and Richard."

"Margaret is coming to stay with us in Devon later in the summer, as you probably know. I'm very much looking forward to it. But I hope she's able to come before the heavens start to open, or it won't be enjoyable for her at all."

"Oh, don't worry, Aunt Bessie. Margaret will enjoy it, whether it's raining or not. Just getting away from the village for a week or so will be a holiday for her. And if it is raining, then she'll likely have her head stuck in a book and be perfectly content – you mark my words."

"Well, we have that in common. As Walter knows, I can't do without books either, especially ones that tell a good story. Lionel has a bookcase full of books about science and politics, topics that don't interest me at all. But he's cleared one shelf for my modest collection of fiction, which is slowly growing in size. I'm sure Margaret will find something interesting to read if the weather does keep us indoors."

I can see Edward frowning at my mention of Lionel and our books – he thinks I'm showing off – but both Joseph and Walter are smiling and nodding their heads in approval.

"And I'm quite sure, Aunt Bessie," Walter says, "that *David Copperfield* has pride of place on your shelf."

"Yes, of course it does, Walter. That's the one title I could never part with."

"Margaret will be thrilled at having such a wide choice of reading material," Joseph says. "Sadly, we have very few books at home that she hasn't read several times over."

"If she likes, she can come with me to Mr Franklin's bookshop and pick out one or two of her favourite titles to bring back with her. He sells second-hand books, as well as new ones. There's certainly more to choose from there than here in Ferndell."

"She'll love that, I'm sure. When she gets the chance, which I'm afraid is seldom, she likes nothing better than browsing in bookshops. Well, I'll leave you now, if you don't mind, Aunt. You're probably planning an early start tomorrow, and you'll have to get up at the crack of dawn if you intend to cook that pheasant. I'll be over to see you next weekend, Uncle Edward, to check that you're not exerting yourself, though I'm sure Walter will be keeping an eye on you. I've heard folk say that this summer flu that's going around is difficult to get rid of, and if you don't look after yourself, the symptoms can linger."

Walter walks with Joseph to the end of the lane. They are just months apart in age and have always been close. Both joined the Territorial Force when it was established in 1908 and have gone together to the annual camp almost every summer since then. It's more difficult for them now, since they are both working full-time and Walter often has to travel for work, but they always try to participate if they can. They look upon the military training as a well-deserved holiday and, indeed, the camp's preferred locations are often within walking distance of the seashore. Of course, I prefer not to think about what would happen if a war did break out. Both my nephews would be expected to serve on the home front, but I'm sure they'd both volunteer to fight overseas if that became a priority. My heart is beginning to flutter just thinking about such a frightening prospect.

Edward goes outside to smoke his pipe – a treat that was denied him while he was confined to his bedroom – while I make a start on the washing up. I still have to pack my suitcase, but that won't take long. I'm beginning to feel a bit sad about leaving, though I am anxious to get back to Lionel. It's just that this house harbours so many memories, both good and bad, and I can still picture Father smoking *his* pipe – in the exact spot where Edward is sitting now – and Mother with her wicker basket, gathering flowers in the garden. In fact, when Edward sat outside earlier today, I thought for a fleeting moment that he was Father. How I wish that were true! Now that Edward's older, he resembles him so much physically, although I have to confess that their characters couldn't be more different.

I must stop this reminiscing or it will make me weepy. After all, even if we could wind back the clock, would any of us wish to relive our younger days? That's a hard question to answer truthfully. Thankfully, before my memories start to get the better of me, Walter strides into the kitchen and, without being asked, picks up a tea towel and begins drying the dishes. Sensing my wistful thoughts and intent on bringing a smile to my face, he tells me that his uncle is staring yearningly at the key to his workshop, turning it over and over in his callused hands, as if the very feel of it brings him comfort. We both chuckle at Edward's expense. He doesn't need a woman to provide contentment; a piece of wood and a handy saw can give him more than enough pleasure and satisfaction in life.

13

"Bessie, Bessie, over here!"

I am so relieved to hear my husband's voice. When I alighted from the train a few minutes ago, I was aghast to find the platform empty. But thankfully, here is Lionel striding towards me, quite out of breath. I realise now how much I've missed him. He's so apologetic about being late, even though he wasn't even certain which train I'd be travelling on.

"I'm sorry, my dear," he says, giving me a tight hug. "I was just about to lock up – it was well past closing time – when old Mr Gifford arrived, desperate for his medicine. I didn't feel I could send him away. He's the talkative type, as you know, and wanted to tell me all about his latest complaint. In the end, I had to be quite rude so as to get rid of him."

"You're never rude, Lionel," I say, not wanting to disengage from his arms, "and you're not late. But I was beginning to wonder if you'd received my letter and was trying to work out the route I'd take if you *didn't* turn up. I think I do remember the way through the fields, but going in the opposite direction always confuses me."

"You wouldn't have got lost, that's for sure, but you'd have had to carry your suitcase and that would have been hard for you, tired as you must be from your journey. Anyway, all is well now. I can't tell you how pleased I am to see you. You've been away, what, six days? It's not long, but I've missed you terribly. The house just isn't the same without your cheerful presence, Mrs Bessie Fielding."

"Oh, Lionel, I'm not always cheerful, as you well

know. I'm sure you won't believe me, but I've missed you just as much. The first evening and the last day of my visit were the nicest, as Walter was at home. Edward wasn't much company once Walter left for Gloucester – he was quite difficult and complained incessantly. I had to draw heavily on my dwindling reserves of patience at times. If he hadn't been so poorly, I'd have snapped at him several times a day."

"How is Edward now? Fully recovered?"

"Yes, I think so. It must be the first time in his life that he's been really unwell, and it was a shock for me to see him so thin and pale, but each day he looked a bit better. The doctor came only once while I was there and was pleased with his recovery. I'll tell you more when we get home. I'm dying for a cup of tea!"

It's such a pleasure to be back in my own home, which is so clean and tidy that I can only conclude it must be *me* who always makes it messy. Lionel insists that he hasn't done any cleaning since I left, but I'm not sure I believe him. He tells me to put my feet up while he makes a pot of tea and prepares a cold supper. I tell him that I've been sitting on trains most of the day and am not tired at all, but he says it's not often that he waits on me, so I should just relax and enjoy it. He's more capable than most men in the kitchen, though not as accomplished or methodical as Walter.

"Tell me about your visit to the Goodes, Bessie," Lionel says, as he pours me my tea. "You said in your last letter that you and Walter were planning to call on Blanche and her mother."

"Yes, we did visit, though we didn't stay long. Poor Mrs Goode is not at all well, and it wasn't easy having a conversation with her. Hilda's name wasn't mentioned, but she was at the back of all our minds. Blanche told me in confidence that her aunt has a soft spot for her brother-in-law, Fergus Doyle, who lives in New York, and that he may have been the main reason for her voyage to America. The Goodes doubt that Hilda's son Ernest is soon to be married. Because of this suspicion, Mrs Goode had a serious falling out with her sister before her departure. Harsh words were spoken, which Mrs Goode now regrets most dreadfully."

"Hmm, no wonder she's so distraught," Lionel says. "It's terrible when your last words with a loved one are spoken in a fit of rage. It makes the pain of loss even more acute."

"Yes, that's so true. By the way, Lionel, what do you think about Mrs Goode's insistence that she'd know instinctively if her twin sister had perished? Is there such a bond between twins – even if they're different in every other way? Would they really be able to sense it if one or the other were in danger?"

"Well, there is evidence that twins sometimes find themselves doing the exact same thing at the same time, even if they are miles apart. But as for anticipating or sensing danger or death, I don't know. I think it's unlikely. Mrs Goode is insisting that her sister is still alive, as she doesn't want to believe otherwise. That's a normal reaction when a family member is missing, presumed dead, whether it be a twin or other sibling, a parent or a child. Incidentally, has anyone tried to contact this Fergus fellow? If it *was* Hilda's intention to meet him, then perhaps *he* could throw some light on whether or not she's still alive."

"No, I don't think they've thought to contact him. He's only been in America for a short while, apparently, and I doubt that anyone, except for Hilda, would have an address for him. In any case, she denied that she had plans to meet him, even when her sister confronted her about it."

"I think that our best source for information continues to be our bookshop friend, Bertrand Franklin. He's a reliable fellow and I'm sure he'll do his best to contact Ernest. With any luck, we might hear from him in a week or two. In the meantime, Bessie my dear, you need to resume your reading sessions with Andrew. His mother forgot that you were away and came to the pharmacy with him on Wednesday. He was most upset to learn of your absence. Mrs Frost had an urgent errand to run, so she left him with me for half an hour. She asked if he could just sit quietly in the back room, but I thought I'd make use of a second pair of hands. I showed him how to measure out and bottle the prepared liquids for my tonics, and I must say he was a good little helper. He may not be able to read, but he memorised all the measurements and didn't make a single mistake."

"Oh, I am glad, Lionel. I can't believe he actually *wanted* to come to our reading lesson. But I'm pleased – it's a good sign. And how trusting of you to allow him anywhere near your tonics. I'm sure that gave him a boost of confidence."

"I believe it did. In fact, I think I might enlist his help again, perhaps for an hour or so on a Saturday morning. I can give him a thruppenny bit for his efforts, which I daresay will please him even more."

"That's a good idea. He's different from most boys his age, but I believe he has some hidden talents. It's now up to you and me to find out what they are."

Andrew shows me one of his handicrafts at our next meeting. Using a variety of shells, sea glass, pebbles, dried seaweed and driftwood, he has crafted a picture of a lighthouse on a stiff square of cardboard. The body of the lighthouse is a piece of driftwood, with red and white stripes fashioned from bits of old ribbon; it stands on a base of small pebbles and seaweed, and its light is a fragment of white sea glass. The picture is framed with seashells. It's a clever work of art and I am very impressed.

"Have you shown this to your parents, Andrew?" I ask him. "They should see what you've created. You're really talented."

'No!" he exclaims. "They'll be cross if they find out that I'm going to the beach and searching for stuff to make pictures with. I know Mother will say it's no wonder I'm unable to read. No one at home must know about my hobby – they'll just make fun of me."

"But I really think that they ought to be aware of your artistic ability. It's not something to be ashamed of. Do you want *me* to speak to your mother?"

"No, please don't, Mrs Fielding. Mother will just be angry and the others will tease me. Even my father will be upset with me for spending time on art, instead concentrating on my lessons."

"Well, all right. But perhaps when you've made a bit more progress in your reading, we can tell them about your other skills. Really, your picture is excellent, Andrew. But for the moment, we'll keep it a secret. Now, have you practised the verse you copied down during our last meeting? Some of the words are quite hard, but perhaps you've memorised them? The ones with the long and short *i* vowel sounds?"

"Yes, and I know how to spell *lighthouse*. Actually, I think I can recite the whole verse. Josephine read it out to me a couple of times and I memorised it."

"That's excellent. If you're able to memorise a verse just from hearing it recited, then I'm sure you'll be reading fluently by the end of the summer. Now, can you read the verse and try to point to each word as you do so?"

I have to help him find some of the words on the page, but he's able to identify the ones he's learnt, like *lighthouse*, *ships* and *sailors*. They are all words that affirm his love of the sea. I feel that we're making some progress, however slight it might be. For now, though, I think we need to persevere with phonetics, even though this may not be the best method for teaching a boy like Andrew.

Together we look for words containing the *o* vowel and copy the more straightforward ones in two columns, one for the short vowel sound and one for the long, just as we did with *i*. I try to make it as easy as possible and ignore exceptions to the rule. I don't feel I can introduce the difficult *a* or *e* vowels just yet; learning more than one vowel in one lesson is bound to confuse him.

Instead, I ask him to choose another verse to memorise. He takes a few minutes to turn each page, looking carefully at the pictures, and finally chooses *P for Pirate*. I read the verse out loud.

> "*The naughty Pirate, fierce and bold,*
> *Oft sailed the seas in times of old*
> *To seize our ships and climb aboard*
> *With marlin-spike and knife and sword,*
> *And then he whacked, and cut and hacked*

Until the helpless ship was sacked.
But now no Pirates over-run
Our seas, we've conquered every one."

The picture shows a group of pirates, equipped with dangerous-looking weapons, about to attack a ship, thus causing the sailors to cower in fright. Andrew is smiling as he looks at the picture and asks if he can draw it.

"Yes, but not right now," I say. "Would you like to take the book home with you, then you can draw as many of the pictures as you like?"

"I would like to," he says. "But I don't have any paper. Unless I can tear some pages out of this notebook. Mother says drawing is a waste of time."

"Well, *I* think it's a talent that you should be proud of. I'll ask Mr Fielding if he has some paper he can give you, even if it's only brown wrapping paper that you can cut into squares. For now, though, I'd like you to copy the entire verse into your notebook, and I'll read it again while you're doing that."

"Have they really conquered all pirates?" Andrew asks. "I don't believe they have. Cyril says pirates don't exist nowadays, but I think they still do, don't you, Mrs Fielding?"

"Yes, I'm sure they do. But piracy was probably more common in the eighteenth and early nineteenth centuries, at least in the seas around America, which is perhaps what the author was thinking about when he wrote the verse."

"Why do I need to copy out the verse when I'm taking the book home with me?"

"Because when you write words down, you get a sense of how they're spelt and that will help you to recognise them later on, especially if I read the verse aloud at the same time. Also, you need to practise your handwriting. A couple of words here are also in the lighthouse verse. Can you tell me what they are?"

He's still looking at the picture and marvelling at its detail. Reluctantly, he turns to the verse.

"*Ships, seas*. I think that's all."

"Excellent. You see, that's two words you know how to spell already."

"What's a marlin-spike, Mrs Fielding?"

"I think it's a sort of sharp pointed tool that sailors use when tying and untying rope, and separating strands. Presumably, it can be used as a weapon as well – at least these pirates seem to think so."

"I wish I had one. Perhaps I'll be lucky one day and find one. All sorts of fascinating things are washed up on the beach, especially after a storm."

Once Andrew has finished copying out the verse, I decide to call it a day. His penmanship could use some improvement, but we'll tackle that some other time. I don't want him to find the sessions too tedious, or he might not be so keen on attending them.

His brother isn't due to pick him up for another ten minutes, so I take him into the pharmacy to see if Lionel has any simple chores to give him. It turns out he has. He's just received a delivery of supplies, so he asks Andrew to unpack one of the boxes and transfer its contents to a cupboard under the counter, making sure that the labels on the packets are clearly identifiable.

Andrew is happy to help and is soon on his knees behind the counter. I remind him to learn his list of words for our next session and to take good care of the book, which has been thrust carelessly to one side. Lionel picks it up, wraps it in several sheets of brown paper that Andrew can use later for drawing, and places it next to his jacket and satchel. He then asks him if he'd like to come and help in the pharmacy on Saturday morning from eleven to twelve. The boy's brown eyes light up at the suggestion. He asks if he can stay longer than an hour.

"No, you mustn't neglect your homework," Lionel says, "so an hour will be sufficient. And only if your mother agrees. I'll write her a short note. Please make sure you give it to her."

"Yes, but I know she won't mind. She hates it when we're all in the house during the weekend, especially when Father is home as well."

Poor Andrew. No wonder he spends so much time on the beach, searching for treasures along the strandline. His mother would no doubt be a lot happier if all six of her children were out from under her feet on a Saturday morning.

The next couple of weeks pass uneventfully. My sessions with Andrew continue and I see some further progress, more in his attitude than anything else. He no longer thinks that he's never going to be able to read, and this new self-confidence is helping him overcome some of his initial inability to recognise and make sense of often simple words. His time at the pharmacy on Saturday mornings is also helping. Lionel is teaching him to read the labels on some of the tonics and medications, so as to lessen his fear of the written word, and entrusts him to measure out quantities of powders, tablets and liquids – a task that he undertakes easily, as he has no difficulty at all in understanding numbers.

We've received no news from Ferndell and I'm beginning to feel doubtful as to whether any of us will ever find out the truth about what has become of Hilda Doyle. But no sooner do I express my despondency to Lionel than a letter arrives from Mr Franklin in America. The news he gives us, however, is quite puzzling. His letter reads as follows:

Dear Friends,

It is I, Bertrand Franklin, writing to you from New York. I arrived here at the beginning of the month and, once I had settled into my lodgings, I set out in search of young Ernest Doyle.

When I rang the bell at his Brooklyn address – a tall, soulless apartment building in a run-down neighbourhood – I received no response. I therefore enquired as to Ernest's possible whereabouts from his immediate neighbour, a Mr Matthew Johnson. He told me that Ernest is no longer living in Brooklyn; he left his apartment in April – quite suddenly, in fact. It is Mr Johnson's belief that he managed to acquire a passage on a steamer leaving for Ireland, but he does not know the exact date of his departure.

I asked about Ernest's fiancée, but Mr Johnson was unaware that he had a sweetheart, let alone one to whom he was engaged to be married. Being a naturally curious person, I also asked whether Ernest had been gainfully employed while living in the city. Mr Johnson said he had been working as a handyman and, although it wasn't permanent employment, he usually managed to pay his bills. He was, however, becoming increasingly disillusioned with life in America.

Unfortunately, Mr Johnson had no forwarding

address for Ernest, and he has no idea what has become of the letters sent by his family that were delivered after his departure in April. The apartment is still vacant, so he presumes that they are piling up in the mailbox in the lobby, or have been discarded by the landlord.

Of course, this information leaves your good selves no further forward in your quest to learn the fate of Ernest's mother. Perhaps, however, his aunt might wish to get in touch with relatives in Ireland with whom he may have made contact upon his arrival in that green and pleasant land. Incidentally, I took the opportunity to consult with the authorities here regarding the list of Titanic *survivors – in case it had received an update – but, again, there was no mention of Mrs Doyle's name. I also requested a copy of the passenger list and can confirm that she boarded the ship in Southampton. Might it be possible that she disembarked at Queenstown, Ireland, if she had received last minute news that her son was no longer in New York?*

I'm sorry if my letter gives rise to more questions than answers, but clearly New York is not the place where answers can be found. If there is anything else I can do, however, please let me know. I will be staying at the above address for another two weeks.

Respectfully and sincerely yours,
Bertrand Franklin

Lionel and I look at each other in bafflement. Still, the possibility that Hilda may have left the ship at its last port of call, and is presently alive and well in Ireland, makes me more hopeful than I've been in quite a while. Lionel knows just by looking at me what I'm thinking.

"Bessie dear," he says, "you do understand, don't you,

that what Mr Franklin has suggested is pure speculation? We don't know the exact date in April that Ernest left New York, so it's more than likely that Hilda did *not* receive news of his departure before leaving Southampton. And – as you suggested earlier – he may not have known that his mother was on her way to America, especially if her intention was to meet Fergus Doyle, as the Goodes suspect. If she *did* plan to meet her brother-in-law in New York, then don't you think she'd have stayed on board, even if she knew of Ernest's departure? Would she really spend good money on a ticket to New York and then not complete the journey? Besides, I can't believe she would fail to inform her sister if her plans *had* changed, especially once she'd heard news of the *Titanic*'s sinking. She'd surely have known that her family in Ferndell would be sick with worry."

"I know, Lionel, but we can't just dismiss the possibility that she *might* have disembarked at Queenstown. I'll write to Walter straight away and suggest that he find out if the Goodes know anyone in Ireland to whom they can write. But I doubt that they have any contacts over there. Clearly, Hilda's late husband had relatives in Dublin, but it's unlikely that the Goodes would have addresses for any of them."

"If Mrs Goode has access to her sister's house, then perhaps she could see if there are any old letters from relatives in Ireland, or maybe an address book. It's a bit like spying on the poor woman, but it would be for a good reason."

"Yes, that's a thought. I'll mention it to Walter and let him decide what to do. He probably won't want to say anything to Mrs Goode just yet, as it will only give her fresh hope – hope that might later be dashed. If Blanche or Daisy can find a key to Hilda's cottage, it would be best if they did the search, and Walter can help them."

"Very well, Bessie. You write your letter and I'll post it on my way to work in the morning. In the meantime, I'll write to Bertrand Franklin in New York to thank him for taking the time to look for Ernest, and informing us of the outcome so quickly."

After copying out Mr Franklin's letter word for word, I tell Walter about Lionel's suggestion that the Goodes try to obtain access to Hilda's cottage so as to search for an address in Ireland. But I insist that it's for him to decide how to proceed. I hope that by now Blanche has told him about Hilda's fondness for her brother-in-law, as I can't help thinking that *he* may be able to shed some light, however faint, on a number of puzzling matters. Perhaps they will also find his address in New York and can write to him directly. There must have been some communication between Ernest and his uncle, and he may know the reason why Ernest left for Ireland when his mother was just setting out for America. I do so hope she received news of Ernest's departure before she left Southampton, and then decided to disembark the *Titanic* at Queenstown. Despite what Lionel says – and I know he's only trying to protect me from disappointment – I can't help feeling that there's now a glimmer of hope where before there was none.

Another letter arrives the following day, this time from closer to home – the sender is Mrs Winifred Smith, whom I met on the train. Her letter is long and rambling – she tends to write exactly as she talks – and her spelling is poor, but I manage to extract some points of particular interest to me. First of all, she kept her promise and contacted Mr Barlow, her late son-in-law's friend on the *Titanic*. Unfortunately, however, he did not make Hilda Doyle's acquaintance on the ship, so knows nothing of her fate, although he did say the name sounded familiar. It doesn't surprise me. It must have been so chaotic for passengers struggling to reach safety once they knew the ship was sinking, and thus quite unlikely that they would know what had become of persons they *were* acquainted with, let alone folk they'd never met.

Mrs Smith tells me that her daughter Maud and the two grandchildren are settling in as well as can be expected, and that the children are enjoying living so close to the beach. She says her grandson William is about the same age as the boy I spoke about on the train, and it's quite possible that they have similar interests. If I would care to bring the lad to her house once school finishes for the summer, then she will be pleased to welcome both of us. She says that Stanley, her husband, will be happy to take the boys to visit the lighthouse. This is good news and I'm sure Andrew will be thrilled, but first I must inform Mrs Frost of the invitation and obtain her permission to take him with me.

"I really like Winifred Smith," I say to Lionel, showing him the letter. "She reminds me a lot of Mrs Radford, Michael and Harriet's former neighbour, who witnessed the dreadful fire at their house and cared for the children immediately afterwards. She seems just as sincere and ready to lend a helping hand to anyone in need. Despite her own troubles, she took the time to enquire about Hilda from someone she's never met. I wish she lived a bit closer and we could meet regularly. As I've said before, I do miss having heart-to-heart conversations with a good friend."

"Am I not enough for you, my dear?" Lionel says, faking offence.

"Oh, Lionel, don't be silly. You're more than enough. I wouldn't change my life here with you for the world. But it would be good to have a female friend to meet up with occasionally for a cup of tea and a good natter."

"Well, she doesn't live too far away. Didn't you say she lived at Larkin's Cove? Any time you want to get away from me, just say the word, Bessie. No, seriously, you ask me for so little. I'm more than willing to increase your housekeeping allowance so that you can have the odd day out now and again."

"Thank you, Lionel. But there's no need to increase it – I always have money left over at the end of the week. For now, Mrs Smith – or Winifred – and I will continue our friendship by correspondence. She has her hands full at the moment with her widowed daughter and two grandchildren. They need time to come to terms with the terrible loss of a dear husband and father. But I'll go with Andrew – if Mrs Frost allows it – when he no longer has school. Who knows, after spending an afternoon in Winifred's company, it might turn out that we don't get along well at all!"

"Then it'll be her fault, not yours. I cannot imagine anyone of good character not getting along with you, Mrs Bessie Fielding."

14

Walter has written to tell me that Daisy and Blanche wasted no time in searching for a key to Hilda Doyle's cottage. Luckily, they found what they were looking for within minutes. A spare key was located underneath a flowerpot in the back garden – where Hilda had always kept it – allowing them access through the kitchen door.

Lionel is shocked that Hilda would hide a key in such an obvious place. But it doesn't surprise me. The villagers are honest folk and no one would think of entering the property of another without permission. Accustomed to many years of living in London, my husband is not convinced.

"What about travelling salesmen and the like?" he asks. "If no one answers the door and the coast is clear, might they not go round the back and look for a key in such a common hiding-place, and then help themselves to the poor woman's valuables?"

"Oh, Lionel," I say, "I've never heard of such a thing happening in Ferndell. The travelling salesmen or rag-and-bone men that pass through the village are mostly known to all and sundry. They come every year and folk know them by name and greet them like long-lost friends. And the gypsies that often camp nearby are welcomed and trusted as well. You can't go through life being wary of everyone."

"Well, I admit that we Londoners are a bit more sceptical about the honesty of our fellow men than those who are born and bred in the countryside. But don't be too naïve, my dear. You can't blindly trust everyone you meet. I want you to be able to recognise those who might be dishonest and take advantage of your good nature."

"I think I'll continue to trust people unless there's a good reason not to, Lionel. But let me read to you what Walter says next.

Once Daisy and Blanche were inside the cottage, he writes, *they soon found a notebook with the names and addresses of Hilda's family and friends. There were two Doyles listed as living in Dublin; one was Fergus Doyle, who is now believed to be in New York, and the other was Brian Doyle, whom Daisy says is the elder brother of Fergus and the late Declan Doyle. Since the Dublin address for Fergus is clearly not a current one, she is planning to write to Brian to tell him about Hilda and the probability that she lost her life when the* Titanic *went down. She will ask him if he has received any news from Ernest, who is now thought to be in Ireland, or from Fergus in New York, or even from Hilda herself, should she still be alive. I've suggested that she give him my address for any response, so that Mrs Goode doesn't get wind of the correspondence. It doesn't feel right to be going behind her back, but we think it's in her best interests. As you witnessed yourself when we visited her, Aunt, she isn't at all well. She begins a conversation and then stops mid-sentence – it's as if she's suddenly forgotten what she was talking about.*

There, that's it. It's clear that Mrs Goode is no better than when I met her recently."

"Poor woman," Lionel says. "Emotional shock or trauma can affect people in different ways. She probably isn't sleeping well and is unable to think about anything other than the whereabouts of her sister. The sooner she receives some reliable news, the sooner she can start living normally again."

I'm reminded of my late fiancé Arthur and the shock and grief I suffered on learning that he'd met his death by falling off a roof during a sudden storm while repairing a thatch. I was much younger then, of course, barely twenty, but for weeks I was unable to concentrate properly on any task I undertook, and I didn't feel like talking to anyone. But Arthur's widowed mother must have suffered more; he was an only child and her pride and joy – in fact, her only reason for living – and within a year she was laid to rest next to her son. The shock of losing her beloved Arthur was too much for her heart to bear, just as – a few years later – the deaths of Ethel and her baby were fatal for my mother's poor heart.

But it's good news that Daisy and Blanche have found the address of one of the Doyle brothers in Dublin, to whom they can write. If Ernest *is* in Ireland, then it's likely that he would have headed straight to the home of his uncle. Hopefully, one step at a time, we'll discover whether or not his dear mother is still alive.

Lionel suggests that we go for another Sunday afternoon walk on the beach. He says we should make the most of the good weather while it is still with us. When I told him about Farmer Townsend's prediction of persistent rain in the late summer, he said he didn't doubt it for a minute. He has great faith in the accuracy of weather forecasts by those who work on the land.

The sun beats down relentlessly as we cross the fields that lead to the dunes, and there is not a breath of wind today, which is an unusual occurrence. Wildflowers abound – foxglove, harebell, meadowsweet, valerian, buttercup and field poppy – to name but a few. I try to recognise as many varieties as I can to impress Lionel, who is able to name only the ones that can be used for medicinal purposes. And even those, he'll know just the scientific term and be ignorant of its common name.

"Ah, Bessie," he says, pointing to a weed-like plant with small white flowers. "I bet you don't know the name of that one."

"I do, actually," I say. "It's called *Shepherd's purse*."

"Really? What a silly name! Well, I know it as *Capsella bursa-pastoris*. It can be used to reduce bleeding, although not always reliably so. But let me know if your monthly curse is unusually heavy, my dear, and I can prepare a tincture for you to take with your tea. It won't do you any harm, and it might help stem the flow."

"I'm sure that won't be necessary," I say, blushing.

"You never know. I prepared it for Mathilda once and she said it helped. But she may have just said that to please me."

Lionel often speaks openly about personal matters, and I rarely know how to respond without embarrassment. I sound like a prude with my stuffy responses, but I can't help it. I should be used to his remarks by now – he is my husband, after all, and his work makes him aware of all kinds of bodily functions – but his openness still continues to shock me. I've never spoken to anyone about my 'monthly curse', as Lionel calls it, except my sister Ethel. Mother, of course, did her duty in telling me what to expect, but did so with a great deal of awkwardness, and then announced that I should be the one to explain the menstrual cycle to Ethel, when her turn came. For some reason, it was considered too shameful to be spoken about. In contrast, Lionel's daughter Mathilda was only fourteen when her mother died, leaving her father to guide her through puberty. He must have spoken freely and frankly about such matters as menstruation, without any trace of embarrassment – so different from the attitudes of folk in the village when I was a girl.

The tide is out when we reach the beach, so we walk on the sand for half a mile or so, then sit to rest on rocks that are pleasantly warm from the sun. It is still not crowded by any means, but a few families have spread out blankets and are enjoying a picnic, or just relaxing with a book or newspaper. Groups of children are building sandcastles, collecting shells, or playing with their balls. A few older children – boys mostly – have ventured into the sea to bathe, or are filling buckets with seawater for their younger siblings. Parents, eager for a rest, are reluctant to accompany their smaller children into the water while the tide is so far out.

Suddenly, a child's high-pitched scream disturbs the sleepy grown-ups. Everyone – Lionel and myself included – is now alert and running towards the sea and the sound of the wailing child. But before we reach the water's edge, a boy appears carrying a toddler in his arms. I recognise the lad instantly; it's none other than Andrew Frost.

A young woman rushes to retrieve the little boy. She wades into the shallow water and grabs the child from Andrew's arms. Tears stream down her cheeks as she kisses the toddler's head over and over again.

"Oh, I'm so grateful to you," she says to Andrew. "I only closed my eyes for a second, but I must have dozed off. Thank God you rescued my darling boy. He could have drowned! I would never have forgiven myself!"

Andrew looks embarrassed, not only because of the woman's extreme gratitude, but also because quite a crowd has now gathered.

"I don't think he would have drowned," he says. "The water wasn't deep at all – it barely reached his knees. But he fell over and was frightened. That's what made him scream. He could easily have crawled out by himself. I just gave him a helping hand."

"You deserve a medal," she says. "Please tell me your name and address so I can write to your parents and tell them of your brave deed."

"No, please, there's no need. If I hadn't helped him, someone else would have."

Clearly not wanting to draw any more attention to himself, Andrew turns and runs away from the crowd. I feel like calling after him – he hasn't seen Lionel or myself – but think better of it. If he doesn't want his actions in helping the child to be acknowledged, then we should respect that. I'm not so sure that the little boy would have made it to safety without his assistance. He can't be more than about two years old and was clearly startled by the fall that left him soaking wet.

The poor mother, who looks too young to cope with a parent's hefty responsibility, is now being reprimanded by those who have gathered for not keeping a closer eye on her toddler. I feel sorry for her. She is small in stature with a heart-shaped, pensive face, and long dark brown hair that has escaped from her bun and fallen over her shoulders. Her distress is being made worse by the accusatory remarks being hurled at her by the older parents. Lionel decides to intervene.

"Leave her be," he says to the group. "Can't you see

that she's already stricken with guilt, and will have learnt her lesson the hard way. It's Sunday, so let us remember what Jesus said, 'Let he who is without sin cast the first stone'. Now, show some compassion and be away with you."

The grown-ups disperse, muttering amongst themselves. Lionel turns to the young woman and enquires whether there is anything we can do to help her.

She thanks him, but says there is nothing. Lionel is not convinced. "Where are you living?" he asks. "Is it far away?"

"I'm staying in town," she says hesitantly. "I shouldn't have come so far, but..."

"Listen, Mrs..."

"Blackwell, Miss Marjorie Blackwell."

"Miss Blackwell. I'm Lionel Fielding and this is my wife, Bessie. May I suggest that you come home with us? We live just across the fields. It's not far from here. Both you and your child have had a nasty shock. Bessie can make you a cup of tea and give your little boy a glass of milk, and you can both have a bit of a rest before heading back to town. I don't think you should be walking all the way there until it cools down a bit. It's still hot and the sun's rays are strong today."

"I don't want to be a bother..."

"It's no bother, Miss Blackwell," I say. "Why don't you go and collect your things while I hold your little one. I daresay he's sleepy after his adventure and ready for a nap. What's his name?"

"His name is Clive," she says, handing him to me. "But he's going to make you wet. Are you sure you don't mind?"

"Not at all. I can wrap him in my towel."

Thankfully, Clive is too drowsy to notice a new pair of hands. He rests his head on my shoulder and starts sucking his thumb. Miss Blackwell runs to pick up a towel that's been spread out on the sand, a bucket and spade, and a large carpet bag.

"Why on earth does she have that carpet bag?" I whisper to Lionel. "Surely she doesn't need that for an afternoon on the beach with her child?"

"I don't know. It does seem strange. Perhaps we'll find out more about the two of them once we're back at the house."

"Would you like me to carry your little boy as well?" Lionel asks, taking hold of Miss Blackwell's bag. "He looks like quite a heavy load."

"No, thank you, it's all right," she says, retrieving Clive from me and placing him on her hip. "I'm used to it. If he wasn't so sleepy, he'd probably want to walk. But the excitement of the seaside always tires him out."

Clive is wide awake and walking by the time we reach the house. He is curious about his new surroundings, although he holds tightly to his mother's skirt. Lionel finds some toys that he recently bought for Geoffrey – a wooden train engine, a spinning top and some colourful building blocks – and sits down on the floor to play with him while I make a pot of tea. Miss Blackwell seems glad that someone else is keeping her child occupied.

"Did you grow up here?" Lionel asks her.

"No, I'm from Wiltshire," she says. "I don't know this place very well, which is why I got a bit lost today."

"But you said you're staying in Brampton-on-Sea, right? Are you on holiday?"

Miss Blackwell hesitates, as though wondering how to

answer. I have the impression that she has nowhere to stay, hence the carpet bag full of her belongings.

"Listen, Marjorie, my dear," I say, handing her a cup of tea. "You don't mind if I call you Marjorie, do you? You can call me Bessie. Please treat us as your friends, and we can try to help you. If you need help, that is. Where were you and Clive planning to spend the night?"

Marjorie's eyes fill with tears. She wipes them away with her sleeve. Once again, I notice that she is struggling to find the right words.

"I *had* to leave him," she says finally. "I couldn't stay any longer. He said I shouldn't have come, but he's Clive's *father*. He promised me he'd look after both of us, but then he left and came back here before Clive was even born. *He's* from here. I would never have known how to find him if his sister hadn't written to me. But Billy doesn't want me any more – he has another sweetheart now. So we have no choice – we have to go back home. What else can we do? I went to the station this morning, but it's Sunday and there weren't any trains we could have caught, and I don't have enough money for another night in a guest house. I decided we'd spend the day on the beach – Clive loves playing in the sand – and then find shelter for the night in one of the caves. Tomorrow we'll go back. Not that my parents want us. Father keeps saying I've shamed the whole family."

"Oh, Marjorie," I say, "I'm so sorry to hear of your troubles. But I'm sure that you're wrong about your father. Mark my words, he'll forgive you and welcome you back with open arms. He probably misses you terribly, despite his harsh words. Did you tell your parents where you were going?"

"No, but they will know by now. Whenever I told

Father I wanted to find Billy, he laughed and called me a stupid girl. That made me even more determined to leave. Father never liked him and said that if I thought he would marry me if I turned up with Clive, then I was more of a fool than he took me for. Anyway, I borrowed some money from Mother's purse and left in secret. I wrote my parents a note saying I was sorry, but that Clive needed to be with his father. I know Father will be angry and might even have started looking for us. He was so sure that Billy would want nothing to do with me or Clive. The worst thing is that he's been proved right – Billy never had any intention of marrying me. What's more, he flatly refuses to admit that he's Clive's father. How can he say that? He knows there's never been anyone else."

"In that case, I think you're better off without him, Marjorie. He doesn't sound like the type of man you can respect or trust, or would want to spend your life with. How did you meet him? You say he lives here, but you told us *you're* from Wiltshire."

"He was living close to my village for almost a year. His aunt gave him lodgings and he found work as a bricklayer's apprentice. He doesn't get along with his father and, after his mother died, he decided to move to the place where she'd grown up. But he didn't finish his apprenticeship and came back here to live with his sister when she got married. Before leaving, he said that once he was settled, he would send for me. We would then get married and find a place of our own before our baby was born. But I only ever received one letter from him, with no return address."

"His behaviour is unforgivable. I can't believe he left you on your own like this. But you'll see, once you return home and admit your mistake, your father will show compassion. He'll be so happy that you've both returned safely. What about your mother? Did she also think that you were being foolish?"

"Mother always agrees with everything Father says. They both warned me against Billy, but he has a way of charming everyone he meets and getting want he wants. I know now that I should never have taken him seriously. And I shouldn't have come here. But I thought that if he could just spend some time with Clive, he'd surely fall in love with him, especially since he's his own flesh and blood."

"Go home to your parents, my dear, and tell them you're sorry. I'm certain they'll forgive you and help you look after Clive. Your child is the most important thing in your life right now, and he needs stability. I can see already that you're a good mother and will put his welfare first and foremost."

"I do want to do what's best for him, but my worry is that, if I go home, I will have to agree to let Clive believe that Mother and Father are his real parents and that I'm his big sister. That's the only way they will agree to our living with them. Since I wasn't married, I had to keep my pregnancy hidden – my parents were terrified that people in the village would find out. And once Clive was born, Mother pretended that he was *her* baby. She told friends and neighbours that she hadn't known she was expecting until her third trimester and, since she's always been on the plump side, no one questioned her explanation. I accepted all this, thinking that once Billy sent for me, as he'd promised, everything would be fine. We would marry and live a normal life. Clive would know that I was his mother before he was old enough to question it. He calls me 'Ma', but only because my name is Marjorie and people call me 'Mar' for short. Mother insists that he should call *her* 'Mama', but he's still too young to understand. I waited and waited, but heard nothing from Billy. Then, out of the blue, I received his sister's letter and decided to take matters into my own hands. But I've failed miserably."

"I can understand how hard this must be for you, Marjorie. But perhaps it's for the best. You're still young and will likely meet someone who will really care for you. If it becomes known that you're a single mother, it will be harder for you to find a future husband. When you do eventually meet a man who really cares for you – and I'm certain that will happen – you can tell him about Clive and, if he truly loves you, he will accept him as his own son. In the meantime, I think you should let your parents do as they think best."

Marjorie nods, but my words don't make her feel any better. The truth is, she doesn't have much choice, and she knows it. She can't support herself, and both mother and child will likely end up in the workhouse if she refuses to live with her parents and follow their rules.

Lionel proposes that Marjorie and Clive spend the night with us; he says he'll put them on the train in the morning. He asks Marjorie if she has enough money for the journey. She tells him she only has a shilling left, as Billy wouldn't give her a penny towards her one night in the guest house, but she insists that it's enough for the train fare. Lionel gives her an extra shilling, just in case she needs it. She promises to repay him, but he says there's no need.

Fortunately, I made a shepherd's pie this morning and it's enough for the four of us. Clive eats only the mashed potato with a drop of gravy, but is happy to tuck into stewed apple with custard for pudding. Marjorie appears ravenous, and I give her seconds of everything. I suspect she hasn't eaten a proper meal since her arrival in town. When we are finished and Clive starts to suck his thumb again – a sure sign that he is about to fall asleep – I take our guests to the largest spare room, where both single beds are already made up for any surprise guests. Marjorie says it's been a long day and asks if she can join Clive in retiring for the night. I suspect she feels awkward in our presence without the distraction of her little boy.

"My goodness," Lionel says, pouring himself a glass of port once we're alone in the kitchen. "Our afternoon at the beach didn't turn out at all as we expected, did it? Who would have thought we'd have a mother and her child staying with us tonight? And what about our young hero, Andrew? He ran off before anyone could properly acknowledge his gallantry."

"Yes," I say. "It's been quite a drama, hasn't it? Poor Andrew was horrified to find himself the centre of attention and tried to downplay his heroism. I feel so sorry for Marjorie, Lionel. The poor girl has brought a beautiful baby boy into the world and is now unable to claim him as her own. It must be so hard for her."

"I know, but it does seem as if her parents want to help her. If she rejects their help, she could find herself and her child at the mercy of the workhouse's so-called guardians. That would be the worst possible outcome. I do believe that Mr and Mrs Blackwell mean well and they deserve some sympathy too. Their good reputation will be ruined if it becomes known that Marjorie has had a child out of wedlock. Not only that, but Clive's future will be doomed if he's allowed to carry publicly the stain of illegitimacy. I don't need to tell *you* how it is in small towns and villages, Bessie. And you were right in telling the girl that she stands a better chance of marrying in the future if she's thought to be childless."

"Yes, but it does seem deceitful, and I'm pretty sure Marjorie thinks so herself. Why, for reasons of respectability, should she have to deny ever having borne a child?"

"I'm afraid that's the world we live in, my dear. It's a cruel place, especially for women. Why, I ask myself, do we only hear about fallen women and never fallen men? Society should look upon the young man who abandoned Marjorie and Clive with the same amount of shame. But sadly, men are allowed to get away with it. Did Marjorie tell you her age, Bessie? And is she an only child? I couldn't hear all that she was saying. She's so softly spoken."

"She's seventeen and Clive is just twenty months. She must have had him when she was only fifteen. Still a child herself. And she has an older brother and a younger sister. They seem to be a respectable family and are obviously intent on remaining that way. Mr Blackwell runs a hardware shop in the nearest town and they live in one of the villages on the outskirts. It sounds a bit like Ferndell, where everyone knows the affairs of their neighbours."

"No wonder the girl's parents are keen for Clive to be seen as their own. But if anyone saw her catching the train on Friday morning with just the child, then they're going to become suspicious. I can't believe she planned to spend the night inside a cave on the beach! Thank goodness we brought her back with us. She obviously has no idea that, at high tide, the water often reaches the caves. It would have been terrifying for both of them!"

"You were so kind to her on the beach, Lionel. And the way you sent the crowd away with words from the New Testament – I was impressed. I didn't know you knew your Bible so well."

"I don't really, though I studied it in my youth, as we all did. Some passages stuck in my mind, I suppose. But it wasn't really an appropriate thing to say. Those people weren't about to stone the poor girl, and they would have helped to rescue Clive if Andrew hadn't got there first. I feel a bit guilty about what I said. I hope nobody from town recognised me."

"Well, they deserved to be told off. They were upsetting Marjorie and she already felt terrible about letting Clive out of her sight. What you said did no harm and it put a stop to all the unkind remarks."

"Hmm… if you say so. Anyway, I'll see them off on the train tomorrow before I go to work. I know she's reluctant to return, but even in the unlikely event that Clive's father relents and wants to do the right thing, I would still advise her to go back home. I suspect he's not much older than she is, and is clearly not mature enough to accept the responsibility of fatherhood. But he shouldn't have treated her the way he did – it was a shameful thing to do. It saddens me when people talk about a baby being an accident, as one is tempted to do in these cases. As you say, Clive is a delightful child, and he's intelligent too. He knew how to sort the blocks by colour and size, and how to build a structure with them. I'm certain that once the dust settles, little Clive will bring a great deal of joy to the lives of the Blackwell family."

15

I rise early the next morning, having slept very little, and make a pile of sandwiches for Marjorie and Clive to eat on the train. Just as I'm buttering the last slice of bread, our two guests enter the kitchen. Yawning and rubbing her eyes, Marjorie admits that she also passed a restless night, although Clive slept like a log. She does have an appetite though, and consumes several slices of toast, spread generously with blackcurrant jam, while Clive makes rather a mess of a soft-boiled egg and some bread and butter.

I was planning to let Lionel go alone to the railway station with Marjorie and Clive, but at the last minute I decide to accompany them. It's rare that I take an early morning walk, but today I'm hopeful that the fresh air will cure me of my drowsiness.

Marjorie and I each hold one of Clive's hands and swing him along. He squeals with delight and won't let us stop. Lionel carries Marjorie's carpet bag, which now contains the wooden train engine that Clive so enjoyed playing with. Marjorie didn't want to accept the gift, but Lionel insisted, telling her that it will keep Clive amused on the journey home.

We arrive at the station a few minutes early, just as a train going in the other direction grinds to a halt and one passenger alights. As it moves away, Marjorie gives a gasp and the colour disappears from her cheeks.

"That's my father over there," she whispers in a quavering voice. "He's come to find me."

"Then we must go and greet him," Lionel says cheerfully. "Don't worry, Marjorie. He'll be glad that his journey's not been in vain."

We quickly cross the bridge connecting the two platforms and catch up with Mr Blackwell, who has just exited the station and is looking left and right, wondering which direction leads into town. He's a thin, wiry man with receding black hair, and is wearing a three-piece suit and Windsor eyeglasses. When Clive spots him, his little face lights up with glee, and he frees his hand from Marjorie's and rushes towards his grandfather. "Papa, papa!" he cries, causing Mr Blackwell to turn around in surprise.

Before saying a word to his daughter, or to Lionel and myself, Mr Blackwell bends down and picks up his grandson. Hugging him tightly, he kisses him on the forehead and says, "Don't worry, little one, Papa's here now."

Clive is unable to hide his joy at being in the arms of his grandfather once again, but Marjorie – overcome with conflicting emotions – bursts into tears. I put my arm around her and Mr Blackwell produces a handkerchief, telling her – not unkindly – that there is nothing whatsoever to cry about.

At this point, Lionel makes the introductions and explains the unusual circumstances in which we met Marjorie and Clive.

"They were on their way back to you," he says. "The train will be here in a minute or two. There's still time to catch it, if you want to return right away."

"Thank you, Mr Fielding," Mr Blackwell says. "I'm so relieved that we all ran into one another – another minute and I would have been out of your sight. I spent the night at Exeter's railway station and don't know if I could have faced another night away from home. So yes, we'll catch the train back right away. I do appreciate your kindness and am sorry that my daughter has caused you so much trouble. I feel so ashamed. Believe me, she had no good reason to run away – my wife and I have done everything in our power to protect her and Clive."

"I'm sure you have and, trust me, it's been no trouble at all. We've enjoyed the unexpected company. Please, say no more about it. It's been a difficult couple of days for you and Mrs Blackwell, and for Marjorie and Clive as well. But, to quote our great poet, *All's well that ends well.*"

Mr Wright delivers a letter from Marjorie two days later. She's enclosed the shilling Lionel gave her, carefully wrapped in a piece of cloth. She thanks Lionel and myself for looking after Clive and herself in their time of need, and apologises for not returning the money to Lionel at the station. She also tells us how much Clive loves playing with the train engine and thanks us again for the gift. Lionel is rather put out by the receipt of the coin, saying he didn't expect to be recompensed. But I point out that it's probably her father who has insisted that she refund him, and that *he* would likely have done the same himself in similar circumstances. He wouldn't have wanted a stranger to be out of pocket because of a wrongful deed by a member of *his* family. I've little doubt that Mr Blackwell continues to feel ashamed by Marjorie's conduct and embarrassed that we came to be involved in her unfortunate predicament.

Lionel says that there's no need for me to keep up a correspondence with Marjorie, but I think it only courteous that I reply to her letter, which is short and doesn't give any details about the reaction of her parents upon her return. Society is so hard on young, unwed mothers like Marjorie, I think to myself. I'm sure she never imagined that she would find herself in the family way at the age of fifteen, and that all her hopes and dreams for the future would be shattered as a result. But, as Lionel said, Clive's existence should be looked upon as a blessing rather than a curse. No doubt, when Marjorie is a bit older, she'll feel indebted to her parents for raising her son, even though, at the present time, she sees their involvement as an affront.

A loving family is so important, I reflect, especially when one or both parents are lost to us. My dear Walter, for instance, lost both his mother and his father at the age of five. When his mother died in childbirth, his father should have been there for him, providing emotional support and stability. Instead, Frederick Blanch left the village, bound for the north of England, where his brother found him work in a cotton mill. Although he had promised to come back for little Walter, he was never seen again. Thankfully, Edward and Mabel came to Walter's rescue and took him in. If they hadn't done so, then I'm certain my younger brother Harold and his wife Dorothy would have been more than willing to raise him. But Edward, being the eldest, said it was his duty to give Walter a home, though Harold would have done so out of the goodness of his heart, without any talk of duty. I would have liked nothing more than to bring him up myself – but how could I? I was a single woman, bound to domestic service for the foreseeable future.

Talking of family, I know that Lionel misses his little grandson, Geoffrey, even though he won't admit it. This truth was brought home to me when I witnessed him playing with Clive and enjoying every minute of it. I won't say anything to him, as the last time I raised the topic, he dismissed it with a laugh and changed the subject, as he is wont to do when he doesn't want to discuss or acknowledge something. I shouldn't feel guilty, as it was *his* decision to move away from London when he was offered the position of pharmacist in Brampton-on-Sea. Of course, I was delighted at the prospect, though I wouldn't have objected if he'd wanted to stay in the city. My home is wherever Lionel feels happiest. I admit that London didn't really agree with me, but if we were still there, he'd be able to see both Mathilda and Geoffrey whenever it pleased him. He's missing so much of Geoffrey's precious childhood and, with a new baby soon to arrive, the tug on his heartstrings will be even more acute.

Mrs Frost has again brought both Andrew and Violet to the pharmacy. She says Violet insisted on coming, as she wanted to return my book, *The Wind in the Willows*. I take the opportunity to step outside with Mrs Frost and ask her if she'll allow me to take Andrew on a visit to a lighthouse once school finishes for the summer.

"My friend's husband is a lighthouse keeper," I say, "and will be happy to show Andrew around the lighthouse, along with his grandson, who's of a similar age. I think this will be a chance for Andrew to learn what a keeper's job involves, as it's become clear to me that he has a keen interest in all types of lighthouses, on land or on rock."

Mrs Frost stares at me in disbelief. She appears quite amazed that anyone should be willing to take such an interest in her son.

"But why Andrew?" she asks finally. "I'm sure Cyril,

my eldest son, would be far more interested in the workings of a lighthouse. Even little Paul would be more attentive and willing to listen and learn than Andrew. Isn't it enough that he's assisting Mr Fielding in the pharmacy? Cyril is already envious of that privilege and would no doubt be a much better helper than his brother. Goodness knows how much patience your husband is having to exert with Andrew getting in his way on a busy Saturday morning!"

"My husband has nothing but good things to say about Andrew's help in the pharmacy. He certainly doesn't get in his way. And, believe me, Mrs Frost, your son has shown a real curiosity about lighthouses and is already quite knowledgeable on the subject. Besides, it's Andrew I'm teaching, not Cyril. I'd take all the boys if I could, but my friend has only invited one child."

That's not strictly true. But I certainly don't want to take three boys on the train with me. It irks me that she doesn't acknowledge or appreciate Andrew's talents, but I decide not to say anything more for the time being.

"What about the train fare?" Mrs Frost says hesitantly. "I'm not sure…"

"Don't worry about that," I say quickly. "It's Andrew's reward for helping my husband in the pharmacy."

"Very well. But you'll need to keep a close eye on him. He has a habit of wandering off."

"I'll take good care of your son, I promise."

Mrs Frost bids me good afternoon and I breathe a sigh of relief. I can easily pay for Andrew's ticket out of my housekeeping money; it will only be a half fare, after all. Now I need to find a way to tell the boy about the excursion without his sister overhearing us.

Violet actually has no intention of returning my book.

She says she's only got as far as the chapter where Mole and Rat find Mole's home and spend the night there after being entertained by the field mice carol singers. She asks me if she can keep the book for another week, as she would like to read a few more chapters.

"Yes, of course, Violet," I say. "I'm pleased you're enjoying the story so much. Why don't you keep the book until you finish it?"

"Oh, thank you, Mrs Fielding. I really want to find out what happens next."

"I love that scene at Mole's house, don't you? The Rat was so kind when he insisted that they search for Mole's home, even though he was longing to return to his own comfortable dwelling on the riverbank. And he was especially encouraging when Mole was feeling downhearted and ashamed of where he lived. Didn't he exclaim what a capital little place Mole's home was, and how they'd make a jolly night of it? Such a loyal friend. We can learn a lot about friendship from that book."

"I like both Rat's home and Mole's," Violet says thoughtfully. "But I like Badger's most of all. All those rooms and passages. I wish I lived in a big place like that."

"Hmm, I'm not sure I would like it. A cosy little home like Mole's suits me more, I think. We should all be thankful that we have shelter and a place to call home, whatever its size. Many folk – and animals too, I suppose – are not so lucky."

"I'm sorry for those who haven't got a home. But I can still dream about living in a mansion, can't I? If I married a prince, I could live in a palace. A palace with lots of rooms and a banquet hall, a dance floor, a big garden with lots of flowers and a pond, and…"

"And an underground cell to lock you in when you're

being annoying," Andrew interrupts. "Like you are now. As if a prince would ever want to marry you, Violet Frost."

"You're so mean. You'll probably end up living in an old cowshed, since you can't even read and will never get a job."

"I *will* get a job. I'm going to be a lighthouse keeper and live in the lighthouse. That's the perfect home for me. So there!"

"That's enough," I say, trying not to smile, as their bickering reminds me of Edward and myself when we were children. "Now Violet, can you please sit quietly and read while Andrew and I have our lesson? Have you brought the alphabet book with you, Andrew? Did you learn the verse about the pirates?"

"Yes, and I drew a picture. What do you think of this, Mrs Fielding?"

He shows me a drawing he's made in charcoal of the pirates climbing aboard the ship. I look at it admiringly. It's a skilful representation of the illustration in the book.

"That's excellent," I say. "You really are quite an artist, Andrew. Now if we can get your reading up to the level of your drawing and your arithmetic, you'll have nothing to worry about in school or elsewhere."

"Cyril's friend lent him a book called *Treasure Island*," he says. "I asked if I could borrow it to show you, but he refused. He said I might lose it or damage it, though he knows I never would. Anyway, the story is about a boy called Jim Hawkins, who goes in search of buried treasure and meets some pirates. That's all I know. Cyril says he has to return the book this week, and he refuses to read even one chapter to me, or let me copy any of the pictures."

"Yes, I've heard of *Treasure Island*. It's by Robert Louis Stevenson, who also wrote a book of verse for children. Let me try and find a copy of the novel for you, then we can read it together at the end of our lessons."

"Really? Could you? I would love that."

"I'm not making any promises, Andrew, but I'll try. Now, shall we remind ourselves of words in the pirate verse that contain the *o* vowel? Can you spot them?"

Andrew has learnt the verse off by heart and is able to recognise most of the words containing the *o* vowel. I can tell he is now bored with it, so I ask him to choose another verse. He turns straightaway to the one dedicated to *G for Gunner*; the picture below the verse is of a massive cannon about to be fired.

"Can you read this one to me?" he asks.

"Yes, of course. We'll start on the *a* vowel now that you're beginning to understand *i* and *o*. It's a more difficult one though, so you'll need more than two columns for the different sounds."

I would have preferred almost any other verse to this one, but I begin to read:

"Hurrah for the Gunner, the Navy's pride
Stalwart and faithful when wars betide.
Before his calm and deadly aim
War-ships crumble or burst aflame
Or, foundering, soon find their graves
Beneath the cold, engulfing waves.
Trains he the cannon, which belch and thunder,
Filling our foemen with fear and wonder."

"Actually, I think I'd like to be a gunner in the Navy when I leave school," Andrew says, his eyes shining, "and then later on, when I'm older, I can be a lighthouse keeper. I would love to fire a cannon like that."

"You'd only be able to fire the cannon if we were at war, and let's hope and pray that this country won't be at war during our lifetimes. War causes such a lot of unnecessary deaths and leaves many families grieving for their menfolk whose lives have been cut short."

"I suppose so. But if we *do* go to war, then I'll join the Navy and train to be a gunner."

I find the verse disquieting. The lines *…soon find their graves beneath the cold, engulfing waves* reminds me of poor Hilda who, along with so many others, may have met her end in a watery grave less than three months ago.

"Well, you clearly love the sea," I say. "But it's hard work aboard a ship and you could be away from home for many years. One of my nephews is an able seaman in the Royal Navy and he hasn't been home for at least five summers. Perhaps, when your reading has improved, I can ask him to write to you to explain what life in the Navy is really like. I know he's been to many countries, so probably has lots of tales to tell. But, Andrew, you don't have to decide what you want to do in life right away – you're only nine years old. By the time you leave school, your interests may have changed completely.

"Now, I'd like you to copy out the verse to familiarise yourself with the words, and I'll read each line out loud to you, just like we did before. The more times we read it, the easier it'll be for you to commit it to memory. Then we'll make lists of words with the different *a* vowel sounds."

When Violet excuses herself to go to the outhouse at the end of the lesson, I seize the moment to tell Andrew about our forthcoming outing, during which he'll have the opportunity to visit a lighthouse. He can hardly contain his excitement. I tell him that his mother has agreed to the excursion and that we'll go on the train soon after the last day of school. I advise him not to talk about it with his siblings just yet, as they will no doubt be envious. But I doubt that he'll be able to keep such thrilling news to himself for long.

"By the way, Andrew," I say, "I was on the beach last Sunday with Mr Fielding, and we saw you helping a little boy who was in distress. The child's mother was so thankful and wanted to reward you. You shouldn't have run off the way you did."

"I didn't do anything, really," he says, looking embarrassed. "The boy wasn't in any danger of drowning. He was frightened when he fell over and started screaming. I helped him to his feet, but then he wouldn't let go of me. So, I picked him up and carried him out of the water. I don't know why so many people came to see what was going on."

"I think because the child was crying so loudly. But well done, Andrew. You were certainly a hero in his mother's eyes."

Violet returns and we pack away our books. Just as I'm giving each child a liquorice stick, Mrs Frost appears in the doorway, quite out of breath.

"Andrew, Violet," she says, "come along quickly. We need to hurry. Your father will be home within the hour, and he'll expect his meal to be on the table the moment he walks in the door. Goodbye, Mrs Fielding, and thank you. I hope these two weren't too much trouble."

"Not at all, Mrs Frost," I say. "Your children are a credit to you and your husband."

"I'm not sure my husband has anything to do with it. He's seldom at home and, even when he is, he doesn't do much to help with the children. I apologise for being in such a rush, but I'm sure a married woman like yourself will understand how demanding our menfolk can be."

"Have you ever met *Mr* Frost?" I ask Lionel, as we walk home together.

"No, I haven't," Lionel says. "Why?"

"Well, Mrs Frost said that he's hardly ever home and doesn't help much with the children when he is."

"I would take that remark with a pinch of salt, Bessie," Lionel says, chuckling. "Have you ever heard Rose Frost say a good word about anyone? Personally, I feel sorry for her husband. I think you're wondering, Bessie, if Mr Frost is anything like young Michael's late father, who drank excessively most evenings and made life intolerable for his children when he did return home. But though I've never met him, I've heard that Dick Frost is a decent, hard-working sort of fellow, whose sole purpose in life is to provide adequately for his wife and six children."

"But if he's never home…"

"He's away a lot of the time because of his job. He works at the ship-building yard, which is some way along the coast. A lot of the men who work there are only able to go home at weekends. I don't deny that it's hard for his wife being on her own with so many children, but he's the one who puts bread on the table and keeps a roof over their heads. And the children never appear hungry and are always nicely dressed, aren't they?"

"Yes, you're right about that. Mrs Frost isn't an easy woman to get along with and perhaps her husband is glad his work takes him away from home. I didn't like the remark she made about Andrew's inability to read, and the way she compared him unfavourably to his siblings, but she must care about the boy or she wouldn't have responded to our advertisement, would she?"

"No, she wouldn't. She's a woman who loves to complain. But, compared to some families I've met – and I'll mention no names – the Frosts are good, respectable folk."

Lionel takes my hand and gives it a squeeze. "Let's have fish and chips for supper," he says. "It's been a long day for both of us and we deserve a treat."

"But Lionel. I was going to make…"

"No excuses, Bessie. Whatever it is you were going to make can wait until tomorrow. You've been looking tired ever since you returned from Ferndell. I think you overdid it there, what with nursing Edward, cooking, cleaning and tending to the garden. And I know you're not sleeping well. You mustn't worry too much about Walter and the Goodes. There's nothing more we can do to help them find out what has happened to Hilda. Walter will let you know as soon as there's any news from Ireland. In the meantime, we just need to be patient and not trouble ourselves too much. Easier said than done, I know."

"All right, Lionel. I'll try not to worry. It's just that I thought we'd have heard something by now. It's been almost two weeks since Daisy wrote the letter to Hilda's brother-in-law."

"Well, there could be any number of reasons why he's not responded right away. The letter would probably have taken a few days to reach him, and he may not even be residing at that address any more. But if he's still in

Dublin, then it will no doubt be forwarded to him, and I'm sure a reply will soon be forthcoming.

"Now you go on to the house, my dear, while I pick up our supper. No need to set the table. We'll sit in the garden and eat our fish and chips straight out of the newspaper."

16

A few days after the local school shuts its gates for the summer, Andrew and I board the local train that takes us some thirty miles along the coast. Mrs Smith says she'll meet us at the local station, her house being less than ten minutes' walk in the direction of the lighthouse. Andrew is so excited he can hardly sit still, so it's good that we have the compartment to ourselves. I've brought along some ginger biscuits for us to munch on the journey, and I have a cake in my basket that I baked last night to give to the Smiths.

As we draw into the station, I can see my friend waiting on the platform with two fair-haired children, a boy of about Andrew's age and a girl, a year or two younger. She sees me leaning out of the carriage window and waves. As we step down from the train, I notice that Andrew is staring nervously at the boy, who's quite a bit taller than he is.

"Don't worry, Andrew," I say quietly. "You and Mrs Smith's grandson don't need to become best friends. Just relax and be yourself. I'm sure you'll both get along splendidly."

"Hello Bessie, how are you?" Mrs Smith says, greeting me with a smile. "We *are* on first name terms, aren't we? And this must be Andrew. These two here are William and Wendy. They insisted on coming with me. They haven't been to school since moving here from Bristol, and they're desperate to have some other children to play with."

"We're not *desperate*, Granny," William says. "But I'm happy Andrew could come. And it's a good thing we're no longer going to school. I hated my old school, though I do miss my friends."

"I hate my school too," Andrew says. "I wish I never had to go back."

"It seems like you two have something in common already," I say. "What about you, Wendy? Do you miss your old school?"

"Not really," Wendy says shyly. "But I do miss one teacher – Miss Black. She was always nice to me, but not Miss Crowe. She was horrible to everyone, except Cissie Arnold, who was her favourite."

"Don't mind her," William says to Andrew. "She's forever going on about how much she misses that teacher. I don't miss any of mine."

"Well, we can't stand here nattering forever," Mrs Smith says. "The sooner we get back to the house, the sooner you children can go and visit the lighthouse, and Mrs Fielding and I can have a bit of time to ourselves."

"How is your daughter, Winifred?" I ask, as the children run on ahead. "You said in your letter that she was settling in as well as could be expected. Is that still the case?"

"Oh, please call me Winnie, Bessie. I'm not used to Winifred – it's such a mouthful. As for Maud, I'm afraid she's having a difficult time coming to terms with her loss, which is understandable. I think, in the beginning, she just felt numb, then with the move here – so much to do in such a short time – she didn't have time to grieve properly. But now that the initial shock is over and she has little to do, it finally seems to have hit her that Colin is never coming back, and she questions how she's going to live the rest of her life."

"I'm so sorry to hear that, Winnie. For the sake of the

children, I hope she manages to overcome such a feeling of despair. But I know it isn't easy."

"You say that as if you've experienced something similar, Bessie."

"Well, yes, but it was a long time ago. It's been more than twenty years now, but the pain is still there. I lost my fiancé Arthur in a terrible accident – he was a thatcher and fell off a roof during a sudden storm. He died instantly. For years I couldn't imagine spending my life with anyone else, but then, two years ago, I met Lionel – a widower – and my fortunes changed. For the better, I might add."

"That's a long time to wait for better times to come. Maud is still young – she's not yet thirty – and yet she seems to think life is over for her, as I'm sure you did when you lost your betrothed. But she has the children to think of, as you say. They're also trying to understand why their father was taken from them, though I think being here at the seaside is doing them good. I suggested to Maud that she try to find a job to keep herself busy and earn a few bob at the same time. I can look after William and Wendy, and they'll both be at school come September. She can't keep moping about the house forever. Colin certainly wouldn't have wanted that. He gave his life so that the women and children on the ship could be rescued. I think Maud owes it to him to raise their own children in a way that's a credit to his memory.

"But she says that if she's to go out to work, then she should have stayed in Bristol where more opportunities exist for working women. She's a good typist and worked in the office of a large haberdashery shop before she married Colin. But moving back to Bristol is out of the question. Who would take care of the children while she was out at work all day? She'd risk having them taken away from her. No, I think they're all better off here. No one's going to take those two angels away from their Granny and Grandpa."

The Smiths' house soon comes into sight. It's a small whitewashed cottage with wisteria covering most of the front wall. In the garden, either side of the recently mowed grass – where cricket stumps, a bat and a ball have recently been abandoned – are bushes of pink, white and purple hydrangea. The dunes are just beyond the garden and a sandy beach is within a stone's throw. I believe it's the prettiest and most perfectly located house and garden I've ever seen.

"This is such a lovely house!" I exclaim. "And, I'm sure you're right – living by the sea *must* be good for the children, at least for now."

"Yes, they love being so close to the beach. But I have to be quite strict with them, as I can't risk having them wander off. The sea can be dangerous and neither child can swim. As for the cottage, yes, it suits me and Stanley very well. But it's small, with only two bedrooms. Maud and the children have to sleep all together in one room. So, I'm not sure how convenient it will be in the long term. William is already a big boy for his age."

We go straight into the parlour where Mr Stanley Smith is sitting reading a newspaper. He's a well-built man, and his face is ruddy and weather-beaten; one can see instantly that he's never strayed far from the seashore. Winifred makes the introductions, reminding him that he's to take the children to visit the lighthouse. He stands up, shakes my hand, and says he's pleased to make my acquaintance. I can tell that he's a man of very few words, just like Edward, which is just as well since Winifred is such a chatterbox.

"Would you like a cup of tea before you leave, Stan?" Winifred asks.

"No, I'll leave you to your blather," he says. "I'll take the young'uns off your hands for a couple of hours."

"Yes, be off with you," Winifred retorts. "Blather, indeed!"

Andrew looks at me, as if needing my approval before setting off with Mr Smith and his grandchildren.

"Go ahead, my dear," I say. "I'll look forward to hearing all about it later on."

"Maud is upstairs, lying on the bed," Winifred says, as she makes the tea. "It's what she does most of the time, I'm sorry to say. I'll let her know that I have a guest and if she wants to come down to meet you, she can. But don't be offended if she doesn't show her face. As I said, she rarely leaves that room. Now, what is this cake you've brought? You really didn't need to, Bessie. But thank you all the same. William and Wendy are eating me out of house and home."

"It's just a plain Victoria sponge. Nothing fancy. I'm not an expert in the kitchen. I was in service for nigh on twenty-five years, but mostly attended to housekeeping. The cook and her assistant gave us our meals, so I didn't do much cooking at all after the age of fourteen when I left home. I'm sure Lionel has noticed my deficiencies, but he never complains, bless him."

"Oh, I was in service too, from the age of thirteen until I got married at twenty-one. I was a lady's maid, though the lady in question wasn't much of a lady, if you get my drift."

"I can't really complain about my old employers. They had their little oddities, like most folk, but they were kind and generous. I'm still in touch with Lady Sophia, who married an Italian count and is now living in Rome. I was always a favourite of hers, though I certainly didn't take advantage of the fact."

"Well, I'm glad you're now happily married and no longer 'below stairs', as they say, especially after your misfortune all those years ago. Let me just take this cup of tea up to Maud, Bessie, and then we can sit down and have a good old chinwag."

"Do you have any other children, Winnie?" I ask, once we are comfortably seated with our cups of tea.

"Yes, I have a son, Reginald, or Reggie as we call him," Winifred says, cutting me a large slice of cake. "He's two years younger than Maud and is married with two daughters – Lily, who's five, and Rosie, who's three. Delightful little girls. He works at the ship-building yard not far from here. Long hours, but a secure job, or so I'm told."

"Oh, I think that must be where Andrew's father works. His mother complains that her husband is away a lot, and that she has to take care of all six children all by herself."

"Well, six is a lot, but I often wish I'd had more than two. Oh, I'm sorry, Bessie, that wasn't a very tactful thing for me to say when you've none of your own. Do you ever regret not having had children?"

"To be honest, Winnie, I don't really think about it. When Arthur died, I accepted that I would live a childless life. I wouldn't want to have a baby now – at the age of forty-one, I think it would be far too risky. Lionel says I'm not too old, but I think he's probably glad that I've decided against it. He has a grown-up daughter and a grandson, and there's another grandchild on the way. I don't think he'd want to become a father again in his late fifties, though he's active for his age and is still young at heart. Anyway, we've decided that we're happy the way we are, just the two of us."

"As long as you're both agreed on it. I know a few women who've had children in their forties, and all went well. But it wasn't their first, I'll grant you that."

"Actually, my friend Patty gave birth for the first time last year at the age of forty. It was touch and go for a while, but thankfully, both mother and baby are now doing splendidly."

"Well, thank the good Lord for that. Now, tell me, Bessie, have you had any news about the poor lady who is missing, presumed dead?"

"No, not really, though there's a slight possibility that she may have disembarked at Queenstown, Ireland, which was the last port of call before the tragedy. We found out from an acquaintance in America that her son Ernest departed New York for Ireland – his late father's birthplace – in April, the very month the *Titanic* went down, though no one has heard a word from him. Hilda was supposed to be travelling to attend his nuptials, but she may have changed her mind at the last moment if she'd heard that he had left for Ireland and there was no longer a wedding taking place. But if that were the case, how could she not have told her family, who are so terribly worried about her?"

"Isn't there anyone in Ireland the family could contact?"

"Yes, Hilda's two nieces have managed to find an address for one of her brothers-in-law, and have written to him in Dublin to enquire if she or her son have been in touch with relatives there. Lionel thinks it's unlikely that she would have received a message from Ernest at the very last minute, but in the absence of official confirmation that their aunt *has* perished, her nieces don't want to leave any stone unturned. They've not told their mother, Hilda's twin sister, of this lead – if that's what it is – as it might not come to anything."

"I suppose not knowing is in many ways more painful than knowing the worst. Those who have confirmation that a loved one has died can at least move on with their lives, difficult though that may be. But not knowing... Well, I say that, but Maud has not even begun to think about moving on with *her* life. I suppose there's no one way of dealing with grief, and for some it takes more time to come to terms with loss than for others.

"By the way, Bessie, we received another letter from the fellow who befriended Colin on the ship, Mr Alfred Barlow. He wrote to *me* this time, as I was the one who replied to his letter to Maud, thanking him for letting us know Colin's fate. Maud was in no fit state to put pen to paper, and I didn't want him to think we weren't grateful for his letter. Anyhow, he told me in quite some detail what had actually happened on that dreadful night. Between you and me, I didn't show the letter to Maud. It would have upset her no end to learn what Colin endured. Mr Barlow did apologise for giving me all the horrific details, but he says it helps him to write about it, rather than keeping it all bottled up."

"Yes, I can understand that. I find writing therapeutic, too."

"That's a big word, Bessie. Your husband's learning must be rubbing off on you. Now, don't blush – I told you I've habit of blurting things out. Anyway, Mr Barlow claimed that there weren't enough lifeboats on board – I think that fact has now been confirmed – and the first and second-class passengers were given priority. Many third-class passengers were actually blocked from reaching the boat deck. I suppose the officers thought there might be some kind of stampede if they let everyone go up at once. It beggars belief, I must say. The women and children had a better chance of reaching safety, as they were allowed onto the boat deck before the men, but many were reluctant to leave their cabins – that is, until the third-class quarters became flooded, and then they had no choice. The crew repeatedly told them that no one was in danger, as they didn't want passengers to panic, and perhaps they really did think there was nothing to worry about. The *Titanic* was supposed to be unsinkable, after all. But such tactics led to a greater loss of life, I'm certain of that."

"Well, if Hilda was still on the ship when it struck the iceberg and the alarm bells sounded, I don't think she'd have been one of those rushing to get to a lifeboat, especially if the crew had advised passengers to stay calm. Folk from my village are generally trusting and not the least bit pushy, so I'm sure she'd have let others go before her. How did Colin's friend manage to get to a lifeboat in time, assuming he was also in third-class?"

"Yes, Mr Barlow explains that in his letter. Poor man, he feels terribly guilty about the fact that he survived when so many others lost their lives. He said he and another fellow made it to the boat deck before the barriers came down. They'd overheard a conversation between two of the stewards, so guessed that there was a disaster waiting to happen. Colin could have gone with them, but my dear son-in-law always did think of others before himself and refused to leave steerage. He said that if the ship and its passengers *were* in danger, then he felt duty bound to stay and help the women and children. Perhaps if he *had* gone with his friend, he may also have been rescued. Mr Barlow made it onto one of the last lifeboats – one of the collapsible ones. He was lucky because male passengers only had access to the lifeboats once all women and children – at least those who were on the deck, as many still weren't – were installed. For the most part, the men were patient and the fortunate ones secured a place. Mr Barlow stressed that he would willingly have swapped places with a married man like Colin – as he himself is a bachelor and all alone in the world – but it was too late. Colin had not yet reached the upper deck and the lifeboat was already being lowered into the water."

"Goodness me, Mr Barlow is lucky to have survived, but I'm sure he's reliving that dreadful experience every minute of every day."

"Yes, he says he now wishes that he'd stayed below deck and gone down with the ship. He's having nightmares about what happened that night, and believes this feeling of remorse will stay with him for the rest of his life. I shall have to write to him and tell him not to be so silly – he's a young man still and can do good in the world, if he has a mind to. The fact that he feels he needs to atone for his behaviour that night might make him a better person in the long run. Why should he feel guilty about surviving? Apparently, many of the first lifeboats to be lowered were half empty, which is a crime in itself. I hate to say it, but if only Colin hadn't been so honourable and intent on helping others, he could be sitting here with us now."

"You're right, Winnie. Mr Barlow shouldn't feel guilty. He has as much right to life as anyone else. Another ship came to rescue those in the lifeboats, didn't it? At least that's what Lionel told me."

"Yes, the RMS *Carpathia*, but it didn't arrive for several hours. There was a ship that was much closer – the *Californian* – but they say it ignored all distress signals. Can you believe that? It's still a mystery as to why that was. Those in the lifeboats were finally rescued by the *Carpathia*, and the crew really went out of their way to care for them. But the lifeboat experience was terrifying, according to Mr Barlow. In some of them – at least the one he was in – there were no trained sailors who were able to row, so in the end, he took one of the oars and a well-built woman took the other one. Somehow, they managed to get away from the *Titanic* that was sinking rapidly. But, oh my goodness, he could actually see the ship going under with all those people still on board, some of them just jumping into the ocean, hoping they'd be saved.

"The lifeboats that still had room in them were supposed to go back to take on more passengers, but most of the occupants felt it was too dangerous to turn around and were desperate to move away from the sinking ship as fast as they could. By the time the *Carpathia* arrived, the *Titanic* was no longer visible and almost all the passengers who'd jumped into the water had perished. Stanley, who knows about these things, says that those who were wearing lifebelts wouldn't actually have drowned, but they would not have been able to survive the freezing waters of the North Atlantic for more than ten to fifteen minutes, so would almost certainly have succumbed to hypothermia."

I wish Winifred had not told me all these details. Now that I know more about the tragedy, I will never stop thinking about Hilda and how she may have met her life's end. If she *were* aboard, she must have been absolutely terrified and would most likely have been powerless to do anything to save herself. I know if it were me, I'd have been in a state of paralysis, unable to think straight or summon any self-preservation skills. I just hope that some fellow passenger may have shown her kindness on that terrible night, and that she did not die friendless.

"Goodness, Bessie," Winifred says. "You've gone quite white and you've hardly touched your tea. I'm sorry if I've upset you with all this information. I'm so selfish – I just felt the need to share it with someone, just as Mr Barlow felt the need to share it with me. Stan read the letter, of course, but he doesn't want to talk about it. Being close to the sea himself – a sea creature is what I call him – and having seen more than a few shipwrecks at first hand, though obviously not on such a massive scale, he's more philosophical about the tragedy. He often quotes the statesman Edmund Burke, who said, 'the ocean is an object of no small terror'. Not that Stan wasn't deeply saddened by the sinking of the *Titanic* – especially when we heard that poor Colin had perished – but the actual catastrophe didn't shock him as much as it did most other people. He says that no ship is unsinkable, whatever the White Star Line or the ship's captain might have said.

"But let's not talk any more about it. I don't want to give you nightmares. I myself haven't had a full night's sleep for weeks. What with worrying about Maud and the children and what's to become of them, I'm lucky if I manage two or three hours of shut-eye a night. And there's Stan next to me, snoring away as if none of this has happened. Believe me, sometimes I feel like digging him in the ribs!"

"I'm not sleeping well, either," I say. "And I don't have half your cares. But I am concerned about my nephew Walter and when he'll be able to wed his sweetheart, Blanche Goode, Hilda's niece. I'd like to see him settled, as he's like a son to me. His mother – my sister Ethel – died when he was just five years old, and although my brother Edward and his wife gave him a home, I always tried to spend as much time with him as I could, and we became close. Blanche's sister, Daisy, is engaged to my other nephew, Joseph – my younger brother Harold's eldest son – and their wedding in September has had to be postponed until it becomes clear what has happened to Hilda. There's no date yet for Walter and Blanche's wedding. The girls' mother is terribly upset and quite unwell at the moment. Understandably, no one is in the mood for a joyous event like a wedding. Waiting for news is such a strain on everyone's nerves, my own included. Still, when I compare my worries with what you and your family are having to cope with, I feel quite ashamed of myself."

"There's no need to feel ashamed, Bessie. We all have our crosses to bear. I'm sure the young couples will find a way forward, as will Maud, eventually. We older folk can only pray for them and hope that they make the right decisions. We can give them advice but they don't always want it, and often prefer to do things their own way. Now, let's talk about more cheerful topics. I want to hear all about your time in London and how you came to meet your esteemed husband. It's not every day that someone who's from a humble background lands a professional gentleman from the city. I'm sorry if that sounds rude, but you did tell me that you'd been in service, and I remember only too well that working below stairs can lower a young woman's expectations."

"No, don't apologise, Winnie. No one could have been more surprised by my good fortune than I was myself. It's true that Lionel and I are from different social classes, but he's always said that he doesn't believe in a class system. The number of times he's scolded me for even mentioning it. He's a gem of a man and I'm not really worthy of him, but for a reason I've yet to understand, he chose me as his wife. I've already mentioned that he's older than me – sixteen years in fact – but age means as little to him as class or colour, or any of the other prejudices that exist just to cause misery to mankind, or so it seems. I thank God daily that He saw fit to bring us together at a time when both of us were in need of a change in our lives."

For another half hour or so, Winifred and I share information about our respective lives. The horrific details of the sinking of the *Titanic* aren't mentioned again, although she does tell me the reason why her son-in-law was aboard the ship.

"Colin worked for a tobacco company in Bristol," she says. "You will have heard of Wills Tobacco, no doubt. They're merging with other companies to form Imperial Tobacco, apparently, and wanted Colin to go to America to talk with some representatives over there. Don't ask me what about, even Maud doesn't know, but they trusted him and knew he would make a good impression. The thing is, his bosses were prepared to give him a second-class ticket, but Colin said he'd rather save the company some money and travel third. That's the type of man he was – never thinking of himself."

"I know what's on your mind, Winnie," I say. "That if he'd travelled second-class, perhaps he would have made it to safety. But I daresay it wouldn't have made a scrap of difference. He'd still have wanted to save other people's lives before his own."

"You're probably right, Bessie. But still, things *might* have turned out differently if he hadn't been so stubborn."

Before we know it, the children are back, chattering excitedly and ravenous for cake and lemonade. Mr Smith says he'll walk us back to the station, as Winifred has had a busy day and is feeling tired. William insists on coming too; it's clear that he and Andrew are already the best of friends. Neither of them wants Wendy tagging along, despite Winifred's protest that they should let her come if she wants to. But Wendy says her feet are aching from all the stairs she's had to climb and wants to lie down next to her mother, who still hasn't emerged from the bedroom.

"You do that, my precious one," Winifred says. "And please, do persuade your dear mama to come down for her tea, which will be ready in about an hour. I can't keep treating her like an invalid, and she must be sick and tired of being cooped up in that room, all day and all night."

17

"What did you think of the lighthouse?" I ask Andrew, once we're settled in our compartment on the train and the guard has blown his whistle, signalling departure.

"Well, it was fun because William came too," he says, "but the sort of jobs Mr Smith has to do weren't really what I was expecting. He says he keeps a daily log, recording weather and sea conditions, and boring stuff like that. It sounds like he does a lot of writing. I didn't think I'd need to know how to read and write to be a lighthouse keeper. I thought it would just be things like keeping the light burning, operating a fog signal, and looking out for unusual sightings at sea."

"Writing a daily log won't be a problem for you, Andrew. You'll have learnt to read sooner than you think, and writing will follow. I can see already that you're a fast learner and you have an excellent memory, so you'll progress quickly once you've fully mastered the basics."

"I hope you're right, Mrs Fielding. Will says he reads lots of books and has already read *Treasure Island*. But guess what? He doesn't know how to swim! I said I'd teach him if we visit again."

"We'll have to wait and see if we're invited another time. But the sea probably isn't the best place to teach someone to swim. It's rarely calm enough on this coast, and the waves are so strong. It can be dangerous for a beginner, as you know, Andrew. Remember the little boy you rescued?"

"He was a baby! And I already told you, I didn't rescue him. Will is my age, nine, almost ten – he's not going to be scared. I'm sure I can teach him to swim. If the sea's too rough, he says some of the large rock pools, which are also quite deep in places, would be perfect for swimming lessons. We can start in one of those. But I'm not teaching Wendy. She's even more annoying than Violet."

"Come now, Andrew. That's not a nice thing to say. I thought she was a sweet little girl. If we go again, then perhaps your mother will let Violet come with us, and she can play with Wendy. Then you'll have Will all to yourself. It's a shame that the two of them haven't yet had a chance to make any friends locally."

"They haven't been living with their grandparents for very long. Did you know that their father drowned at sea?"

"Yes, it was a terrible accident in the North Atlantic Ocean. You may have heard of it. The ship, the *Titanic*, struck an iceberg on its way to New York, and it sank within a few hours. Many people lost their lives. I think I'm right in saying that it was the worst shipwreck ever recorded. I'm surprised that Will isn't afraid of the sea after what happened to his father."

"No, I don't think he is, though Wendy might be. She was even frightened to go to the lantern room at the top of the lighthouse. Will says the sea doesn't scare him, but he never wants to go on a big ship like the *Titanic*, and definitely not one that's going to America."

"I don't blame him. I don't want to, either."

"How did you enjoy the company of Mrs Winifred Smith?" Lionel asks me upon my return.

"Oh, I enjoyed it very much," I say. "She's certainly good company. It's difficult to get a word in edgeways, as she talks non-stop. She wanted to talk about the

Titanic's sinking, which I can understand, but it was hard for me to listen to what she had to say. Apparently, the fellow who survived the sinking – the friend of her late son-in-law, Colin – has written to her and told her a lot of the details."

"Is that so? What did he tell her?"

"Well, Mr Barlow – that's his name – said that most men in third class were barred from accessing the boat deck, but he managed to get up there before the barriers came down and was able to secure a place in one of the last lifeboats being launched. He tried to persuade Colin to come too, but he refused. He felt he should stay below deck and help the women and children, most of whom did not believe they were in any danger. Mr Barlow now feels terribly guilty that he survived when so many others perished, and wishes he'd not been so selfish. He's a bachelor so didn't have a family waiting for him at home, like Colin."

"In a moment of panic, who knows what any one of us would do? Rumour has it that the officers were strict about who should or shouldn't be given a place in the lifeboats. There weren't always enough women and children on deck to fill them – some women refused to leave their husbands – and yet they still denied a place to the men, even younger ones who had their whole lives ahead of them. It's unforgivable that so many lifeboats were launched only half full, especially when there were so few available to begin with. I don't think this fellow should feel guilty unless he supplanted a woman who actually wanted a place."

"No, I don't think he did. He waited until the last moment and even when his lifeboat was about to be lowered, he continued looking around the deck to see if he could spot any more women. And if Colin *had* made it to the upper deck, he would willingly have given him his place."

"Did you meet Colin's widow?"

"No. Apparently, she's still in a state of profound grief and stays in the bedroom most of the time. Her mother certainly has her hands full, what with caring for Maud *and* two energetic children, but Winifred is a capable woman and nothing seems to faze her."

"And her husband? Did you meet him too?

"Yes, he walked us back to the station. He's a quiet man, as if often the case when the other half is extremely talkative. It's clear that Mr Stanley Smith is well suited to his job, which requires spending a lot of time alone at the lighthouse. Andrew got along well with William, the Smiths' grandson. He wants to teach him to swim if we visit again. I told him we'd need to receive another invitation first, but I'm happy that he's made a friend. I don't think he has many at school."

"That's excellent, Bessie. Oh, before I forget – a letter arrived for you in the second post. Here it is. It's from Ferndell, but I don't recognise the handwriting."

I can see straight away that it's from Margaret, my niece. I told her to write to me once she had obtained permission to take some time off from her job in the local bakery, and then we'd fix a date for her visit. She is my only niece and I'm fond of her, though I don't know her as well as I'd like to. But that will change once she comes to stay with us.

Margaret says she'd like to visit the following week, if it's convenient for Lionel and myself. She says if she travels on Sunday, then her brother Joseph will accompany her on the train to Brampton-on-Sea. I don't think Margaret has ever been on a train before, so the family would be hesitant to let her to travel alone. They will need to make an early start, as Joseph hopes to return to Ferndell the same day. He plans to come and pick her up the following Sunday, so she will stay with us for a full week. I am thrilled at the thought of her visit and Lionel has no objection whatsoever, so I immediately write back telling her that this arrangement suits us both.

Lionel and I are again at the railway station, this time waiting for Margaret's train to arrive. It's another sunny, cloudless day and I'm hoping that it will stay this way for the rest of the week, though even folk in Brampton-on-Sea are saying that the good weather can't last much longer.

The train is right on time and Joseph and Margaret alight, Joseph carrying Margaret's small suitcase. I hug the two of them, becoming quite emotional at the warm touch of my own flesh and blood and on hearing the familiar village accent for the second time in less than a month.

"I'd love to stick around, Aunt Bessie," Joseph says, "but I need to return right away. A train bound for Exeter is due to arrive in about a quarter of an hour. If I miss that one, then I won't get home until tomorrow."

"Oh, Joseph, what a pity. I was hoping you'd have time to come to the house for a cup of tea and a bite to eat before catching the train back. But I do understand. Perhaps next week you might have some time to spare?"

"Walter said yesterday that he might be able to come and collect Margaret next week, unless he has a sudden job that takes him far from home. But at the moment it looks like he may be free."

"Well, it will be lovely to see Walter again, but I'm sorry we can't see more of you. Thank you for bringing Margaret to us. I've been looking forward to her visit so much. You'll give my love to the family and to Daisy and her sisters, won't you, Jospeh? And, of course, to Mrs Goode."

"I certainly will, Aunt. Goodbye until next time. Goodbye, Mr Fielding."

"It's Lionel to you, Joseph," my husband says, picking up Margaret's suitcase. "We're family now. I'm just as sorry as your aunt is that you can't spend more time with us. But rest assured, we'll take good care of your sister."

What a pity Joseph has to leave right away. But I can understand that he wants to be home by the end of the day, especially as he has to rise before dawn each morning to care for the livestock on Mr Townsend's farm. In a way, it's a good thing that Walter has offered to come next week to accompany Margaret back home, otherwise Joseph would be spending two Sundays in a row on the train when I'm sure he would rather be in the company of his betrothed.

"How are your parents, Margaret?" I ask my niece, as we walk home arm in arm. "And, of course, young Richard. How is he spending the summer?"

"Mother and Father are both well, thank you," Margaret says. "Father is working hard, as usual. Old Mr Collins finally retired, so Father is now the head wheelwright. He's taken on an apprentice, Charlie, who's only a little older than Richard. Father tried to persuade Richard to learn the ropes of his trade – since Joseph had not shown any interest – but Richard also says he doesn't want to become a wheelwright. For the rest of the summer, he's helping Joseph on the farm. He loves the outdoor life, just like his older brother."

"I suppose that's a disappointment for your father. Your grandfather was a wheelwright, as I'm sure you know. But perhaps with automobiles becoming the transport of the future, or so I'm told, wheels for carriages and other horse-drawn vehicles won't be needed as much by the time Richard is a grown man. In any case, if I know my brother, he would never try to force a particular line of work on any of his children. And you, Margaret, are you happy working at the bakery?"

"Oh yes, and I'm learning such a lot. Mr and Mrs Bakewell are very kind. Isn't it funny that they run a bakery and their name is Bakewell? They insist that I take home any bread or cakes that are left over at the end of the day. Mother doesn't need to do much baking these days, so she's pleased about that."

"And the young man you're stepping out with? Edgar, isn't it? How is your courtship progressing?"

Lionel gives a laugh.

"Margaret, my dear," he says with a twinkle in his eye, "you don't need to answer that question. Your aunt is being far too inquisitive. She should know that young people don't like older folk poking their noses into their personal affairs."

"Listen to you, Lionel Fielding," I retort. "I'm sure you interrogated Mathilda like nobody's business when she was courting Ronald!"

"No, I kept out well of it. In fact, I was the last one to know when they became engaged."

"I don't believe that for one minute. But perhaps you're right. Margaret doesn't need to answer me if she doesn't want to."

"Oh, I don't mind at all," Margaret says with a smile.

"Things couldn't be better between me and Edgar. We see each other every Sunday. We go for a walk by the river, if the weather's fine, and then have tea either at my home, or at his. His parents already treat me like one of the family. They have five sons, ranging in age from six to nineteen, but no daughters. They're originally from Italy – their surname is Perrotti – and they run the village greengrocer's. Everyone says that the quality of fresh produce has really improved since they took over the shop. Edgar's name is actually Edgardo, but only his parents call him that. We haven't talked about marriage yet, as we both feel too young to settle down, but perhaps next year we'll feel differently."

"I don't remember an Italian family running the greengrocery. How long have they been living in the village? Were you and Edgar at school together?"

"They've been living in Ferndell for quite a few years now, but have only been running the shop for the last couple. Yes, Edgar and I were in the same classroom for two years. I never spoke to him at school, though. The boys sat on one side of the classroom and the girls on the other, as you'll remember, Aunt. Boys and girls didn't mix at all. But last year, Edgar and I kept bumping into each other – it may have been intentional on his part, I don't know – and he finally suggested that we go for a walk together. When I told Joseph, he said he felt he should accompany me, but I refused to let him. I don't know what century he thinks we're living in. It's 1912, not 1812!"

I smile, remembering how Mrs Grist's son Phillip insisted on accompanying Walter's former sweetheart Edie to her lodgings when she visited me in London. There was a dense fog that evening and Edie would surely have lost her way without Phillip as a guide. I wanted to accompany them, but they were both emphatic in telling me that there was no need. I thought at the time that perhaps it was only in London that young people walked out together unaccompanied, but – from what Margaret says – it's now normal practice in the countryside as well.

As soon as Margaret's suitcase is deposited at the house, she and I go for a walk on the beach while the sun is still shining. It's the first time my niece has set eyes on the sea and, like others before her, she is filled with wonder at the sight. It gives her great pleasure to take off her shoes and stockings and paddle in the incoming water, which is ankle-deep one minute and knee-deep the next. Margaret's laughter is infectious, so I join her and we spend an amusing half hour trying to out-run the waves and avoid getting our skirts wet.

I'm concerned that Margaret might be feeling hungry, although she denies it. I can tell that she doesn't want to leave the beach. But I assure her that we'll return tomorrow, and the next day, and the day after that. The sea is going nowhere. By the end of the week, I tell her, she'll be tired of it and longing to return to the countryside.

For tea, I've prepared macaroni cheese and it just needs baking in the range oven for about twenty minutes.

"Do you eat a lot of macaroni at Edgar's house?" I ask, as I lay the table.

"Yes," she says, "but they don't call it macaroni. They call it 'pasta'. Pasta comes in many different shapes and the Italians cook it with lots of different sauces made from fresh ingredients. Many of the sauces have a tomato base and contain unusual spices that add a lot of extra flavour. Sometimes they add mince to make it more nourishing and, once the dish is served, they sprinkle sharp-tasting grated cheese, which they call *parmigiano*, over the top. Mrs Perrotti makes her pasta from scratch and it's delicious. The Perrottis have even started selling some different types, which come in a shipment from Italy. But I think the villagers are a bit suspicious of foreign foods and don't know how to make the sauces – though Mrs Perrotti is happy to explain. She's such a good cook, but she spends hours in the kitchen every single day. Mind you, she does have a large family to feed – Mr Perrotti, Edgar and his four brothers. Edgar is number two. Both he and his elder brother Franco – or Frank, as we call him – help their father in the shop, which stays open well past normal closing hours."

It's so pleasant talking with Margaret. She's not shy at all and chats to Lionel and myself as if she's known us all her life. Well, I have known her since she was a baby, but have spent too little time in her company. Now that she's a young lady, I feel I hardly know her at all. She has such a confident manner about her – so different from the way I was at that age – and her personality is just as engaging as her looks. She reminds me so much of my dear sister Ethel, who was the beauty of my immediate family and broke all our hearts when she died young. Margaret has the same wavy, light brown hair, bright blue eyes, a clear complexion and charming dimples that appear when she smiles, which is often.

"Does your father ever tell you that you look a lot like your Aunt Ethel?" I ask her.

"Yes, he says it all the time," Margaret says. "I found it embarrassing when, not so long ago, he said to Walter,

'If you ever forget what your mother looked like, just cast your eye over your cousin'. Walter wasn't the least bit embarrassed though – he just chuckled and said that from what he's heard, his mother was nothing short of a saint, and he doubted whether I would ever be able to live up to such a reputation, or would even want to."

I've spoken to Walter many times about his mother; he was so young when she died and has only a few memories of the time they spent together. I don't want him ever to forget her completely. The fact that Margaret resembles Ethel so much makes me wonder whether my sister's still-born baby, Catherine, would also have inherited her good looks. Walter is a handsome man, but I see more of his father Frederick in his face than the features of his dear mother. How sad that we lost both Ethel and Catherine on that unfortunate day sixteen years ago, and that Ethel was denied the joy of watching her son grow up. But they are both still with us in our hearts, and I have no doubt whatsoever that we will all be reunited one day.

"That certainly sounds like a remark Walter would make," I say cheerfully, as now is not the time for wistful thoughts. "He's used to the family talking about his mother as though she were a saint. They do say that those whom the gods love most, die young. Ethel wasn't a saint, believe me, but it's true, she lives in our memories as if she *were* one. And she was quite beautiful, just like you, my dear. Now, let me not embarrass you like your father did. I'd like you to tell me all the news from Ferndell, good and bad. After that, I swear I won't bombard you with any more questions. But if you want to tell me more about the Perrotti family, then I'm all ears."

18

Margaret's visit has been such a welcome change that I know I'm going to miss her terribly when she leaves. Having a young person in the house, especially one from Ferndell with whom I can share memories and hear all the local gossip, is like a breath of fresh air. Working in the bakery six days a week, she is well acquainted with most of the village womenfolk, who are only too happy to spend a few minutes chatting while waiting for their loaves to come out of the oven. Much to my delight, Margaret has told me quite a few funny stories, making me laugh out loud. That in itself, Lionel says, is like a tonic. He has been rather excluded from our conversations, but he doesn't seem to mind. He's just happy that I'm being entertained and that Margaret feels so much at home.

And I think she has enjoyed her stay with us just as much as we've enjoyed having her. The weather cooperated for the first half of the week and we spent a lot of time on the beach, walking, paddling and looking for shells. By mid-week, however, the long-forecasted rain finally swept in from the south and we were mostly confined to the house, though we did venture out a couple of times to marvel at the enormous waves. Margaret didn't complain about staying indoors. She is as fond as books as I am, so we enjoyed some quiet time reading and sharing our thoughts on various novels, especially the works of Miss Charlotte Brontë, who ranks high among her favourite authors.

On the first rainy day, we walked into town and paid a visit to the bookshop. Thankfully, the pleasant young man who attended us in Mr Franklin's absence didn't mind our prolonged browsing. I bought Margaret a copy of Miss Brontë's *Villette*, for which she couldn't thank me enough. I told her it was a reward for the hours she's spent in the kitchen each morning, baking many loaves of bread and a great variety of biscuits and cakes, for which she received much praise, from Lionel in particular.

But all good things come to an end and tomorrow she will leave us. Walter has written to say that both he and Blanche will be coming to take Margaret home, but will arrive today, Saturday, and stay with us for one night, if that is all right with us. Walter should know he doesn't need to ask that question; he and his fiancée are welcome to stay for as long as they like. Blanche can sleep with Margaret in the larger of our two spare rooms, and Walter can take the smaller one. Margaret tells me she has only met Blanche on a couple of occasions, so this will be an opportunity for them to get to know one another better, especially since Blanche will soon be part of the family.

The weather is still wet and windy, so I would not be surprised if Walter's train is delayed. Lionel says he can go alone to the station, to save us all from getting wet, but I cannot conceive of not being present to meet my dear nephew and his betrothed off the train. So we set off, Margaret included, with our umbrellas, though it's only Lionel's that doesn't blow inside out in the sudden gusts of wind. Fortunately, the train arrives on time and, amazingly, the sun comes out and a rainbow appears just as Walter and Blanche alight from their carriage. If that is not a good omen, I don't know what is!

"Your arrival has caused the rain to stop and just look at that beautiful rainbow," I say, giving them both a wet hug. "That must be a sign that your visit is going to be a happy one, even though it's much too short."

"What about *your* visit, cousin?" Walter asks Margaret. "Has it been a happy one? I trust it hasn't been raining all week?"

"It's certainly been a happy one," Margaret says. "And no, it hasn't rained all the time. The first half of the week was glorious, and Aunt Bessie and I spent many hours on the beach. I've had such a lovely time. I shall never forget my first glimpse of the sea – it was such a spectacular sight! I wish I could stay longer, but I have to go back to work on Monday. The time has gone by so quickly."

"Let's get back to the house before the rain decides to return," Lionel says. "Despite what your aunt says, Walter, I don't think we've seen the last of the wet weather today. It is a pity you and Blanche are staying for only one night, but perhaps you can come back another time and stay a bit longer? We would both be delighted if you could manage to visit us again before the end of the summer."

"We'd very much like to," Walter says, "but it's difficult finding the time, what with my work – which often requires me to travel at short notice – and Blanche's night shifts at the woollen mill. But we both feel like we could do with a holiday, so we'll do our best to return as soon as we can."

I've prepared a late lunch of soup and salad – all ingredients gathered from the vegetable patch this morning – and Margaret has made a mouth-watering strawberry tart for dessert, which I'll serve with fresh cream.

"Margaret's been baking all kinds of lovely cakes and tarts," I say, as we sit down at the table. "The next time she visits, I'm going to ask her to bring some of Mrs

Perrotti's pasta with her, so she can teach me how to make some tasty Italian dishes."

"It's a good thing Joseph isn't here," Margaret says. "He's forever telling me that with all the food I'm enjoying, both at the bakery and at Mr and Mrs Perrotti's house, I'm becoming quite plump. It's more fashionable for ladies to be slender these days, and I'm certainly not that, so perhaps he's right and I ought to start watching my weight."

"Whatever is Joseph thinking, saying such a thing? You're a perfect size, Margaret. Don't listen to him – I'm sure he's only teasing you. Besides, when I was growing up, being a little plump was considered a good thing. If you were thin, it usually meant you had an illness, or weren't getting enough to eat."

Perhaps I should have thought twice before making that last remark. Lionel's first wife died from consumption, which is known as the wasting disease because those afflicted lose weight so quickly. I don't want to remind him of the sad years when he and Mathilda had to care for her, knowing that her end was imminent. But Lionel doesn't appear to be the least bit perturbed by my comment.

"Indeed," he says. "Your aunt is right, Margaret. Don't start worrying about your weight. I'm sure that the Perrottis' meals are healthy with lots of fruits and vegetables. Italians know how to eat well. The pasta is not going to make you gain weight and neither are the baked goods, if eaten in moderation. A varied diet, exercise and a good night's sleep are key to staying in good health *and* in good shape."

Once we have eaten our fill, we sit with our cups of tea in the back garden. The rain has held off, though there's still a mist and a strong southerly breeze.

"Well, I can't keep silent any longer, Aunt Bessie," Walter says, looking at Blanche, who nods. "We've had some news from Ireland and it's both good and bad. First the good news. In fact, it's not just good – it's wonderful news, and we are all so relieved. Hilda is alive. She disembarked the *Titanic* at Queenstown, Ireland, as your friend suspected might've been the case."

Lionel and I stare at Walter for a moment or two, wondering if we've heard correctly. Did he just say that Hilda is alive?

"Oh, Walter, Blanche!" I exclaim, once Walter's words have sunk in. "That really is the best news! I'm so, so happy to know that Hilda is alive and well in Ireland! I'd begun to give up all hope of such an outcome, though I know the family hadn't. But Walter, why didn't you tell us this as soon as you arrived?"

"Well, there's quite a bit of explaining to do, so I thought it best to wait until we were sitting quietly. Obviously, we are all incredibly thankful that our prayers have been answered. But although Hilda is most certainly alive, she's not at all well at the moment. Still, we're hopeful that her illness is just a temporary setback. She's staying with her in-laws in Dublin, at least until she gets better, and Ernest is now with her. We've no idea when she'll decide to return to the village, if at all."

"So, is that the bad news, Walter? The fact that she's not well and might not return? I hope her illness is not too serious."

"We think she'll recover, with time. It's certainly not life threatening. But let me start from the beginning. Or do *you* want to tell the whole story, Blanche?"

"No, you go ahead, Walter. You're better at explaining things than I am."

"All right. Well, as you know, Aunt Bessie, Daisy wrote to Brian Doyle in Dublin. She received a return letter from him two days ago. It appears that Mrs Goode was right all along. Hilda's purpose in setting off for America was not to attend Ernest's wedding, but to meet her brother-in-law, Fergus Doyle, with whom she was exceedingly close.

"Just hours before she embarked on her journey across the Atlantic, however, Ernest sent her a telegram saying that Fergus had returned to Ireland for the funeral of his mother – that would be Ernest's grandmother, though I don't suppose he'd ever met her. He was unsure when his uncle would be returning to New York, believing that he might be planning to stay in Dublin for some weeks. On hearing this news, Hilda decided to disembark at Queenstown and not to continue on to New York, even though she'd bought a ticket for the entire journey. It was a life-saving decision that she made, but sadly it didn't result in happiness. Fergus only stayed in Ireland for three days before returning to New York... on the *Titanic*. He did not survive the sinking."

Walter pauses in his explanation and takes a sip of tea. I don't know what to say. Of course, it's wonderful news that Hilda is alive – she is the one we are most concerned about – but the fact that her brother-in-law lost *his* life instead feels like a sharp rebuke; it's as if we are being reproached for our joy and relief on hearing that Hilda is still with us.

"That is so sad," I say finally. "The Doyle family's grief must be two-fold with Fergus losing his life so soon after the death of his mother."

"Indeed. The good news about Hilda is tempered by the knowledge that Fergus perished less than a week after his mother's funeral."

"But what about Ernest, Walter? Why didn't he let anyone know his mother was in Ireland? She must have sent word to him that she planned to disembark at Queenstown."

"Yes, she sent him a return telegram straight away. And he immediately set sail for Ireland himself. He'd become terribly homesick in New York and was anxious to be with his mother. But on his arrival, he found her in a weakened state. She'd arrived in Dublin exhausted from the difficult journey from Queenstown, which took her much longer than expected, only to discover that Fergus had already departed on the very ship she'd disembarked from. When the Doyle family heard, a couple of days later, that the *Titanic* had sunk – and then received news that Fergus had not survived – Hilda was inconsolable and became quite unwell. For some reason, she blamed herself for Fergus' demise. Brian says she's on the mend now that Ernest is at her side, and is no longer saying that she wishes she'd remained on the *Titanic* so that she and Fergus could have met their end together."

"Goodness me, the poor woman. If only Fergus has waited! It's surely going to take her some time to get over such a tragic outcome."

"Yes, it will take a good while, no doubt. Both Hilda and Ernest are staying with Mrs Maureen McGuire, Hilda's sister-in-law, who's also a widow. Brian said that Ernest sends his apologies for not letting any of us know of his mother's change of plan. He was so worried about her that it didn't cross his mind that family in Ferndell would be thinking she was on the *Titanic* when it struck the iceberg. It just never occurred to him that the Goodes would not have known that she'd disembarked in Ireland.

He's going to write a personal letter of apology to his aunt, and hopes that she'll forgive him."

"I'm sure she will. Do they both plan to come back to England eventually? Or will Ernest return to America? Hadn't he hoped to start a new life over there? What about the girl he was supposed to be marrying?"

"Brian thinks Hilda will come back home as soon as she's well enough. As for Ernest's future, I don't know. He didn't say. But it looks like there's no intended marriage – that was just a fabrication on Hilda's part. Ernest may let us know of his future plans when he writes. I imagine that he'll return with his mother and stay with her for a while longer. It will be hard for her to be alone after what has happened."

"How does your mother feel now, Blanche? Greatly relieved, I imagine."

"Yes, of course," Blanche says. "At first, she was weeping tears of joy that her twin sister was still alive. We all were. She always did say she would have known if Aunt Hilda had died, so it was a case of 'I told you so'. But it seems that when one worry goes away, it's not long before there's something else to be troubled about. Now she's concerned for Aunt Hilda's health and what state she'll be in when she does return. And it's horrible to hear her talk in such an unkind way about Fergus Doyle, for whom she has no sympathy whatsoever. The poor man died a terrible death, but Mother still blames him for Aunt Hilda's present woes."

"Why is it that she disliked him so intensely?"

"Well, she's only met him twice – the first time at Aunt Hilda's and Uncle Declan's wedding, and then at Uncle Declan's funeral – so it's unkind of her to talk ill about the man without having known him properly. She says Fergus claimed to have promised his brother on his deathbed that he'd spend the rest of his life looking after his widow. My aunt apparently took him at his word, hence her decision to follow him to America. I don't think she took that decision alone though – they'd clearly been writing to each other for some months. And I believe she always did have a liking for him. Mother says his promises were all a pack of lies – that he had no intention of looking after Hilda – that any fool could see that he was a ladies' man, flirting first with one and then with another. As for making such a deathbed promise, she says he wasn't even present when Uncle Declan died."

"Poor Hilda. I suppose she hadn't completely recovered from her husband's death and must have found her brother-in-law's attentions a comfort. And, when you think about it, since Fergus *and* Ernest were in New York, it made sense for her to join them. I do hope that Ernest decides to stay with her. It's now that she really needs looking after."

"Yes, I agree. Mother says she can come and live with us if she returns to Ferndell. It's now clear to all of us that, since Father died, we've neglected Aunt Hilda, forgetting that she's lost a husband too and has been on her own for far too long. We do feel guilty about it. And it will be good for her to be under the same roof as those who truly care for her. But I hope Mother changes her opinion of Fergus Doyle before making the suggestion, or Aunt Hilda is bound to refuse."

"I'm sure she will. They are twins after all and I imagine that harsh words spoken in the past will be forgotten once they are reunited."

"Hmm... we'll see. Mother can be quite obstinate at times! And so can Aunt Hilda! For twins, they have very little in common, but stubbornness is certainly one trait they share. If she *does* agree to Mother's suggestion, then it will solve the problem that Walter and I have – where *we'll* live once we get married. Walter doesn't want to leave Uncle Edward alone, and I don't think Mother and Millie will be able to cope on their own. Daisy, of course, will be going to the farm cottage as soon as she and Joseph are wed. I think Walter's already told you of our dilemma, Aunt Bessie, so I won't say any more. I don't want you to think that we're acting out of self-interest, because we're really not. It doesn't matter to us where we live, as long as we're together. We'll have to see what Ernest's plans are first. Of course, both he and Aunt Hilda might decide to stay in Ireland indefinitely."

"I don't see why Hilda wouldn't want to come back to Ferndell once she's regained her strength. She has her home here, after all, and her sister and nieces. She surely feels closer to her own family in the West Country than to her husband's kin in Ireland."

"One would think so, but Aunt Hilda thinks highly of her Irish relatives, even though it pains Mother to admit it. Another reason why Mother hasn't a good word to say about the Doyles is because they're Roman Catholics, and Ernest has in fact been brought up as a Catholic. Clearly, it's Mother who's at fault here, with her petty prejudices. For as long as I can remember, this has been a trigger for fallings-out between my mother and my aunt. I don't understand why religion is so often a cause for animosity."

"My friend Patty in London is married to a Roman Catholic, and there couldn't be a happier couple alive today. Patty's mother was sceptical of the marriage at first, but now she's a great advocate for Catholicism, having witnessed what a kind and honest human being her son-in-law is. It's such a shame when religion leads to discord, especially among family members."

"Yes, it most certainly is. I should add that there's one more thing that has begun to trouble Mother, and that's the Doyles' views on the Irish question. Can you explain this, Walter? I still don't understand it properly."

"Well," Walter begins, "it appears that the Doyles actively support the movement for Home Rule in Ireland. Uncle Lionel, I'm sure that *you've* been following Irish politics in *The Times* and know all about recent events in Dublin."

"Ah, yes, Home Rule," Lionel says, "I did read that the Liberals have drafted a Third Home Rule bill in alliance with the Irish nationalists. If that gets passed, it's going to make a lot of people unhappy."

"Exactly, especially the Ulster Unionists, the majority of whom are Protestants. They don't want to be a part of a self-governing Ireland dominated by Roman Catholics. Apparently, they're forming a military force known as the Ulster Volunteers. But I don't think Mrs Goode really understands the politics any more than you do, Blanche – she just doesn't want her sister to get mixed up in any kind of hostility between Protestants and Catholics, especially since *she's* been raised as a Protestant."

"That's true," Blanche says. "But she's now using the Irish troubles as one more reason for her aversion to the Doyles. She's not fooling anyone. Her dislike of that family has been brewing for many years, long before the present tensions."

"Tell me, Walter," Lionel asks. "Was it Fergus Doyle's intention to find support in America for Home Rule in Ireland?"

"I'm really not sure. It's a possibility, I suppose. Neither Blanche nor myself know much about the Doyle family. Up until now, Mrs Goode has been quite tight-lipped about their affairs. But she probably knows more than she's letting on, or she wouldn't be so against Hilda remaining in Ireland. It's true that there's a huge Irish community in New York, but my guess is that they're not too concerned about what's going on back home. By all accounts, they're struggling to make a living in America and to gain acceptance as citizens."

"Indeed. I've heard that too. They're not always welcome in America and face many hardships that they hadn't expected. What about the other brother? Is he actively campaigning for Home Rule?"

"Yes, I believe Brian Doyle is more into politics than his brothers were. I think Mrs Goode is also worried that if Ernest decides to stay in Ireland, *he* might get mixed up with the supporters of Home Rule. Being a Roman Catholic himself, his sympathies will probably lie with those of his own faith. And if he stays, then Hilda may remain too."

"Oh dear, it all sounds very disturbing," I say. "My dear father always said one should steer clear of politics and religion if you want to remain a friend to all."

"That may be true," Lionel says, "but wasn't it Thomas Jefferson who said, 'I never considered a difference of opinion in politics, in religion… as cause for withdrawing from a friend'?"

"Let's just hope and pray that both Hilda and Ernest will return to the family fold in Ferndell eventually. Blanche, do you know if Daisy and Joseph will finally be able to fix a date for their wedding, now that your mother knows the whereabouts of her sister?"

"Yes, I think so. It looks like they might be able to stick to their original date in September or, if not, then October at the latest."

"Well, that's good news. A wedding in the family is always something to be welcomed, not least because it brings people together. It would be lovely if Hilda and Ernest could return in time for the nuptials."

Margaret, who's been in the bedroom packing her suitcase, comes outside to join us. She says she'd like to show Walter and Blanche the beach now that the sun is finally peeking through the clouds and the threat of rain is no longer a constraint.

"Would you and Uncle Lionel like to come too, Aunt Bessie?" she asks me.

"No, thank you, my dear. You go ahead with your cousins. It's still too windy for me to enjoy the walk. And your Uncle Lionel will just slow you down. You'll need to leave fairly early in the morning, so now is as good a time as any for you to take Walter and Blanche to the beach. Stay as long as you like – don't feel you have to rush back."

"What do you mean, I'll slow them down?" Lionel asks me, as our young guests set off across the fields. "I know I'm old, but not *that* old."

"You're not old, and I know you can walk as fast as any of them, and certainly faster than me. But I just wanted them to have some fun without you and me tagging along. You know how young people are – they'll have a better time if they don't have to be on their best behaviour because of us. Didn't you hear them laughing as they left? They have their own jokes that they can share together without worrying about being disrespectful to their elders. Margaret has been stuck with the two of us for a whole week, so she must be longing for some younger company."

"Oh, that's the reason, is it? I thought perhaps it was because you wanted some time alone with me, ancient though I am. But I might have guessed that wouldn't have been foremost in your mind. Silly old me."

I know Lionel is just joking, but I give him a hug and a kiss to reassure him of my unwavering affection.

"As of tomorrow," I say, "we'll be all alone until our next set of visitors arrives. That suits *me* just fine, Lionel. You know it does."

Later that evening, once our guests are in their beds, I ask Lionel what he thinks about Hilda's situation; whether he believes she will return to Ferndell when she is well enough to travel.

"I don't know," he says. "It won't surprise me if she stays in Ireland. She seems very close to the Doyle family and they *are* looking after her in her time of need. As you mentioned, they've only recently lost their mother, so are grieving for both a cherished mother *and* a brother – yet they've welcomed her with open arms, or so it seems. The Irish are big-hearted people and I'm sure that, in her present state, she appreciates their kindness and honest hospitality. As for Ernest, I can't imagine that he'd want to return to the village that he was only too anxious to leave a few years ago. He may have become disillusioned with life in New York – he certainly wasted no time in getting aboard a steamer bound for Ireland once he heard that his mother intended to disembark at Queenstown – but that doesn't mean he would be willing to live in Ferndell again. Perhaps he'll come to the conclusion that

Ireland is where he belongs, especially since many changes are taking place there at the present time."

"Hmm… you may be right. I was rather hoping Hilda would return and decide to live with Yvonne Goode and young Millie, so that Walter and Blanche can stay with Edward."

"What about her own home? Does she own the cottage?"

"Good heavens, no. She pays a rent. But her husband left her enough to live on, and I believe Ernest helps to pay the bills, when he's working, that is. I can't help thinking… all these women who are not much older than me and now they are widows. Hilda Doyle and the sister-in-law she's staying with – Maureen McGuire, I think she was called – Yvonne Goode, and poor Maud, Winifred's daughter, who's not yet thirty. They must have begun their married lives expecting years of happiness together, and now look at them. I count my blessings, Lionel, believe me. I was lonely for years, but you remedied that. My married life with you is still in its infancy – I hope and pray we can be together until we reach our three score years and ten, at the very least."

"I thought you already considered me an old man, Bessie Fielding. By the time you reach *your* three score years and ten, I'll be well into my ninth decade on this earth! But don't worry, I think longevity is in my blood. I plan to keep you company for many years to come. You may even begin to rue the day you married me when I become a tottering old fellow making unreasonable demands on my youthful wife!"

19

The house is so quiet now that Margaret has left us. Not that I mind, really. For years I lived in a house full of people and often longed for a bit of solitude. I remember when I was living with Mrs Grist in London, I used to look forward to Sundays when she spent the day with one of her sons, or with her sister-in-law, and the cook and the housekeeper had their day off. When I wasn't visiting Patty and Robert, or giving Michael a reading lesson, I was all alone in the house and it was so quiet and peaceful. My nerves were always on edge in Mrs Grist's presence and it was a such a relief not to have to face her disapproving looks, or listen to the spiteful comments of Mrs Hopper and Mrs Evans. Those two never took a liking to me, however hard I tried to be their friend. I couldn't understand it, as I'd always got along so well with the other domestic staff at Farringdale House. Lionel told me it was because I was a lady's companion, which was seen as a superior position to theirs; thus, any friendship would not have been on an equal footing. Naturally, I didn't feel the least bit superior, but it was hard to convince the cook and the housekeeper otherwise.

Lionel suggests that I visit the bookshop this week and inform Mr Franklin, who has just returned from America, what we now know about Hilda. He gives me some money and tells me to buy whatever books take my fancy, so as not to come away empty-handed.

The rain has returned – Farmer Townsend was not far wrong in his weather predictions for the second half of the summer – but I don't let that put me off. I don't mind meeting Mr Franklin again; it was so kind of him to take the time to search for Ernest in New York, and he deserves to know that both Hilda and her son are alive and well, and presently being looked after by the Doyle family in Ireland.

He doesn't see me when I enter the shop, as he's busy at the till with another customer. I find myself gravitating towards the children's section once again. It's Andrew's tenth birthday this week and I'd like to buy him a copy of *Treasure Island*, if I can find one. He won't be able to read it by himself just yet, but we can read it together and he'll get a taste of just how enjoyable reading can be. Lionel will probably scold me for not buying a book for myself, but I think Andrew is in greater need. And I'm in luck – there's a second-hand copy on the shelf and it's reasonably priced. I'll even have some money left over to buy this week's *The Spectator* for Lionel.

As soon as Mr Franklin is free, I greet him at the counter. He recognises me right away.

"Ah, Mrs Fielding," he says. "What a pleasant surprise. How are you and Mr Fielding?"

"We're both well, thank you, Mr Franklin, as I hope you are too. Welcome back to Brampton-on-Sea. Did you achieve all you set out to do in New York?"

"Yes, I think so. Except for tracking down Ernest Doyle, that is."

"Well, we're most grateful to you for trying to find him, and for your kind letter. I have some good news. We've actually located Ernest in Dublin – he's staying with his relatives – and, thankfully, his mother is there as well. By the grace of God, she wasn't aboard the *Titanic* when it sank. She disembarked at Queenstown, as you suggested might have been the case. As you can imagine, it's a great relief for her family and friends."

"Oh, I *am* pleased to hear that. One less casualty. And what a blessing it is that Ernest hasn't lost his mother so soon after losing his father."

"Yes, we're all thankful for that. There is one casualty though, and it's Hilda Doyle's brother-in-law, Fergus Doyle – Declan's brother – who'd been living in New York. He'd been in Ireland for the funeral of his mother, and was returning to America on the *Titanic*. Sadly, he was not one of the survivors."

"I'm so sorry to hear that, Mrs Fielding. How very unfortunate. Declan did tell me he had two brothers, though I thought they both lived in Ireland."

"Yes, Fergus was living in Ireland until quite recently, I believe. But like so many of his countrymen, he decided to try his luck in America. Now there's only one Doyle brother left, along with one sister. It's very sad."

"It is indeed. How is Mrs Doyle's state of mind after such an experience? She must be thanking her lucky stars that she disembarked at Queenstown."

"I agree, that would be the normal reaction. But she's terribly upset about Fergus, whom she'd also hoped to meet in New York. In fact, it was after she heard that Fergus was in Ireland that she decided to come ashore at Queenstown, only to find out later that he'd boarded the very ship she'd just alighted from. If only he hadn't been in such a hurry to return to New York! On hearing the news that Fergus had perished, Hilda became quite unwell, but now that her son is with her, we're hopeful that she'll make a full recovery and return home very soon."

"I hope so too. Do you have Ernest's current address, Mrs Fielding? I'd like to write to him and express my condolences on both the death of his father – though I know that was some time ago – and his uncle and grandmother. I considered Declan a good friend and would like to know what plans Ernest now has for the future. I suppose you don't know yet if he'll be returning to New York? If he intends to get married, I imagine he'll be anxious to get back there."

"No, unfortunately, I don't have an address for Ernest. But I can ask my nephew to send me the address of Brian Doyle, the eldest of the three brothers, who will be able to pass on a letter to him. It's thanks to your good advice that Hilda's niece wrote to Mr Doyle and found out that both her aunt and cousin were in Dublin. As for Ernest's return to America and his possible marriage plans, we think both may be postponed until his mother is in better health."

"Ah well, perhaps that's for the best. Who knows, now that he's in the land of his forefathers, he may decide to stay there. Life in New York isn't for everyone, and he may have found it difficult to make enough money to travel west, as was his earlier intention."

"Well, he has youth on his side, so that's surely to his advantage. I can't thank you enough, Mr Franklin, for taking such an interest in the family. As Lionel was saying the other evening, there's a lot of healing that needs to happen, as they seem to have lost several loved ones in a short space of time."

"Isn't that often the case? My sister lost two of her children and her husband within months of each other. She's never been the same since. They say time heals all wounds, but I'm not sure that's always true. Now, what have you there? Ah, *Treasure Island*. Such a stirring adventure story – one that I never hesitate to recommend.

Is it for the boy you spoke of the last time we met?"

"Yes. Andrew celebrates his tenth birthday this week. He has a great interest in anything to do with the sea, whether it be sailing, lighthouses, or even pirates. The ABC book on the navy has been quite a success, I'm pleased to say. I thought I'd give him *Treasure Island* for his birthday, as I know it's a book that he wishes he were able to read. He still has a long way to go, but I'm going to make sure that he achieves that goal eventually."

"It's an excellent choice. Did you know that both Robert Louis Stevenson's father and grandfather were lighthouse engineers? His father, who designed many of the Scottish lighthouses, hoped that Robert Louis would follow in his footsteps, but because of ill health – he suffered frequently from bronchitis – he was unable to do so and thus decided to devote his life to literature. Bookworms like ourselves have benefited greatly from that decision. But he was an adventurer at heart, as one can tell from his novels."

"No, I didn't know that. He certainly had a wonderful imagination. One of the children at the house where I lived for many years had a copy of *A Child's Garden of Verses*, and I remember being moved by some of his poems. In one, he wrote about being sick in bed and having all his toys laid out next to him on the counterpane. He would make up games and adventures and was 'happy all day long', even though he was confined to his bed."

"Yes, he had the rare ability of being able, as an adult, to understand the minds of children and write in ways that would appeal to them. Let me wrap the book up for you since it's a present. I take it *The Spectator* is for your worthy husband. It looks like the type of periodical he'll enjoy reading."

"Indeed. Lionel rarely reads novels and makes fun of me sometimes for my reading choices. He usually has his nose stuck in a medical journal or a current affairs magazine. I daresay this one will please him greatly."

"Give him my best regards and tell him not to be a stranger. He passes this way often, yet rarely comes into the shop. I know he's a busy man, but can he not spare a couple of minutes to chat with an American friend who is as interested in natural medicine as he is?"

"I'll certainly tell him that. And I won't forget to send you the contact details for Ernest Doyle. Thank you, Mr Franklin. You've been most kind."

I meet with Andrew the next day and give him his birthday present. He is thrilled with the book and wants to start reading it immediately. I tell him that we need to learn a few more words and some new vowel sounds first, and then we'll do a bit of reading. I'm pleased with his progress; he seems to be trying hard to overcome his difficulties. His ability to memorise and recognise words helps a lot and makes up for his deficiencies in mastering phonetics. Lionel has helped him too by letting him assist in the shop, where he has picked up many new word spellings, even if they do mostly pertain to the labels on various tablets or tonics.

When at last I begin to read the first chapter of *Treasure Island*, Andrew listens attentively. Since it's a present, I don't make him follow the words, as it will spoil the pace of the story. I have the feeling he'd like to stay longer and listen to a couple more chapters, but I close the book at the end of the first one and tell him we'll continue the following week.

"Cyril says that the Admiral Benbow is a real inn and

exists today. Is that true, Mrs Fielding?"

"Yes, I believe it's situated in Penzance in Cornwall and was popular with smugglers. Apparently, Robert Louis Stevenson visited it during his travels and decided to use its name for the inn in *Treasure Island* that's owned by Jim Hawkins' parents. But in the book that inn is located in North Devon, not Cornwall."

"I'd also like to visit the real Admiral Benbow one day. Is Penzance far away?"

"Well, it's at the far western tip of Cornwall, not far from Land's End. I think there's a direct train from Exeter, but it's quite a long journey – I would say not less five hours."

"I'm going to make sure I go there when I have a job and my own money. I don't care how long it takes – I love travelling on the train."

"By the way, talking about jobs, Robert Louis Stevenson's father and grandfather were both lighthouse engineers, apparently. I've been told that Mr Stevenson senior designed many lighthouses in Scotland. Lighthouse design might be something for you to think about, Andrew, once you're able to read and write, and if you make up your mind to do well in school. You're certainly not lacking in intelligence. With your drawing and mathematical skills, that sounds like the perfect occupation for you in the future."

"Except that Mother says I have to leave school at fourteen. Cyril has to leave next year and start at the match factory. But he's happy about it and is counting the days until then. Mother's not going to make an exception for me, especially since she believes I'm the dunce in the family. And besides, I hate school as much as Cyril does."

"You're certainly not a dunce, Andrew. Don't let

anyone tell you that you are. And once you're reading fluently, I think you'll find that school isn't so bad after all. Does your father not have a say in these decisions, or is your mother's word always the final one?"

"Father usually agrees with what Mother says. He says he prefers a quiet life and doesn't want to get into any arguments."

"Ah, well, there's something to be said for that. But there's still time for your mother to change her mind – you've only just turned ten. You'll first need to show her that you're doing well in school, though."

Cyril arrives with his usual impatience, not even trying to hide his annoyance at having to pick up his younger brother.

"What have you got there?" he asks Andrew, who's rewrapping his birthday present.

"You'll never guess…"

"I've given your brother a book for his birthday," I say, interrupting Andrew. "He needs to start reading on his own, and this will help him learn more quickly."

"What book is it?"

"It's *Treasure Island*," Andrew says, unable to resist a gleeful smirk. "And *you're* not going to read it."

"You must be joking! You'll never be able to read that book. You don't even know your ABCs."

"Andrew is coming along nicely with his reading," I say before the boy has a chance to respond to his brother's insult. "Once school starts again, he'll be reading on his own. But Andrew, do share the book with your brother if he wants to read it. You should always share your books and toys with your brothers and sisters."

'I don't want to read it," Cyril retorts. "I've already read it."

"And you didn't share it with me!" Andrew exclaims.

"You couldn't read, you ignoramus!"

"Now, now," I say, "no more arguing, please. I'll see you next week, Andrew. And don't forget to bring the book with you, as we agreed."

"Yes, I will. Thank you for the present, Mrs Fielding."

"You're very welcome, Andrew. Have a lovely birthday. Goodbye, boys."

That evening, I write a letter to Winifred, telling her that Hilda has been located in Ireland. I don't give her all the details, though I know she'll want to hear them. I'm not mistaken; by return post, I receive an invitation to visit the following week with Andrew. She says William has not stopped asking her when his new friend can visit again, and Wendy would like to know if Andrew's sister can come too. I don't mind taking the two of them, but am a bit concerned about the train fares. The Frosts are already bearing considerable costs in raising six children on one pay cheque and may not be able to afford an unforeseen expense. Lionel, as expected, says he can pay for all our fares, which is kind of him, but I don't know if Mrs Frost will accept this offer, which she may regard as charity.

"Well, she's already accepting our charity, isn't she?" Lionel says. "You're tutoring Andrew free of charge. But we can tell her that it's an extra reward for Andrew helping in the shop."

"She may not fall for that again," I say, "especially since Violet has also been invited. Besides, aren't you already paying Andrew thruppence every Saturday?"

"Yes, but he's such a good helper, he deserves a rise."

Lionel chuckles and tells me not to worry. He says he

knows how to handle Mrs Rose Frost.

"Just go ahead, Bessie, and tell your friend that you'll bring the two children on whichever day is good for her."

"Thank you, Lionel. Andrew will be thrilled to visit again, though I'm not sure he'll approve of Violet coming with us. But at least that means he'll have William all to himself, while Wendy entertains his sister. Or the other way round. Wendy is quite shy, whereas Violet is anything but. As for me, I can spend another pleasant afternoon chatting and drinking tea with Winifred."

20

"Now, do we go left or right?" I ask Andrew, once we've exited the railway station.

"It's in the direction of the lighthouse!" Andrew exclaims. "So, obviously, it's right."

"Of course! How could I forget that?"

Andrew is pleased to be able to show Violet that he already knows the way to the Smiths' house. But she's not paying him any attention; she's so excited about the visit and is chattering nonstop. I can see that Andrew is irritated by her presence and would be happier if she hadn't come with us, but I expect he'll forget his annoyance once he's in the company of his new friend.

William and Wendy are waiting for us. William leaps over the fence and comes bounding towards us, while Wendy just stands and stares. As I guessed, she's a little shy, but no doubt Violet will help her overcome her timidity.

"I've got something to show you," William says to Andrew. "It's a new train set! It was my birthday last week and my uncle in Bristol sent it to me. It's magnificent!"

"Your birthday was last week as well?" Andrew asks, wide-eyed. "Mine was on Wednesday. When was yours? Did you just turn ten, like me?"

"Yes, ten. Mine was on Tuesday. Ha! I'm a day older than you! What did you get for your birthday?"

"A book, *Treasure Island*. I've already started reading it."

I feel a tinge of sadness at the thought that the book might have been Andrew's only birthday present. But I'm relieved that he has something to boast about, even though it's not a gift that can equal William's new train set.

Meanwhile, Violet takes Wendy's hand and the two little girls begin to get to know each other. Glancing in their direction a moment later, I see that they're already playing hopscotch on the paving stones. A friendship is quickly forming.

I spot Winifred peering through the parlour window as I approach the cottage. She comes to the front door before I have a chance to knock.

"Well, I'm glad to see the children each have their own friend," she says. "We'll leave them to play outside. William knows they mustn't go to the beach unaccompanied, as the tide is on its way in. It'll be high tide in an hour or so. Those swimming lessons Andrew promised him will have to wait until another day.

"I have another visitor, Bessie, whom I'd like you to meet. It's Mr Barlow, the young man who befriended Colin on the *Titanic*. His visit wasn't planned. He arrived unexpectedly, with the hope of talking to Maud. As he said in his letter, he feels so bad that Colin lost his life, while he himself survived. But Maud refuses to come downstairs, even though I told her he was here to speak to her, not to me. I hope you don't mind his being here. I can't really send him away until after tea time, as he's travelled some distance."

"No, of course not, Winnie," I say. "I'll be more than happy to meet him."

She leads me into the parlour and introduces me to Mr Barlow, who stands up and shakes my hand. He's a fine-looking man of about thirty with thick brown hair and a short beard, and is smartly dressed in a dark suit, a crisp white shirt and a black silk Teck tie.

"I'm pleased to meet you, Mrs Fielding," he says. "I'm sorry if I'm intruding on your visit. I should have written to Mrs Smith to ask if it was convenient for me to come. But I was in the neighbouring county and thought I'd take my chances."

"Nonsense, Alfred," Winifred says. "Any time is convenient for me and I'm glad you've come. I'm sure Mrs Fielding doesn't mind either. Now, sit yourself down, Bessie, and I'll put the kettle on. Then you can tell us all your news."

Mr Barlow and I make small talk about the weather and our respective origins, while Winifred busies herself in the kitchen. She returns with a tray laden with cups of tea and slices of Battenberg cake, which she says she baked herself. I am impressed by her baking skill and will try to remember to ask her for the recipe to send to Margaret.

"What made you decide to make the voyage to America, Mr Barlow?" I ask, once we are all seated and sipping tea.

"Oh, please call me Alfred, Mrs Fielding," he says. "I keep asking myself that question. I can't tell you how much I wish I'd never entertained the idea of travelling to New York. But I was at a bit of a loose end earlier this year. I'm what's called a freelance journalist and I wasn't having much success. A friend of mine had made the journey last year and, within a couple of months, was working as an editor for a monthly periodical. He told me it's much easier to find journalistic work in America than in England. So, I thought I'd go over there for a month or two and see if I met with any success. A third-class ticket on the *Titanic* cost me seven pounds, and I had enough money for the return journey if things didn't work out. As it happened, I returned right away. I hated New York from the moment I stepped off the rescue ship, the RMS *Carpathia*, and didn't think that after what had happened at sea, any good would come of my remaining there."

"You're probably right. It certainly wasn't a promising start to your American venture."

"Not at all. Had I stayed there, I would have been forever haunted by what I'd witnessed. As it is, it's going to take me a long, long time to get over it. But I'm pleased to hear from Mrs Smith that your fears of losing a relative travelling on the *Titanic* were unfounded. I'm sure that was a great relief to your family."

"Yes, it was," I say. "The lady in question, Mrs Hilda Doyle, is not directly related to me, but is the aunt of my nephew's fiancée. She was supposed to be travelling all the way to New York, but then decided to disembark at Queenstown, Ireland, and didn't think to inform her family. As you can imagine, when they didn't hear from her, they feared the worst had happened."

"Why did she decide not to continue her journey, if you don't mind me asking? I heard that only a handful of passengers left the ship at Queenstown."

"It seems that on the morning of her departure from Southampton, Hilda received a telegram from her son in America telling her that the gentleman she was also hoping to meet in New York – her brother-in-law – was in Dublin attending his mother's funeral. She knew the ship was stopping to pick up passengers in Ireland, so thought she would meet him there instead, thinking that he might be staying some weeks with his family. She's been a widow for about two years, but is still close to her in-laws in Ireland, hence her decision to disembark at Queenstown. But unfortunately, her brother-in-law left that very day to return to New York... on the *Titanic*. And, sad to say, he lost his life while Hilda avoided losing hers."

"Oh no!" Winifred exclaims. "You didn't tell me that in your letter, Bessie."

"Well, I didn't want to speculate too much on the close friendship between Hilda and her brother-in-law. Since hearing that he didn't survive the *Titanic*'s sinking, she's not been well at all. She's still in Ireland, staying with her sister-in-law."

"But didn't you say she was going to New York to attend her son's wedding?"

"Yes, that's what she told her twin sister, who disapproved of her close friendship with her brother-in-law. Hilda apparently felt the need to invent an excuse for her unexpected voyage, so she told her sister that she was travelling to New York for the wedding of her son Ernest. In fact, he had no intention of marrying his sweetheart. Anyway, when Ernest heard that his mother was in Ireland, he immediately crossed the Atlantic to be with her. It was thanks to his earlier telegram, which arrived only just in time, that she disembarked at Queenstown. Otherwise, she would most likely have been one more casualty. Obviously, she knew she would be losing her fare by not continuing with her journey, but had she cared about that, she'd have lost her life instead. It makes you think, doesn't it? Money is of no consequence when compared to life itself."

"That's very true," Mr Barlow says. "Mrs Fielding, may I be so bold as to ask the name of the gentleman she hoped to meet?"

"Doyle. Fergus Doyle."

"Sorry, did I hear you correctly? Did you say Fergus Doyle?"

"Yes, that's right."

Mr Barlow puts down his cup of tea. "Good gracious me!" he exclaims. "I met that fellow, and so did Colin. There were a lot of Irishmen in steerage, and we got to know a fair few of them. Believe me, Fergus was one of the friendliest. He was a kind, good-natured soul – but, my, could he hold his drink! We were only on the ship a few days, but had a riotous party every night – Fergus would sing, while another Irish fellow played the fiddle. Irish songs, full of love and longing. There was usually a competition between the Irish and the Italians to see which group of singers could gain the loudest applause. It was rowdy, to be sure, but so much fun. And he often mentioned this lady, Hilda. I could swear that when he was singing his ballads, he was serenading her personally, even though she wasn't present."

"What a coincidence! Who would have thought... You say he mentioned Hilda often – what was it he said about her, Alfred?"

"Well, for the first couple of days, he was actually searching for her. He knew that she planned to buy a one-way ticket for the maiden voyage of the *Titanic* and that she was expecting to meet him in New York. She didn't know his mother had died and that he'd had to return briefly to Ireland for her funeral – just as you've said. But he didn't plan to stay in Ireland for more than a few days and made sure that his return ticket was on the *Titanic*, as he wanted to surprise Hilda on board. But try as he might, he couldn't find her, so assumed that she'd had to delay her departure from Southampton and had already sent word to him in America."

I can feel goose pimples rising on my arms as Alfred continues his story.

"One night, when he'd had a few drinks, Fergus told us he was going to marry Hilda once they were together in New York. Colin asked him why he'd waited so long, as it was clear to us that he was no longer a man in his prime. He said his brother had captured her heart more than twenty years ago and had wasted no time in asking her to marry him. Though heartbroken that he'd missed his one chance for happiness, he told himself that as long as *Hilda* was happy, he had no cause to be miserable. He never took a wife, since his feelings for Hilda remained strong as the years slipped by. But now, he said, since his brother had been in his grave for nigh on two years, he believed that at long last it was his turn for marital bliss. He wasn't altogether sure that Hilda would accept his hand in marriage, but he was praying every night that her answer would be in the affirmative."

"And it would have been," I say, blinking back tears on hearing this tender love story that had ended so sorrowfully. "No wonder poor Hilda is in such a state of anguish. She must have been happily looking forward to starting a new life with Fergus. Sadly, fate was not on her side. It's such a great pity that her chance of a future with a man who'd loved her for so long has been snatched away by such a tragic turn of events."

"It's certainly sad," Winifred says. "Tell me, Bessie, why was her sister so against the friendship?"

"I'm not really sure, Winnie. Hilda and Yvonne are twins, and Yvonne is probably over-protective of her sister. She wouldn't have wanted her to leave the village, especially if it meant she'd be living so far away in

America. I don't think she had too high an opinion of Fergus – she thought he was leading Hilda on a wild goose chase and that no good could come of it. But then again, she hardly knew the man. Also, the fact that he was a Roman Catholic didn't endear him to her either, but Hilda's late husband *and* her son were Papists, so you would think she'd have accepted the Doyle family's faith by now."

"Well, if it's any consolation," Mr Barlow says, "I can attest to Fergus Doyle's popularity and subsequent heroism aboard the *Titanic*. As you know, to my shame, I didn't stick around to help those in need. But I heard from a fellow survivor that when water started to flood the lower decks, Fergus knocked on each and every cabin door to tell people to put on their life jackets and not to listen to a word the crew said – that it *was* an emergency. Then he made sure that as many of the women and children as possible were let through the gates, which the stewards were trying to keep shut so that there wouldn't be a stampede. *And* he found extra life jackets – as not everyone had one – and helped the elderly and the women and children to put them on. I believe that he and Colin saved more than a few lives on that terrible night.

"Mrs Fielding, I should tell you, as I've told Mrs Smith, that I've made it my personal quest to visit as many of the grieving families as I can – at least those whose relatives I had the privilege of meeting before the ship went down. I feel that, as a survivor, it's the least I can do. I hope that by talking with the bereaved about their loved ones, and encouraging them to speak candidly about their feelings, they may find healing and strength. At some point in the future, I may – with the permission of the families, of course – publish some anecdotes about the deceased, or even their life stories, so that they are not forgotten by future generations.

"I was hoping to meet Mrs Maud Davies today, but if she's not yet ready to talk to me, I will return another time. How would you feel, Mrs Fielding, if I were to visit Mrs Doyle, if and when she returns to England? Or perhaps I could write her a letter telling her what a popular fellow Fergus Doyle was, how brave he was, and how he was looking forward with great eagerness to their reunion in New York. Do you think this knowledge might be of comfort to her in her grief?"

"That's a kind thought, Alfred, and your mission is a worthy one. I'll be honest with you – I don't know Hilda Doyle personally, though I am acquainted with her sister. Since no one has any idea when she plans to return to her home village of Ferndell – she might even decide to stay in Ireland – I think a letter would be the best course of action. It can't do any harm and, as you suggest, it might bring her some comfort. If you give me your address before I leave today, I can send you the address of her other brother-in-law, Brian Doyle, who is sure to pass on any letters addressed to her. I've already asked my nephew to send me his address and should receive it very soon."

"Thank you, Mrs Fielding. I've already written to and met a few of the widows, and it does seem to help them to talk about their loved ones and to hear how brave and selfless they were. There were so many valiant souls aboard the *Titanic* that fateful night. Your mention of Mrs Doyle's son, Ernest, makes me recall a clergyman by the same name, who sadly lost his life, along with his wife. I'm talking about The Reverend Ernest Carter, an Anglican minister. He and Mrs Carter were travelling second class and, apparently, on the evening before the ship went down, he presided over a hymn service for his fellow passengers. Believe it or not, the last hymn sung was *Now the Day is Over.*"

"*Guard the sailors tossing... on the deep blue sea,*" Winifred quotes. "Really," she says, "I don't know whether the knowledge that the congregation was singing such words on the night the ship struck the iceberg makes one believe more in the Lord, or less. Certainly, if it were a prayer, it wasn't answered."

"Who knows, the Reverend may have had a premonition of the disaster about to happen. Indeed, the band that continued playing while the ship was sinking must have known that many hundreds of lives would be lost that night. They played the hymn, *Nearer, My God, to Thee*, and kept it up until the last lifeboat was launched. I know that's true because I was on one of the last ones to be lowered. I'm told that all eight musicians perished."

Again, I find myself on the verge of tears and searching for my handkerchief.

"We were three days on the RMS *Carpathia*," Mr Barlow continues. "And, of course, everyone was in a state of shock, especially the women who had been separated from their husbands. But there was no distinction between the classes on the rescue ship, like there had been on the *Titanic* – we were all just so grateful to be alive. I heard stories of great heroism shown by those passengers and crew who gave their lives so that others might live. The Reverend Carter's name was mentioned frequently. By all accounts, he was a remarkable man. It seems that he and his wife were offered places in one of the lifeboats, but they refused to leave the ship. His wife, incidentally, was the eldest daughter of Thomas Hughes, the author of *Tom Brown's Schooldays*. I remember reading that book myself when I was at school."

We are silent for a moment or two, awed by the selflessness of good people like the Carters. Mr Barlow's mention of Thomas Hughes reminds me of the time that Robert, Patty's husband, suggested that I use Hughes' well-known book in my reading sessions with Michael. He writes about bullying as a rite of passage for new boys in boarding schools, which Robert thought might help Michael come to terms with the harassment he was then suffering at the hands of his fellow pupils. But in the end, I stuck with *David Copperfield*. I felt that Dickens' novel, which also talks about bullying, would be a more entertaining read for young Michael.

Maud surprises all of us when she enters the room. She is pale and slight, and looks much younger than I had imagined. But she's brushed her long auburn hair and is neatly dressed in an ankle-length black skirt and a long-sleeved silk blouse with ruffles down the front.

"Oh, Maud," Winifred says, "this is Mr Barlow who was with Colin on the ship. Remember the letter he wrote? And this is Mrs Bessie Fielding, whom I met on the train and has visited once before with young Andrew, who's now a great friend of William."

I stand up to greet Maud, as does Mr Barlow. He tells her how pleased he is to meet her and how much he admires her late husband for his courage and self-sacrifice.

"Would you like to go for a short walk, Mrs Davies?" he asks her. "It's such a lovely day and I think we could probably both do with a bit of fresh air and exercise."

Maud hesitates, but then shrugs her shoulders and says, "Why not? It's so stuffy in here, even with the windows open."

Winifred raises her eyebrows at this remark, but she's nonetheless pleased that Maud has consented to leave the house after so many days cooped up in her much stuffier bedroom.

"Well, that's a new development," she says to me, looking out the window. "For more days than I can count, Maud hasn't stepped outside the house. Oh look, Bessie, Wendy is hugging her mother like she hasn't seen her in months. The children have really missed having her around, though they've tried not to show it. Stan and myself have kept them occupied as best we can. Poor little mites. It was as if they'd lost their mother as well as their father."

Winifred goes to the kitchen to refill the teapot and cuts me another slice of cake, despite my objections. We spend the next hour so engaged in conversation that we're both surprised when the clock strikes five.

"I need to start getting the tea ready," Winifred says. "Stan is still at the lighthouse, but will be home shortly. I've invited Alfred to stay for a bite to eat, Bessie, and I'd be more than happy if you and Andrew and the little girl could stay too. You know you're welcome."

"Thank you, Winnie, but we really need to be getting back or I'll be in Mrs Frost's bad books. It doesn't take much, believe me. There's a train at half past five, which I was hoping to catch. But we'll stay in touch. Mr Barlow seems like a good man, and it's clearly helping *him* to talk about the tragedy. Hopefully, his feelings of guilt will become less acute as time passes. I'm sure it'll help

Maud too to hear him speak so highly of Colin and how he helped so many people on that dreadful night."

"Yes, that's what I'm hoping. Here, take a couple of slices of cake for the children to eat on the way home. They'll be starving, as boys and girls usually are."

"Thank you, that's kind of you. Oh, Mr Barlow hasn't yet given me his address. But you have it, don't you? If you don't mind, I'll just make a note of it, then I can write to him directly."

"Here, why don't you take this envelope? It's written on the back. Now, where are those children? If they've been playing in the garden, Andrew and his sister will need to wash their hands before they leave, or I daresay that mother of theirs will have something to say about that as well."

21

Violet falls asleep on the homeward journey. She looks like an angel with her curly golden locks – freed from the pink ribbon that tied them back – falling over her forehead, and her cheeks flushed from so much outdoor activity.

"Look at your sister," I say to Andrew. "She's exhausted from playing with Wendy, not to mention the excitement of travelling by train for the first time. It wasn't so bad bringing her with us, was it now?"

"I suppose not," he says. "But remember, she's been on her best behaviour. You don't know what a pest she can be. She's always telling Mam things that aren't true. By the way, you should never have lent her your *Wind in the Willows* book, Mrs Fielding. You're never going to get it back."

"Why do you say that, Andrew? If she hasn't yet finished it, she can keep it for a while longer. But I do expect her to return it eventually."

"She's lent it to her friend, even though I told her it wasn't her book and that she shouldn't let anyone borrow it. I doubt that she's finished it herself. She just wants to show off to her classmate, who's read a lot of books, or so she claims."

"Well, never mind. I'm sure her friend will return it once she's read it. You're the one telling tales now, Andrew. Do try your best to get along with your siblings, even if you find them annoying. You're Violet's big brother and she needs to look up to you."

"That's never going to happen. It's Cyril she looks up to. She always tries to impress him, but most of the time he just ignores her."

Poor Andrew, I think to myself, always believing he's the black sheep of the family. Perhaps it wasn't such a good idea to bring his sister along, even though Wendy certainly appreciated having a playmate. Andrew only seems happy when he's away from all his family members and doing things independently.

I feel a measure of solidarity with Andrew because I too always thought I was the odd one out in my own family. Edward and Harold could do no wrong in Mother's eyes, and Ethel was everyone's darling because of her beauty and joyous nature. I often felt closer to my father – like Andrew, I suspect – as he would at least praise me for doing well in school. I shall always be indebted to him for encouraging me to read as much as possible, as books have brought me a great deal of contentment in life. I'll never forget the time he told me that he didn't think he could have survived the Crimean War without his treasured copy of John Donne's poems, which he managed to keep within easy reach even during the toughest of times.

That is not to say that I didn't love my mother just as much, though we had little in common and I know she found *me* exasperating. I've always understood why she took me out of school after Father died, and I don't hold it against her. She used to say that my head was continually in the clouds and that such a trait would get me nowhere in life. And I have to admit that, for many years, she was right.

Violet wakes up just as the train is pulling into the station. Mrs Frost is there to meet her children off the train, accompanied by her eldest daughter, Josephine, and the four-year old twins, Paul and Pauline. Violet, exuberant again now that she has fully woken up, rushes up to her mother and gives her a big hug, chattering nineteen to the dozen. She sneaks a look at Josephine, hoping that she's listening, but the older girl is busy showing the twins the 'puffer train'.

"Thank you for taking them, Mrs Fielding," Mrs Frost says, pushing Violet away. "I hope they weren't a nuisance."

"No, not at all," I say. "It was high tide, so they didn't go on the beach, as it would have been too dangerous. Instead, since it stayed dry, they played nicely in the garden with Mrs Smith's grandchildren. They minded their *Ps* and *Qs* and were no trouble whatsoever."

"Well, I'm glad to hear it. It was a treat for them both, that's for sure. And I was able to get my chores done without their constant disruptions."

I'm quite sure that Andrew doesn't disrupt his mother when she's doing her chores. I suspect that half the time she doesn't even know where he is – he absents himself from the house as often as possible, either beachcombing or creating art in his secret place in the garden. He looks glum as I say goodbye to the family, no doubt having overheard his mother's comment, but he gives me a nod and a half smile when I remind him to bring *Treasure Island* with him for our next reading lesson.

Mr Wright arrives with his postbag the next morning and sees me pegging out the washing.

"Good luck with drying that lot," he says. "I'm told it'll be pouring with rain by midday."

"Oh no, not again," I say. "We had such glorious weather last month, but now it looks like summer has deserted us. And the wind never seems to let up, though it's good for drying the washing. That's if it's not raining as well, which it often is."

"Well, the wind is something you'll have to get used to, Mrs Fielding. Living by the sea gives us many pleasures, but gentle breezes are not usually one of them."

He hands me three letters and I see that my name appears on two of the envelopes.

"No postcards today, Mrs Fielding," he says. "But I hope your letters bring you good news."

Mr Wright has told me that I'm the only resident in this coastal town to whom he regularly *delivers* picture postcards, although the post box is always full of cards being sent all across the country by day-trippers or holiday-makers.

"Thank you, Mr Wright," I say. "I daresay I'll receive a postcard in a few days' time when my nephew starts a job away from the village. I do hope you manage to finish your daily rounds before the rain starts again. Another of my nephews works for a farmer who is known for his accuracy in predicting the weather months in advance. He said weeks ago that the second half of the summer would be inclement, and it looks like he's been proven right once again."

"It doesn't make my job any easier, that's for sure, but I suppose we should be thankful for the rain. There was talk of a drought in June!"

I place all three envelopes in my apron pocket and carry on hanging up the washing. I can tell from the handwriting that one letter is from Walter, and the other one that's addressed to me looks like it's from Marjorie.

A short while later, I make myself a cup of tea and sit

down at the kitchen table to read my letters. I open the one from Marjorie first, and read the following:

Dear Mrs Fielding,

I'm sorry for the delay in replying to your kind letter. I have had so many things on my mind, trying to decide on a future for myself. As you know, Clive is now supposed to be my brother, which I'm finding hard to accept, but I understand that I have to put his interests before my own. Mother and Father have always been loving parents to me and my siblings, and I know that they are as devoted to Clive as I am. But they have made it clear that no one in the village should know that he is not their own son. I have therefore decided that I need to embark on a career that will stop me from dwelling on the unfairness of not being allowed to be a real parent to Clive. I have therefore decided to train to become a paediatric nurse. If I cannot, as a mother, take care of my own child, then I will spend my days caring for other people's children.

I have thought long and hard about this, Mrs Fielding. Believe me, it is not just a means by which I might forget my own hurt feelings – I really do want to look after babies and children, and believe I can be a good nurse. My application has been accepted and I will begin my training next month. It will take me away from home and my darling Clive, which will break my heart, but I think it is the best way forward. Mother and Father objected to my plan at first, but they are now beginning to come around to it, though they would much rather I stayed at home.

I hope you are keeping well and enjoying the summer. Please give my regards to Mr Fielding. Thank you again for helping me and, if you ever see the boy who rescued

Clive that day on the beach, please tell him that I think about him often.

    Sincerely yours,

    Marjorie Blackwell

I sit with the letter in my lap, deep in thought for a few minutes. It did occur to me that Marjorie might be embarking on such a career for the wrong reasons, but she was adamant that it was not a spur of the moment decision. I would hate to think that she was rebounding into nursing rather than risk having her heart broken again. But I do understand her need for a career of sorts, and to become a paediatric nurse is a worthy path to follow. She must be finding it so hard to relinquish her role of mother to Clive, and will have to summon immense courage to part from him. I decide to put her in touch with Edie, Walter's former sweetheart, who is training to be a paediatric nurse at the Great Ormond Street Hospital in London. I'm sure Edie will be happy to befriend Marjorie and give her all the advice and encouragement she needs.

When I show Lionel the letter in the evening, he suggests that Marjorie may soon find herself walking out with one of the junior doctors and that her future plans may then take a different course.

"Honestly, Lionel," I say, "you sound just like Mrs Grist. That's exactly what she said when I told her Edie was training to be a nurse. She said Edie would likely meet a young doctor and would no longer be interested in Walter as a future husband. I wasn't at all happy with that remark and found it difficult to hide my feeling of annoyance. Because of that, I never did tell her that

Walter and Edie had ended their courtship, although of course she soon became aware of it. Thankfully, they didn't part for that particular reason."

"All right, Bessie. Keep your hair on – as you're always telling me to do. I fully understand that many young women these days are keen for a life that doesn't just involve getting married and having children. I'm all for it. It's just that Marjorie didn't strike me as the career type, though I could tell she'd had a decent education."

"I think the disastrous outcome of her courtship with Billy made her think seriously about what she wanted in life. Her first choice would always have been to marry her sweetheart and be a mother to Clive, but that was no longer an option. So, I think she's doing the right thing. And if she does meet someone else, then good luck to her. But I think she'll be cautious before she becomes too close emotionally with any young man in the future, doctor or otherwise."

"You're probably right, my dear. Now what did Walter have to say in his letter? Or are you going to keep that one to yourself?"

"No, of course not! The good news is that Hilda has finally written to her sister, apologising for causing such worry. So, thankfully, the lines of communication are open again. According to Walter, she didn't really say much, apart from the fact that she's feeling a lot better and intends to stay in Ireland for a while. Ernest will stay there too, having secured a job in a builder's yard. So, it looks like he isn't planning on going back to America just yet. I suppose that's for the best. Yvonne Goode is a bit put out that her twin sister doesn't plan to return to Ferndell right away. She really doesn't understand her desire to remain in Ireland. But my guess is that Hilda feels a greater connection both to her late husband and to Fergus Doyle in Dublin. And, of course, her in-laws Brian and Maureen are both there to make her feel at home. The fact that Yvonne disapproved of poor Fergus has clearly caused a rift between the two sisters, but let's hope that will only be temporary. It's such a shame when siblings who were always close drift apart, and even more so when they happen to be twins.

"Anyway, here's Walter's letter. You can read what he has to say. It isn't quite as much as I've just told you, as I've been reading through the lines. Don't you think it's strange that we've become so caught up in the lives of people who were sailing on the *Titanic* without knowing any of them personally? I've only recently met Mr Barlow, and I've never met Hilda or Fergus, or Winifred Smith's son-in-law Colin, but I feel so close to all of them, as if they were my long-time friends or neighbours."

"So many lives were lost in the sinking of that ship that many people on both sides of the Atlantic can name someone who has perished, either a relative, a friend, a friend of a friend, a colleague, and so on. Mr Franklin from the bookshop told me today that a business acquaintance of his from New York lost his life too, though his wife survived. He only found out a couple of days ago. People are still discovering the names of those who died more than three months after the *Titanic* went down."

"Oh, you didn't tell me you'd been to the bookshop. Mr Franklin said he wished you'd drop in more often. How is he?"

"He seems well. He asked after my 'good wife' and thanks you for the address you provided for Ernest. I really do think he has a soft spot for you, Bessie. He said to tell you that he's written to Ernest, as he promised to do. Since I was in the shop, I asked him to order me a copy of *British Pharmacopoeia*, a useful reference book. And I have a little present for you, my dear, since every time you go into that shop, you come away with something for someone else and nothing for yourself."

"Oh, Lionel, please don't waste your money on me. I don't need anything – you know that."

"How can the purchase of a book be a waste of money? Here you are. I hope you haven't already read it."

Lionel hands me a brown paper package, which I quickly unwrap. It's a copy of Miss Austin's fourth novel, *Emma*.

"Oh, thank you!" I exclaim. "No, I haven't read this one. You picked well, Lionel, as I've already read *Sense and Sensibility* and *Pride and Prejudice*, and you'll be pleased to hear that I've finally finished *Mansfield Park*. I do so love the novels of Jane Austen. I feel such a kinship with her characters, even though they're mostly from high-class families. Perhaps it's because they remind me of Farringdale House and the Radcliffes. I shall start reading *Emma* this very evening."

"Yes, we'll have a cosy evening indoors with our books, since it's still wet outside. I want to continue with my research into the treatment of diabetes. Did you know, Bessie, that diabetes is described as 'a disturbance of metabolic function' and that a balanced diet is an important factor in its treatment?"

Andrew arrives alone for our next reading session. He carefully takes *Treasure Island* out of his satchel and surprises me by saying that he's read the second chapter.

"But how, Andrew?" I ask. "Surely it was too difficult for you to read on your own. We've not even finished revising all the vowel sounds yet."

"It certainly wasn't easy," he says, "and it took a long time. But I asked Josephine to help me with a lot of the words, so I was able to follow the story. As you know, I already knew how to pronounce most of the consonants from learning my alphabet, but I couldn't read the words because of the vowels. It's easier now. The way certain words are spelt still doesn't make sense to me, but Josie is helping me with those. I'm writing them down and trying to memorise them."

"I'm impressed, Andrew, I really am. You really will be reading fluently by the time school starts again. Your teacher is going to be amazed."

"I don't think my teacher cares whether I can read or not. He has no idea which boys can read and which ones can't. But I'm glad I'm learning. Now I can start reading books and teaching myself stuff. School doesn't teach me anything. And Will gave me his address and told me to write to him. He said that when he replies, he'll correct any mistakes I make. Not only that, but Josie showed me how to look up the spelling of words in a dictionary. Father has a copy of the *Oxford English Dictionary*, which she uses all the time. I'm going to start using it too."

"That's an excellent idea. If both William and Josephine are willing to help you, perhaps we don't need any more weekly sessions. What do you think?"

"I think I can probably learn by myself now. Josie isn't always able to help though, as it depends on how much work she has to do. Mam makes her help a lot with the twins and the housework, so she doesn't have much time to spare. And now that she's started a new job at the Bellehaven Hotel, cleaning rooms, she has even less time than before. Oh, and she's usually desperate to see Billy whenever she *is* able to escape for an hour or two."

"Who is Billy, Andrew?"

"He's Josie's 'sweetheart' – at least that's what she says. Such a silly word, don't you think? She's been seeing him for a couple of months now. Mam doesn't even know about it. Josie made Cyril and me swear to secrecy after we spotted them holding hands on our way home from school. I know that once Mam finds out, she'll stop her from seeing him. But she turns sixteen next month and that's old enough to get married, isn't it?"

There must be more than a few lads by the name of Billy in Brampton-on-Sea, but, of course, I immediately suspect that Josephine's sweetheart is Marjorie's former lover, who behaved so despicably. I'm trying to remember if Marjorie told us his surname. I think she did, but I can't for the life of me think what it was.

"Do you know Billy's surname, Andrew?" I ask, hoping that he doesn't wonder why I want to know.

"Um, no, I don't. Oh, wait a minute, I remember now. It's Peebles. I thought it was funny because it sounds like pebbles. You know how much I love looking for unusual pebbles on the beach."

Yes, Billy Peebles. That *was* his name. I recall Lionel remarking – jokingly perhaps - that his family may have hailed from Scotland, where Peebles is an ancient family name. My mind is racing. Somehow, Josephine has to be stopped from seeing this young man, or she may well find herself in the family way, just like poor Marjorie. I'll talk to Lionel and see what he thinks we should do.

Meanwhile, Andrew is telling me how pleased his mother will be if he no longer needs to take reading lessons.

"Mam is always asking me how much longer I'll need to come to you for lessons. She finds it hard to believe that you don't mind teaching me free of charge. So, perhaps it will be better if I stop coming now that I'm able to learn on my own. But I'd still like to help Mr Fielding on Saturdays in the pharmacy, if that's all right."

"I'm sure it is. As long as your mother doesn't object, that is."

"I don't think she minds about the Saturday mornings, as I've been giving her the thruppence Mr Fielding pays me. She thinks I've earned it. She just doesn't like accepting charity, as she calls it."

"It's not charity, Andrew. It's just two people helping each other. I've enjoyed our lessons and you've gained something from them. Still, since you've made so much progress in such a short time, perhaps it's time to call it a day. But remember, if you find you need help at any time, just tell Mr Fielding and we can meet again. You can keep the Navy ABC book, as I know you enjoy copying the pictures. Now, shall we see what Jim Hawkins is getting up to in Chapter 3 of *Treasure Island*?"

22

It is with a sense of foreboding that I tell Lionel about my conversation with Andrew; how he revealed that his sister Josephine is stepping out with Billy Peebles, without the consent of her mother.

"I shall have to have a word with Mrs Frost," he says after hearing me out. "She needs to know the danger her daughter might be in."

"That's what I was hoping you'd say, Lionel," I say. "But I'd rather you didn't let her know that this information came from Andrew. He's going to get into trouble for telling me and not his mother. Apparently, Josephine made him and Cyril swear to secrecy after they saw her with Billy."

"All right. I'll tell her *I've* seen them together, and that I know for a fact that this young man has fathered a child with a certain young lady and denied all responsibility. It won't be an easy conversation, but Mrs Frost has a right to know about her daughter's unfortunate friendship."

"Would it be easier for you to tell *Mr* Frost, do you think?"

"Probably, yes. But I rarely see him. No, I think it has to be Rose Frost. After all, she takes care of all the family matters, as she's at pains to point out. How did Andrew come to tell you about his sister?"

"He was telling me that she helps him at home with his reading when she has time. But between helping her mother with the twins, her cleaning job at the Bellehaven Hotel, and seeing Billy, she hardly has any free time at all."

"Poor girl. She has so little time to enjoy herself. No

doubt the infamous Billy has given her dreams of a different sort of life."

"I'm sure he has, just as he did with Marjorie. Josephine seems such a nice girl and it's good of her to help Andrew when she can. His reading has really come on in leaps and bounds. Thank goodness he doesn't have that condition you told me about. What was it called again?"

"Dyslexia. No, he'd never have been able to learn to read so quickly if he suffered from that affliction. Most likely, he didn't pay attention when he was younger and, because there were so many pupils in the class, the teacher didn't have the time or the inclination to help those who'd fallen behind. So Andrew came to the conclusion that there was no point in trying to catch up. He told himself that he would never be able to read and there was nothing anyone could do about it. All he needed was someone to tell him that he *could* read if he wanted to, and to help him understand the basics. You've done the boy a real service, Bessie. I'm proud of you."

"Oh, I really didn't do much. His intelligence and excellent memory helped enormously. And once he himself realised the benefits of reading, there was no stopping him. I suggested to him that it might be time to end our reading lessons now that we've more or less accomplished all that we set out to do, but said that if he needs any help at any time, he shouldn't hesitate to let me know. Apparently, his mother will be glad she's no longer indebted to me – though that was never the case. But he wants to continue to help you on Saturday mornings, if that's all right with you."

"Yes, of course. I can always find something for him to do. As you said, he learns quickly – you only have to tell him a thing once and he remembers it. I know he'd like to stay the whole day if he could – he's always so reluctant to leave – but I don't want to be accused of profiting from child labour. I'll make sure he understands that he needs to be out of the door by midday and that he's helping voluntarily, if anyone should ask."

"He really has a hard time at home, poor boy. I do wish his mother would appreciate what a fine lad he is. But she never pays him any attention and puts him down all the time."

"That's often the case with the middle children in large families. The eldest and the youngest get much more attention than those in the middle. You were a middle child yourself, Bessie, and so was I. You've often said your brother Edward and sister Ethel were your parents' favourites."

"Yes, Mother's at least. Father saw the good in all of us – I don't think he had favourites. And Harold, although he was number three, didn't suffer as much as I did from Mother's sharp tongue, as he was always such a good-natured lad. But Mother was never unkind in the way Mrs Frost is, and once her work was done, she showed us all affection in her own way."

"Dick Frost, I think, is like your father. He's seldom at home, but when he is, I believe he treats the children equally. Like I said, I don't see him often, but he did come into the pharmacy last Saturday when Andrew was helping me, and it pleased the boy enormously to have his father witness his usefulness behind the counter. I told Mr Frost what a good job he was doing, and he said he was pleased. He really did look as though he was proud of the boy, so I imagine all is well between father and son."

"Oh, I am glad. Andrew does need a bit of encouragement now and again – all children do. And little Violet, she needs so much more attention than she actually gets. She tries hard to catch the eye of her mother and eldest brother Cyril, but most of the time they pay no attention to her whatsoever. She's the opposite of Andrew – he copes by distancing himself from the family, but she wants to get close to all of them. It breaks my heart that those two children are so misunderstood."

"Don't worry about that family, my dear. They'll all survive. But we do need to make sure that young Josephine doesn't get herself into trouble. I'm sure you'll agree with me that our own family members don't always measure up to what we might expect of them – we don't choose those with whom we're related, do we now? The Frosts have their shortcomings, like most other families struggling to make ends meet. But at the end of the day, they'll all be there for each other. You mark my words."

Lionel is about to put up the 'closed' sign on the front door of the pharmacy when a customer rushes in. From my seat in the back room, with the door slightly ajar, I recognise the shrill voice of Mrs Frost as she greets Lionel.

"Mrs Frost," Lionel says. "What a pleasure. How are you today?"

"Oh, not so bad," she says, "although this headache of mine won't go away and I've run out of the powders you sold me a month or so ago. Can you let me have another packet, please, Mr Fielding?"

"Ah, yes, Mr Laidlaw's headache powders. This is one of the few pharmacies outside of Scotland that sells them. But do they do you any good, Mrs Frost?"

"I think so, though the pain always returns after I stop taking them."

"Well, perhaps you should see the doctor about the root cause of the pain. The powders will only ever relieve it temporarily, so you do need to find out the reason why you're getting such headaches in the first place."

"I'll go to the doctor when I've a bit of free time. But now that Josephine is working at the hotel, I don't get as much help at home anymore, and the twins are driving me up the wall."

"Actually, I wanted to speak to you about Josephine, Mrs Frost. Don't look so surprised – I know she's a fine young lady. I certainly don't want to interfere, but I've seen her a couple of times in the company of a young man by the name of Billy Peebles. I don't know if you're acquainted with the family – I can't say that I am myself, being a relative newcomer to Brampton-on-Sea. But I do know that this fellow got a girl of about Josephine's age into trouble a couple of years ago, and then abandoned both mother and baby. Fortunately, the girl's parents – who are not from these parts – are helping to care for the child. I think we would all hate it if a similar misfortune were to happen to Josephine."

There is silence for a moment or two. Mrs Frost must be shocked by what Lionel has just told her, and is thinking of a way to respond without losing face.

"Mr Fielding," she says finally. "I thank you for telling me this. I know that Josephine has befriended one or two young men of uncertain background, and I've told her on more than one occasion to stop seeing them. However, I don't think my daughter is at any risk of behaving in a wanton manner with this particular young man, or with any other. I have not brought her up to conduct herself in such a way. Still, you can rest assured that I will speak to her again about her questionable choice of friends."

"I'm relieved to hear that, Mrs Frost. Now, those powders – let me think where I told Andrew to put them."

When I hear the bell on the shop door signalling Mrs Frost's departure, I join Lionel behind the counter. He is looking quite pleased with himself and is humming a tune as he empties the till.

"You must have heard my conversation with Rose Frost, Bessie," he says. "What do you think? It didn't go too badly, did it?"

"Yes, I heard every word. You're right, it didn't go too badly, but I dread to think what Mrs Frost is going to say to Josephine. The poor girl is really going to be in for it when she gets home from work. I don't think her mother had any idea she was friendly with Billy Peebles, despite what she said. I just hope things haven't gone too far already."

"Hopefully not. But I wouldn't be surprised if Mrs Frost forbids her from seeing any of her *questionable* friends for some time to come."

"Poor Josephine. She seems such a pleasant girl too."

"Now, Bessie. I don't want you getting involved in this affair. Let the Frosts look after their own. I know you mean well, but you can't keep worrying other people's problems. We've done our bit. I've told Mrs Frost about Josephine's friendship with the troublesome young man, and I'm pretty sure she'll put a stop to it. We're out of the picture now – do you understand?"

Lionel is right. I do tend to worry about other folk's troubles, and I've had no end of sleepless nights as a result. I always think I have it within my power to resolve everyone's problems, but of course, I don't. And my interfering can sometimes make matters worse. Thank goodness Lionel has seen fit to caution me before I start 'barking up the wrong tree', as Father used to say.

It's late afternoon and I'm in the back room of the pharmacy once again, this time sorting through the books that Lionel has acquired from Mr Franklin for my lessons in reading. Although he is well aware that I have no pupils at the moment, he's put the advertisement back on the pharmacy door and has already had one or two enquiries. The books, he says, cost him next to nothing, as Mr Franklin was doing a clear-out to make room for his next shipment from America.

"I've had an idea, Bessie," Lionel says, joining me. "Let me explain it to you and then you can tell me what you think."

"Oh no," I say, "when you ask me what I think, it usually means you've already made up your mind."

"Now, Bessie, you know that's not true. But my idea is as follows. This room, as well as being the place where you will hold your lessons, could be turned into a lending library. When I bought all these surplus books from Mr Franklin, it struck me as being just the thing Brampton-on-Sea needs. If children – and adults too – can come to borrow books at no cost to themselves, then their literacy is bound to improve. Without access to books at home, children can't be expected to learn to read fluently. I thought we could put another notice on the door – this one stating the times that the library will be open – and *you* can assume the role of librarian."

"What? Me? A librarian!" I exclaim. "No, Lionel, I don't think I could possibly take on such responsibility."

"Oh, Bessie, all that you will need to do, besides keeping the books in good order on the shelves, is to write down the borrowers' names and addresses, and the titles of the books they've taken home with them. They should be asked to return the books within three weeks, otherwise we might have to charge a small fee. It'll be a straightforward task and an interesting one, since I know you love books, and you'll be doing the community a service at the same time."

"I'm not sure, Lionel. You know how shy I am, and I'd have to talk to so many people. And where are all the books going to come from? Mr Franklin has kindly let you have these at a bargain price, but there's hardly enough here to start a lending library."

"First of all, it will do you good to meet people. You'll find that the townsfolk are not as frightening as you seem to think they are. And I've already given some thought to increasing our supply of books. I've spoken to Bertrand at length about this. He thinks that setting up a library is a wonderful idea and has promised to donate books on a regular basis. We've got some books at home that we've no use for, and I know that Mathilda and Ronald have a study that's stacked with books of many different genres. You've seen it yourself. Mathilda is sure to be more than willing to part with some of them. And I was thinking also of Fanny Grist. You've told me many times how impressed you were by the number of books in her drawing room. I thought I'd ask her if she'd be willing to donate a dozen or so."

"I see you've got it all worked out, Lionel. But I'm surprised Mr Franklin supports the idea. Won't he end up a sight worse off if folk come here to borrow books, instead of buying their reading material from his shop?"

"I think those who buy from his shop will continue to do so. We would be targeting those who can't afford to buy books either for themselves or for their children. And once children develop a love of reading, then I'm sure Bertrand will profit from their improved literacy in the long run. Besides, he's not a poor man by any means – the bookshop isn't his only source of income, believe me. His frequent trips to America are not solely to buy books, as he claims."

"Really? Well, you know him better than I do. But you're right about Mrs Grist. She has an enormous number of books. She was always so strict about them being arranged on the shelves by author, in correct alphabetical order. She told me off several times for putting a book back in the wrong place, even though I'd never lifted it from the shelf to begin with."

"Fanny Grist took advantage of your obliging nature, my dear. You should have answered her back more often, then she might have treated you better. But Bessie, do you agree that this is a good idea? I need your approval before I set the ball rolling."

"I know only too well, Lionel, that once you get an idea into your head, you'll persist with it, with or without my approval. But yes, it is a good idea. I'm just not so sure about *my* role in it. And I don't agree with charging a fee for late returns. If I *am* the librarian, I don't want to be pressing the needy to give me money. They're not likely to come back to borrow more books if they think they might have to pay another fee later on."

"All right, then we won't charge for late returns. But you'll have to be quite strict with the borrowers and scrupulous in following up on those who are guilty of not respecting the three-week lending period."

"Yes, and I won't let them borrow any more books until they've returned the ones they already have."

"Exactly. You see, you've already come around to the idea. I'm confident that you'll excel in your new position of Brampton-on-Sea's first librarian, Bessie."

Well, that's certainly taken me by surprise. Admittedly, I was hesitant at first, but I'm now beginning to feel quite excited about the prospect of becoming a part-time librarian! I love being surrounded by books and can recall with nostalgia the library in the school where Robert works, where I used to hold my reading lessons with Michael when the weather was too cold or wet for us to sit in the park. The spacious room, in which you could hear a pin drop, was furnished with floor to ceiling bookshelves, lined with books on every conceivable topic, some of which hadn't been touched for decades. It filled me with awe to find myself in such a distinguished place of learning, and instilled in me the ardent wish that the privilege of secondary education could be afforded to all children, boys and girls alike.

23

Sadly, Yvonne Goode's expectation that her twin sister would soon return to Ferndell has been dashed. Hilda has made it clear that she wishes to remain in Ireland. Yvonne received a long letter from her last week and, rather than summarise it, Blanche copied out a portion for Walter to send to me. It reads as follows:

Yvonne dearest, I know you took a dislike to the Doyles when you met them at my wedding, believing that such exuberance in folk was unseemly. But, as you know, I have always found their high spirits appealing. It certainly wasn't something we grew up with, I admit that, but those were hard times and I was happy to forget them. Declan was the quietest and most serious of the Doyle brothers, but I admired all three when I first met them at the fairground in Minehead all those years ago. I will never forget that day. It was dear brother John who made the introductions while you and Mother were taking tea on the promenade. Both of you were so disapproving of my new friends. But I suppose you had a right to be. I've always known that Fergus was fond of me, but Declan proposed to me first and I accepted without hesitation. He left his close-knit family in Dublin and was content to settle down with me in Ferndell, where nothing much happens and job prospects are limited. But he never complained and, when Ernest came along, no man could have been prouder. We were happy together and I still miss him terribly.

Fergus, bless his heart, never once interfered in our marriage, but when Declan died, he could not remain silent any longer. We corresponded for more than a year before he moved to America, where he was in the process of setting up an import-export business. He was anxious for me to join him. With Ernest already in New York, not much persuasion was needed. I knew you would object, Yvonne, so I thought I'd wait until later before telling you the truth. I'm truly sorry that I lied to you about Ernest getting married. I've known all along that you didn't believe me – you've always been able to read my mind, as I have yours. Anyway, you know the rest of the story. I narrowly missed losing my life, while dear Fergus lost his in his rush to return to New York, convinced that I was on my way there. That knowledge is not something I can easily live with and I still feel that I'm to blame, although the Doyles insist that I should not feel at all guilty about the tragic turn of events. It seems there was nothing anyone could have done to dissuade Fergus from returning to New York so soon after his mother's funeral.

There is more to tell you, Yvonne. You are probably unaware of this, but Ernest is the only living Doyle of his generation to carry on the family name. Fergus never married, as you know, and Brian's two sons both died in infancy. So, you see, Ernest is very special to his father's family and they have encouraged him to stay in Ireland and consider marrying an Irish lass, once he feels ready to settle down. He has no objection; his American romance was never going to lead to marriage, and he has no desire to return to the so-called land of opportunity. He found it hard to find permanent employment and was unable to make any lasting friendships in New York. And now that he knows he will no longer have his Uncle Fergus' shoulder to lean on, he cannot bear the thought of returning there.

Declan and Fergus' remaining siblings are both good, honest folk. Brian Doyle has been a widower for some ten years. His wife died giving birth to a daughter – who was stillborn – so he was left childless. His life has not been an easy one, but he has never felt sorry for himself and is no less cheerful than his two late brothers. He has been a good friend to me and has welcomed me into the family fold. I am finding much consolation in talking to Brian and his sister, Maureen McGuire, about both Declan and Fergus, rather than keeping my heartache to myself, as was considered the respectable thing to do in our family. Maureen is one of the kindest women I have ever had the pleasure of knowing, and she has asked if Ernest and I would consider staying with her and her daughter Cathleen indefinitely. I have given it a lot of thought and believe that, for the time being, Ireland is the place where I want to live. I have therefore accepted Maureen's kind offer. I hope that you will not judge me too harshly, Yvonne, and will appreciate that this will be a new beginning for both Ernest and myself.

Of course, it is difficult for Yvonne to accept the news that Hilda has no plans to return to Ferndell, but Daisy and Blanche are urging her to see her twin sister's point of view. Walter says she has now written back in a sympathetic tone, apologising again for her harsh words when they were last together; words that subsequently caused her so much anguish. Clearly, both sisters are anxious for a reconciliation, and it's everyone's hope that their past grievances will soon be forgiven and forgotten.

Farmer Townsend was certainly right in his weather prediction. It's turned out to be the wettest August since records began, which makes life hard for Joseph on the farm. But thanks to the hard work of migrant labourers, and fellow villagers who are only too keen to lend a hand, much of the harvest has been salvaged. It does seem inevitable, though, that some families will go hungry this winter, but we can only hope and pray that those who need help will receive it.

Despite working long, difficult hours, Joseph is putting on a brave face. After all, he and Daisy have an October wedding to look forward to. While he puts his heart and soul into weathering the storm and rescuing the harvest, his betrothed has been putting all *her* efforts into making the old farm cottage spotlessly clean, comfortable and as finely furnished as their budget will allow.

With Hilda's decision to stay in Ireland for the immediate future, there is presently no occupant in her Ferndell cottage. So as not to lose the lease, Walter and Blanche have written to ask her if they can live there after they are wed, paying the rent on her behalf. They are confident that she will agree and are now ready to face the future in a more positive light.

The news that wedding bells will soon be ringing, not just for Joseph and Daisy, but also for Walter and Blanche, fills me with immeasurable joy. I was thrilled to learn that a double wedding for the two sisters and two cousins is planned for Saturday, the 12th of October, at the Ferndell parish church. In fact, I'm so excited that that I can barely sleep at night and am unable to concentrate on my daily tasks. Lionel has told me that if I intend to make a habit of tossing and turning in bed each and every night, then he will be forced to move into the spare room.

Mrs Goode insists that she can manage perfectly well

alone with Millie once both Daisy and Blanche leave the family home. Her health has improved enormously since hearing that Hilda is in the land of the living, and young Millie is becoming more sensible by the day. Edward will be alone, but he won't mind that – he'll probably take pleasure in it – as long as the village girl comes every few days to clean and cook for him. And, of course, Walter and Blanche will make sure he doesn't skip meals, as he is wont to do when left alone. I will also make an effort to visit every couple of months, whether he likes it or not, so that I can give the house a thorough clean and check that he's looking after himself.

Despite the wet weather, Mathilda, Ronald and little Geoffrey have come to stay for a few days. Mathilda said she'd threatened to leave Ronald if he didn't agree to take some time off work and accompany her and Geoffrey on a short holiday. It's lovely to see the family again, and I'm delighted that they've brought with them the baby's nanny, Marie-Thérèse, who is able to tell me all the news about our mutual friends, Patty and Robert, baby Agnes, and Michael's sister, Harriet.

Mathilda is in her second trimester and is looking a picture of health – although, understandably, too much time with eighteen-month-old Geoffrey does tire her out. She says Marie-Thérèse, with her quiet but firm nature, has been a godsend these last few months. Understandably, Lionel is over the moon to see his little grandson again and, when he's not working, is more than willing to take it upon himself to entertain the child. They play endless games together and I'm not sure who is having the most fun, Lionel or Geoffrey.

When Ronald hears about Andrew and Violet, and our

visits to the Smiths, he offers to take us there, along with Marie-Thérèse and Geoffrey, in his brand-new motorcar! This unexpected day out causes great excitement, both for Andrew and Violet, and for me, as none of us has ever been in a private motorcar before. I don't have time to write to Winifred beforehand, so we plan to arrive unexpectedly in the shiny red automobile. I am sitting in the back between Andrew and Violet, with my arms around both of them. It is not exactly comfortable, as Violet is fidgety throughout the entire ride. She chatters nonstop and tells me that she feels like Toad of Toad Hall. Well, I have to admit, I feel a bit like the Toad myself!

William and Wendy are thrilled when they see us arriving in such a swanky mode of transport, and Winifred cheerfully disregards our apologies for the impromptu visit and immediately goes to put the kettle on. Ronald, however, declines a cup of tea; he says he'd like to show the children the car and take them for a short ride, if Winifred doesn't mind. He promises to drive carefully.

Through the open window, I can hear William asking Ronald numerous questions; first and foremost, he wants to know what make of car it is.

"It's a Wolseley-Siddeley, a 1910 A3 model," Ronald says, and goes on to explain how the engine works and what all the gadgets are for.

"By the time you children grow up," he says, "there will be many more motorcars on the road than there are today, believe me. You boys will probably find yourselves driving a much faster model than this one. Now, how about I take the four of you for a drive in the countryside? Would you like that?"

"Oh yes, please!" William says, jumping up and down in excitement. "I've never been in a motorcar before!"

"Hop in then," Ronald says. "Why don't you two boys squeeze into the front passenger seat, and the girls can sit in the back."

We can hear the screeching of tyres on the gravel driveway, as Ronald makes a three-point turn and slowly drives away. Meanwhile, Marie-Thérèse, whom I suspect has never been to the seaside before, asks me if she can take Geoffrey to the beach and let him play in the sand. Although I wish she had asked his father first, I agree, knowing full well that she'll take great care of the child and will not let him out of her sight for a single second.

With everyone out of the house, Winifred and I have an hour or so alone together, and she tells me some good news. Ever since Mr Barlow's visit, Maud's state of mind has improved considerably, and she no longer confines herself to the bedroom. She is taking more interest in the children and is helping Winifred in the house and garden, as well as doing most of the shopping. In fact, her absence that afternoon is due to the fact that she's gone into town to buy a late birthday present for William.

"And, finally, she's eating normally," Winifred says, "and gaining a bit of weight. I don't know what Alfred said to her when they went for that walk together, but whatever it was, it seems to have worked wonders. She won't tell me anything about their conversation, but I suppose it did her good to hear someone talking about Colin and praising his bravery. If it were not for Alfred, she'd have known nothing about what Colin did for others that night. I think it's definitely helped her come to terms with the loss, heartbreaking though it is for the whole family."

"Oh Winnie," I say, "I'm so glad to hear that Maud is turning a corner. That's the best news. By the way, I've sent Mr Barlow the address of Hilda's brother-in-law, and I'm hopeful that his promised letter to her will have a similar effect. Fergus Doyle, by all accounts, was a hero too, putting the lives of his fellow passengers before his own. And he made no secret of his love for Hilda and his desire to marry her. The knowledge of his outspoken passion will surely be of comfort to her, as she mourns his passing."

Well, thanks to Ronald and his motorcar, the afternoon has been a rare treat for all of us. Even the rain has held off for a few hours, though threatening black clouds do appear overhead on our return journey. Thankfully, we make it to the house just in time, and Geoffrey, flushed and covered in sand from playing on the beach, rushes into his mother's arms.

"What a pity there wasn't room in the car for you and Mathilda," I say to Lionel when we're finally alone together. "Winifred was completely unfazed by our unexpected visit and was her usual entertaining self. I do wish you could meet her."

"Oh, that's all right, Bessie, Lionel says. "I'm sure I'll meet her eventually. Today I was more than content to stay home with Mathilda. We've had a good old chit-chat, just like you and Winifred. It was quite like old times."

Lionel and I are just beginning to settle back into our normal routine when I receive a letter from Lady Sophia, or *Countess* Sophia I should say – though I can never think of her as a Countess – inviting us to visit her and the Count, and their baby, Giacomo, in Rome. Once I recover from the shock of receiving such an important invitation, my inclination is to write back immediately, thanking her profusely, but declining the kind offer. Lionel, however, seems to have other ideas.

"Remember, Bessie," he says, "after our marriage, we travelled to Ferndell to visit your brothers and their families, who couldn't attend the wedding. I know that is what most newly married couples call a honeymoon, and it *was* enjoyable, but it wasn't exactly a holiday, was it? We've not had a *real* holiday together since we've been married, have we, my dear?"

"But Lionel," I argue, "for me, living here by the sea with you is like being on holiday all the time. And since moving here, we've twice been back to London to visit Mathilda and Ronald, and baby Geoffrey. Isn't that enough? Do we really need to go abroad? Even though Lady Sophia has invited us to stay at their villa, the travel itself will be such a big expense. How would we afford it?"

"Don't you worry about the finances, Bessie. Neither of us are big spenders. Even when I try to give you money to buy something for yourself, you refuse it. So, yes, we can afford it, thanks to your parsimoniousness."

"Still, Lionel, I can't help feeling that, whether or not we have the means, it's an unnecessary extravagance. I don't think we should be seen as folk who are able to travel abroad for pleasure, while others have barely enough money to feed their families. I know you're going to ask why it should matter what people think, but it *does* matter. It matters to me a great deal. I can just imagine what Edward will say if he hears that you and I are to travel to Italy for a holiday. His scathing remarks will upset me no end. And even though Walter and the

Goodes, and Harold and his family, wouldn't dream of voicing their opinions aloud, most likely they'll be thinking the same thing. It's not something I feel comfortable with, Lionel."

"Listen, Bessie. The invitation is addressed to you, not me. So, if you don't want to go, we'll say no more about it. But please, give it some thought. Let me tell you something. In his present job at Westminster, Ronald often reads reports from government sources that are not made public, and he's told me confidentially that we cannot take for granted long-term peace in Europe. He wouldn't tell me the basis for such a remark, but would not have mentioned it if it were not something to be taken seriously. What I do know, from reading the newspaper, is that the balance of power in Europe is shifting. The Ottoman Empire is weakening, as can be witnessed from the ongoing tensions in the Balkans. Even Italy has its own conflict with the Ottomans in North Africa. Developments such as these don't bode well for peace in the near future."

"Oh no! Lady Sophia didn't mention that. Would it be safe for us to travel to Italy if they're fighting... Where did you say it was?"

"North Africa. Don't worry, Bessie. I don't think for one moment that the conflict there will affect our stay in Rome. In fact, I'd be surprised if ordinary Italian citizens have heard anything about it. But the point I'm trying to make, my dear, in light of Ronald's remarks, is that if we are ever to travel abroad together, perhaps now is the best time to do it. We don't know for certain if this country will escape future hostilities – this period of relative peace might be the calm before the storm. Plus, given my age, we should think about travelling abroad sooner rather than later. I don't know about you, but I've always wanted to go to Italy – it has so much to offer in terms of history, culture, scenery and, of course, good food."

Begrudgingly, I promise Lionel that I will think about it. In fact, I can now think of little else. The idea of travelling to Italy has been so much on my mind that I'm beginning to dream about it. By day, we will explore the city of Rome, to which all roads lead, and where ancient monuments exist on every street corner, or so I'm told. And by night, well, that still remains a mystery. I know that Lionel is teasing me when he says that, by night, we'll be transformed into young lovers. He only makes such remarks to embarrass me, and it works every time. He's obviously convinced that I will change my mind, so is already starting to learn the Italian language. He says he wants to be prepared for all possibilities – romantic or otherwise – and says that when in Rome, we'll 'do as the Romans do', whatever that is supposed to mean.

I suppose it just remains for me to overcome my worries about what others might think, and try to ignore the guilt that I feel about our facing no economic hardship, while many in Ferndell and elsewhere are having to watch their pennies and do without what Lionel and his family would consider 'the necessities of life'. But life has never been fair, and my declining a trip to Italy is not going to make any difference to that unfortunate fact.

I decide to ask Walter – who has always been my trusted confidant – how he feels about Lionel and myself accepting Lady Sophia's invitation. He replies to my letter right away, saying that he cannot believe I would seriously consider turning down a once-in-a-lifetime opportunity to set foot on the continent of Europe.

Besides, Aunt Bessie, he writes. *For years now, I've been sending you postcards from almost every place I travel to for work. Don't you think it's about time you sent me a postcard? I can't tell you how much it would mean to me to receive a picture postcard of the Eternal City from my favourite aunt!*

Well! After a remark such as that from my own dear Walter, my long-overdue response to Lady Sophia will surely have to be in the affirmative.

"I'll write to Lady Sophia this evening to inform her that we're coming," I tell Lionel when he arrives home from work.

"*Grazie a Dio per quello*!" he exclaims.

I give him a puzzled look. He informs me that he has just said, 'Thank God for that' in Italian, and that I've made him the happiest man in Brampton-on-Sea. I can't help thinking that the phrase sounds quite blasphemous, but I say nothing. My husband's childlike enthusiasm amuses me and his fervour is becoming contagious. I won't tell him just yet, but now that we've finally come to a decision, I do believe I'm beginning to feel something akin to excitement about our impending Italian adventure!

About the Author

Susan E Jones grew up in Stroud in Gloucestershire, but chose Penzance in Cornwall as her home when she returned to the UK after years of living and working abroad. She was then in a position to devote more of her free time to writing, which had long been her ambition. Daily walks along the South West Coastal Path continue to give her both a sense of wellbeing and an opportunity to think about ideas for her next work of fiction.

Before the Storm can be read as stand-alone, or can be read as a sequel to Susan's earlier novel, *After the Rain.* Both books were inspired by the contents of her Great-Great-Aunt Bessie's postcard album. Susan writes, "I know nothing of Bessie's life, apart from the fact that she was in service of some sort and seemed to move around a lot, but the heartwarming postcards she received from her nephew Walter and close friend Patty touched a chord in me. I'd like to think that the fictional lives I've given these characters would cause them no distress and might perhaps flatter and amuse them."

www.blossomspringpublishing.com